THE
EVERWEED
STATE

REBECCA BAUMGARTNER

Crescent Valley Books

THE EVERWEED STATE

Copyright © 2014 by Rebecca Baumgartner

CRESCENT VALLEY BOOKS

For information visit www.everweedstate.com

Book and Cover design by Derek Murphy

ISBN-13: 978-0692320259

ISBN-10: 0692320253

First Edition: December 2014

10 9 8 7 6 5 4 3 2 1

To Tracy and Sam:
You both made this book possible.

And thank you Mike Sirota:
You are an amazing friend and literary guru.

PROLOGUE

S amuel VanDerhout stood in the empty field, the wailing drone of sirens growing nearer. He managed to spare a thought for the rows of towering cannabis around him, straining against rotor wash and debris kicked up by the helicopter hovering above the scene. The plants would be cut down and burnt; herbicide would be folded into the earth, a precaution against any stray seeds or nascent life. Sam knew he was now part of a drama mixed with farce, funded by taxpayer money. He would reluctantly begin playing his part in seconds.

Earlier in the day, Sam had reached up to give a huge marijuana plant a final, artful clip with his gardening scissors. It had been a perfect Pacific Northwest growing season and the plants thrived in the communal garden, nestled deep in the Olympic Peninsula, surrounded by forest and otherwise inaccessible except by a steep, now abandoned logging road.

This particular piece of land was poised on a natural meadow near the remains of a clear-cut in an otherwise heavily forested region; a glacier-fed river ran through the edge of the property and the soil had proven rich and productive. The dreadlocked community that had established this herbal enclave had enjoyed a fruitful harvest of cannabis for the last three years. Sam had met the founding members of this particular pot farm, brothers Mickey and Duane Miller, while conducting a series of hands-on lectures in sustainable gardening for the Seattle Parks Department. He had found them eager students and was happy to help them in their quest to obtain a measure of autonomy from urban civilization.

The marijuana crop gave the cooperative its hard cash, but a glistening host of vegetables grew alongside the cannabis, manifesting the group's commitment to living off the land as much as possible.

Sam always enjoyed autumn in Washington, especially lovely here in this forest oasis. Summer often came late, spilling well into October, and made enduring the other nine months in the rainy Pacific Northwest worthwhile. Well, mostly.

As he worked the area of the garden containing a few dozen massive marijuana plants, Sam felt the slanted rays of the sun on his neck. He stood and stretched his strong back. "Kaitlin, I didn't see you standing there." He stepped back from the pretty young woman who had been silently watching him work.

She moved her hair back from her face. "I love the way you work with plants, Sam. You seem so in tune with them." She smiled, her cheeks flushing as she stopped to brush the tall cannabis with a sun-browned hand.

Sam smiled at the lovely girl. "I appreciate that. I'd ask you to help me a bit, but you know the rules." Sam had forbade any of the under-aged people to help with the marijuana crop.

She sighed, gazing at Sam with open affection. "I'll be twenty-one in another year or so, you know." She moved closer to Sam. "Maybe we could break the rules just once."

Sam gazed over her head, seeing Mickey's young wife, Betsy, now hugely pregnant, carrying a basket full of small pumpkins. "Excuse me, Kaitlin." He walked toward Betsy, grateful for an excuse to end the conversation. "Let's try and avoid having you go into labor out here. You shouldn't be lifting like that." He took the basket from the pregnant woman.

"I'm okay, Sam." The young woman followed him as he brought the pumpkins to the rusty red van the group used to haul their produce. "I've still got another month to go."

Sam smiled as he watched the industrious group working around him. It gave him great pleasure to see people working in concert with the natural environment. Pulling a beat-up military surplus canteen from its worn canvas cover, he enjoyed a mouthful of the cold, mineral-rich water that had been glacial ice just a short time before.

As he drank, Sam wondered again how he had been persuaded to break his own golden rule by helping this rustic bunch grow marijuana for the marketplace. He did not doubt the majority of these happy pot farmers were seasoned felons; they had certainly demonstrated substantial experience in this kind of endeavor. Sam, on the other hand, had a spotless record; he had adamantly refused to grow weed for sale. He gave his pot away to friends or donated it to medical marijuana facilities, keeping just enough for his own enjoyment, and his research.

Finishing another mouthful of the icy water, Sam slid the canteen back into its faded green cover as he heard the faint thud-thud-thud of a helicopter coming up the valley in his direction. It wasn't unusual for the occasional Forest Service chopper to scan for fires, even in autumn. But this one didn't sound like the older helicopters the Forest Service used. As it came closer, Sam realized with a sinking feeling that this was a Sheriff's Department chopper, scanning for people doing exactly what they were doing at that moment.

"It's a bust! Should we run, or what?" someone yelled as the sound of the chopper grew louder.

Sam thought quickly. He loved this group of gentle, hardworking hippies and considered them part of his extended family. He already knew the answer to his question: "How many of you are looking at a third strike for pot on your record?" Virtually every adult hand in the group shot up.

"Damn. Fucking damn." Sam turned to the shirtless Mickey. "Get everyone out of here right now!"

Mickey hesitated as the rest of the group started running toward the thick forest surrounding the field. "What about you, Sam?"

"Let me worry about that, Mick. Go make sure Betsy's okay." He watched as the last of the group disappeared into the surrounding woods, leaving him alone in the field.

Sam raised his hands just as a Sheriff's drug enforcement vehicle skidded to a stop in front of him, the chopper hovering just overhead. "It's okay, officer. I'm alone here. It's just me and my marijuana."

1

Sam was awakened earlier than usual by one of the guards at the minimum-security prison facility. "Thanks, Dave," he said, yawning as he took the large manila envelope offered to him.

"I hope it's good news for you." Dave Swanson held the early shift at the lockup; he gave Sam a thumbs up as he ambled away.

Sam walked back to his small desk and sat down, turning the envelope over in his hand before carefully opening it. It contained a letter and some legal documents. Sam read the letter first, his face breaking into a grin as the import of the words became clear. He was being released today, almost two months early. Taking full responsibility for a substantial marijuana growing operation had cost him a significant fine as well as a six-month sentence. Still, Sam was satisfied to know he had saved his friends from hardship. Mickey and Duane Miller, the actual proprietors of the marijuana farm, had moved their commune to Oregon and were apparently thriving. Mickey had informed Sam during a prison visit that he and his wife Betsy had named their first-born daughter after him.

"Thank god." Sam closed his eyes, allowing the feeling of imminent freedom to sink in for a moment. He continued reading the letter: apparently his attorney had secured his release. He immediately rose from his desk and waited for Dave to make his way around to the cell again.

"I'd like to use the phone. I need to call my attorney."

"Sure, Sam. Good news in the envelope or what?" Dave unlocked the cell door.

"I think so. I really think so." Dave led Sam to the phone bank, where he placed a call directly to his lawyer's cell.

"Nick! How'd you do it?" Sam spoke excitedly, a huge smile pasted on his handsome face.

"It wasn't altogether me, Sam." Nick Ballatoire had been the VanDerhout family attorney for almost thirty years. He had worked to keep Sam's sentence as light as possible and to get him placed in a relatively pleasant, white-collar facility. "Some folks from California apparently have pull with the Feds. I can't tell you the specifics, but it's a corporate entity of some kind very interested in your research." Nick's voice lowered. "One of the terms they laid down was that you were to be initially released into their custody."

"What?" Sam was immediately on guard. "Someone will have 'custody' of me?"

"It's not what you think. Hear me out. Firstly, your release is a full pardon based on the terms in those documents. No parole, and the whole thing wiped off your record. Secondly, the so-called 'custody' thing simply involves a meeting with you in

California. I'm told it's just for a meeting, nothing more. Then, you're completely free to do as you choose."

Sam remained quiet for a moment, then said, "I guess I have to do it. Having a full pardon is not something I can pass up."

"Damn straight. Hey, I'd like to call your mother and give her the good news, if that's okay?" Nick sounded harried, as usual.

"Sure. Tell her I'll call her once I get back home. Oh, and can you call my friend, Marty Stout, for me?"

Sam hung up the phone and sat quietly for a moment. Things were moving too quickly for him to think much about the mysterious "corporate entity" that had secured his freedom. He called for a guard and was escorted back to his cell, where he spent an hour signing documents and packing his few belongings into a daypack. Soon, Dave arrived back at his cell with several other guards.

"We're all going to miss you, buddy," Dave said as he swung open the cell door and stepped aside.

The guards applauded as Sam took a deep breath and exited the cell, a free man. "Can I say goodbye to a couple folks?"

He made a few farewells with some of his friends in the lockup. Most were there for various petty crimes and assorted business malfeasance; Sam had found them a generally decent bunch, if somewhat morally challenged.

He swung by the main desk and picked up a few more of his personal items and his cell phone, uncharged. Walking out of the gray facility into the open air, Sam stopped to thank the universe for his freedom. A late winter snow was falling, and he lifted his head for a moment, enjoying the feeling of snowflakes melting on his cheeks.

He jumped slightly when a black Range Rover with dark, tinted windows pulled up next to him. The front passenger-side window slowly slid down. "Samuel VanDerhout?"

Sam bent his lean, six-foot frame down to peer at the well-tailored man behind the wheel and smiled politely. "That would be me, but most people call me Sam. Nice suit, by the way. Brooks Brothers?"

"Get in please," the driver said in an authoritative tone.

Sam assumed this was all part of the strange deal he had accepted and slid into the passenger seat. Without another word from the mysterious chauffeur, the supercharged Range Rover left the gravel parking lot of the minimum-security prison and squealed onto the paved road, which led back to the main highway.

"Hey, you mind if I spark up?" Sam carefully extracted a well-rolled joint from where he had expertly sewn it into the waistband of his Levis. In spite of the fact the nameless man driving the black Range Rover had not said a word since he had entered the car, Sam felt it only polite to ask; some people frowned on that kind of thing. Hearing no objection, or any response at all for that matter, he pressed the cigarette lighter down to heat it, and promptly lit the joint. The driver glanced at him darkly, a look of disgust moving across his face.

Sam merely shrugged and adjusted the seat warmer, settling deeper into the comfortable leather. He thought about getting back home, to his island.

Finishing his joint with one last exhale, Sam decided it was time to ask some questions. "So, do you know anything about this? I'm kind of curious to know exactly where we're headed."

He regarded the grim-looking man to his left with an amiable blue gaze.

The man was built like a pit bull, short and heavily muscular; his tailored suit seemed odd on such a tough-looking fireplug of a man. The driver remained silent, grimly focused on the road ahead. Sam had the feeling this guy could get nasty if provoked. Shrugging, he settled back into his seat, hoping he had made the correct decision to leave prison on these terms.

As the Range Rover merged at high speed, Sam noted the Green Washington State sign, *I-5 North — Seattle* as it blurred by. He gazed out the window, enjoying the feeling of being in the outside world again, in spite of his unusual circumstances. When they took the exit toward Sea-Tac airport, Sam ventured another question to the silent driver. "So, where in California am I going exactly?" The question hung unanswered in the air as the vehicle smoothly navigated the twists and turns of the airport entrance, following the signs toward the parking garage.

"I think it's only fair to give me some idea of where I'm going and why." Sam was growing annoyed. "I'm perfectly capable of getting myself on a plane and—"

"Look," the driver interrupted, "I've been contracted to get you from point A to point B. That's all I know, and I don't give a shit otherwise." The man turned to glare at Sam as he shut off the engine. "I'm not being paid to talk to you, entertain you, or enlighten you. Understood?"

Sam sat back in his seat as the driver quickly pressed the central unlock button on the console. Athletically exiting the Range Rover, he strode rapidly around the vehicle to the front passenger door where Sam sat, grabbing the door handle as he attempted to pull it open.

Sam calmly re-locked all the doors of the vehicle with one deft move, pointing casually to the keys, still swinging in the ignition.

The driver patted his pockets "Shit!" The sound of his expletive reverberated throughout the cavernous structure.

"You slacker asshole! Unlock this goddamn car!"

Sam looked at the man in a friendly manner as he cracked the window. "I guess you'll have to go get the spare set of keys then. That, or tell me what you know about all this."

After a quick discussion, the two men made their way through Sea-Tac and boarded a plane for Los Angeles.

As Sam took his seat on the flight, he wondered why the nattily dressed driver had such a hard time telling him this was a trip to L.A. to meet some dude from a pharmaceutical company.

"You could have just told me when I asked initially." Sam had tried to make peace with the angry man sitting next to him on the plane. "I had every intention of going with you peacefully."

"Shut up." The driver didn't look up from the menu.

Sam shrugged and smiled at the pretty flight attendant as she finished taking lunch orders in first class. "Do you have anything organic?"

"No sir, just what's on the menu." The flight attendant smiled back, her eyes lingering for a moment on Sam's handsome face.

"Okay. Then I'll take the turkey sandwich and a Tree Top IPA, please." Sam watched her appreciatively for a few moments as she moved gracefully back up the aisle with the orders, enjoying the sight of an attractive woman for the first time in four months.

Sam finally settled into his seat and began trying to prepare himself for dealing with a pharmaceutical company. His past experience with that industry had left a bitter aftertaste and he had no intention of sharing his research with them. He was grateful the essence of his work, the research he considered truly important, remained well hidden from the outside world. At least he hoped so.

Soon after his landing at LAX, Sam found himself quickly shepherded to Fields Pharmaceuticals' enormous, generic-looking research campus and practically shoved into a huge, luxurious office.

Sam glanced around. "Do you play tennis in here on your breaks or something?"

2

A tall, exquisitely suited man stood up from behind a gleaming desk and introduced himself with hand extended. "Ah, you must be Dr. VanDerhout. I'm Tim Mallory, VP of New Product Development here at Fields Pharmaceuticals."

Sam shook the hand. "I understand from my attorney that I have you to thank for arranging my early release and pardon." He took a deep breath, feeling an urgent need to sharpen his senses quickly.

"Yes, well…I apologize for getting you here on such short notice, but we thought perhaps you would be interested in what we have to say." Mallory gestured toward a round table.

After crossing the office, the two men sat down in comfortable chairs. Mallory loosened the button on his expensive-looking double-breasted suit jacket in a well-practiced, genteel manner. "Sam…may I call you Sam?"

Sam nodded, focusing on the man seated next to him. Mallory reminded him of a sleek jungle cat circling its prey. His muscles contracted instinctually, readying himself to evade attack.

"Well," Mallory said, flashing a white-toothed smile, "it has come to our attention you are somewhat of an academic phenomenon up there in Washington State." He picked up a file folder from the table, glancing at the contents.

Sam remained quiet, shifting slightly in his chair and looking around the room. He felt the air conditioning kick on, and he realized he was sweating.

Mallory continued, reading casually from the file: "We are aware of your career, your botanical work in the Amazon, and your many research papers." He looked up as though to gauge Sam's reaction.

"Well, thanks for the compliment," Sam said in an even tone, "but you may have noticed I haven't published anything for a very long time." The word *cannabis* was unspoken, but he knew what the man meant. Most of his published work involved medicinal marijuana.

"Your lack of recently published work doesn't pose a problem, Sam," Mallory said. "As a matter of fact, we're prepared to offer a mutually beneficial arrangement, which I think you'll like very much."

Sam sighed. "My attorney led me to believe my release and pardon were somehow dependent upon this meeting with you. I'm thinking, though, that it's a bit more informal. I mean a pardon's a pardon. No strings attached once it's done. Correct?" He had let the predator know his prey could escape.

Mallory nodded. "That is true. Your cooperation with us, once you walked out that prison door, was entirely your choice. You had no legal obligation to make this meeting."

"Good." Sam sat back in his seat and smiled, feeling the power shift in the room. "I just wanted to make that clear. But I am certainly in your debt, and I did give my word to meet with you. So I'll happily listen to what you have to say. Please, continue."

Mallory's eyes narrowed. "Yes, well. It's come to our attention you have somehow biologically engineered certain strains of cannabis that may inhibit the growth of cancer." He glanced down at the file again, a slight smile crossing his face.

Sam remained silent for a moment, his heart pounding in his ears. *Not that.* He had retracted that paper just before its publication.

"May I ask how you are aware of this supposed research?" Sam attempted to calm his voice, inhaling deeply and slowly releasing his breath.

Mallory appeared amused. "These days, if something has been written, it can be found."

"Well, sorry to inform you of this, but you've obviously gone to a lot of trouble for nothing." Sam now knew it was futile to deny the paper itself. "It was a purely speculative project. I challenge you to find data that backs up any purported results." He fought back a rising panic. *I hope to god they don't look for the data.*

"Listen, Sam. We are offering you a very generous sum up front for your research." Mallory waved his hand dismissively. "Let's call it a signing bonus. If you are willing to join the Fields

Pharmaceuticals team, share your methods and perhaps some samples, we are prepared to make it very worth your while."

"So let's say I do that." Sam shifted tactics. "I mean, let's assume I have what you claim I have, and I just give you what you want. What are you going to do with it?" He fixed his eyes more firmly on Mallory.

Mallory leaned forward in his chair. "Dr. VanDerhout, we are in business to make treatments for people who need healing and hope. All I am asking is that you join us; lend your efforts and obvious talents to accomplishing a world free of dreadful disease and suffering. This is our overarching mission at Fields, to make people's lives better."

"I'm sure it is, Tim." Sam said. "But please do me the honor of saving your bullshit for someone else. It's insulting to think that I would respond to that kind of canned corporate-speak."

"Is it a matter of money, Sam? We can—"

"It's not about money," Sam interrupted. "Not everything's about money."

"Then what is it about? There's a good chance you are sitting on something extremely important. It's not going to benefit anyone unless it's developed, vetted with the FDA and put into the marketplace for people to use." Mallory's face had flushed, his voice becoming louder and more emphatic.

Sam could see that Mallory was growing impatient, even angry. It pleased him to have broken through the man's corporate veneer, even slightly.

Mallory visibly composed himself. "Well, what do you say, Sam?" He guided a typed check for a generous sum across the edge of the table with the tips of his fingers.

Sam picked up the check and gazed at it for a moment before sliding it back to Mallory.

"You could print me a check for any amount, and I still wouldn't do it." Sam rose from his chair and gathered his daypack from the floor. "I mean, sure, you guys at Fields Pharmaceuticals or whatever can help a lot of people, but you'll be sure and help your stockholders and yourselves first. You are making billions off the backs of hurting people." Sam looked over his shoulder at Mallory. "I can do better than that." The door closed firmly behind him.

Mallory sat, dumbfounded for a moment at Sam's abrupt departure before reaching angrily for his phone. "Yes, Richard. Looks as though we will have to move to the next phase. Yes. I'm ready to do whatever it takes."

3

M an that sucked," Sam said under his breath as he exited the jet way into the north satellite of SeaTac airport. During Sam's research project for his doctoral dissertation years ago, he had often traveled to far-flung corners of the planet and had grown to heartily dislike airports. As he made his way to the taxi pickup area, he could feel his excitement build: it had been four months since he'd been home to his beloved island, and the house he had built.

Since it was just before dawn, Sam hailed a cab almost immediately. He slid the small daypack off his shoulder and hopped into the backseat, cheerily saying, "This is your lucky day. We're going for a ferry ride!"

"Yes sir. Lucky for me, not so lucky for you, I'm afraid. The meter must continue to run while we're on the ferry."

"That's okay, I understand. We need to get to the West Seattle Fauntleroy ferry dock so we can cross to Southworth. My home is about forty-five minutes from there."

"No problem, sir!" the driver replied cheerfully.

Arriving at the ferry dock, Sam could see the first boat of the day was almost finished loading. The driver threaded the cab onto the massive steel craft and parked where directed by a tired and obviously impatient ferry employee.

"I need to use the restroom," Sam told the driver. "I'll be right back." He opened the cab door and stepped out onto the pulsating steel deck of the purpose-built car carrier. He immediately filled his lungs with the familiar salty air and exhaled, long and slow, through his nostrils. "Ah. The wonderful salty scent of home."

Sam wove through the maze of closely parked vehicles and made his way to the stairs leading to the upper decks, the restrooms, food vendors, and other conveniences offered onboard. After exiting the restroom, he saw the intermediate stop at the north end of Vashon Island approaching. He stepped out onto the upper deck area overlooking one of the open ends of the ship used to load and unload vehicles. He watched as the ship began its turn toward the ferry dock. The powerful diesel-electric propulsion system went into neutral for a few moments, then into reverse, causing the massive ship to shudder as it slowed, casting up a thick spray and foaming froth of Puget Sound salt water. The ferry nudged into its berth, unloaded about thirty vehicles, loaded five, and then continued on to the town of Southworth.

As he enjoyed being alone for the first time in months, Sam watched the familiar lights of the small town approaching. He made his way back to the cab and climbed in just as the ferry vibrated and bumped its way to a stop against the cable-wrapped constellations of creosote-soaked log pilings and began to disgorge its load of people and vehicles onto the awaiting ramp.

The driver started his cab in concert with the cars ahead. "Where to?"

Having made this trip by cab several times before, Sam knew less was more when trying to describe how to get to his island. "I'll have to give you directions, turn by turn, but we're going to Manchester State Park."

"Okay, sir."

After half an hour, Sam could see they were approaching the park. He leaned over the seat, pointing. "Turn in there."

The driver brought the fast-moving cab from seventy miles an hour to almost zero in a few heartbeats, cranked the steering wheel hard to the left, and entered the speed bump-festooned State Park.

Sam scanned the parking lot, hoping he would see his old friend Marty, who also happened to be the ranger for Manchester State Park. Manchester was not far from the island Sam had inherited, and where he had built his house.

After paying the fare, plus a generous tip, Sam grabbed his daypack and exited the cab. Examining the parking lot again, he saw his Volvo wagon tucked away in the corner of the lot. As he walked toward his car, he felt the soft cushion of cedar, fir, and hemlock debris silencing his footsteps, scenting the air with a rich, sweet smell.

Arriving at his car, Sam noticed it had been washed and lacked all of the small woodland fragments that tended to bury everything on the forest floor; nature's first step in its process of reclaiming anything man-made. He pulled his keys from the daypack, inserted them in the ignition while saying a short prayer, and gave the keys a hopeful turn. The Volvo wagon eagerly sprang to life.

As the car warmed, Sam sensed someone approaching. Looking to his left through the still open car door he saw his friend, Marty Stout, burst from the thick brush surrounding the parking area, lunging forward in Sam's direction, stopping just short of the car.

"Shit!" Marty yelled. "Sam, you scared the hell out of me! I thought someone was stealing the Sammy-mobile. I'm just glad my Park Ranger training kicked in, and I was able to stop my assault in time."

Sam surveyed Marty who was dressed, as usual, in his perfectly pressed Park Ranger uniform. He had never been able to decide whether Marty looked more like an oversized wood-elf, or a boy scout fresh from Woodstock.

"I would have picked you up myself, but your attorney said you already had a ride."

"Yeah, I had a rather unanticipated trip to Los Angeles."

"It's cool...wait. *What trip to Los Angeles?*"

Sam told Marty about his experience with Fields. Marty appeared alarmed by the story.

"Jesus, Sam. What were you thinking? You can't go around pretending the world is all warm and fuzzy. It's dangerous out there." Marty frowned and took a moment to look him up and down. "You remember the hand-to-hand training I gave you, right?"

"Thanks for the concern." Sam recalled Marty's martial arts instruction and managed to hide a smile. "Luckily I didn't have to kill anyone with my bare hands. How are things on the home front?"

"All's well. After I sprang the Volvo from police impound, I made sure to start it up regularly, and I washed it in anticipation of your return. I have followed your watering and fertilizing instructions to a 'T' in the greenhouse, and took the liberty of dusting the house a bit. You will find I stocked the fridge with a few items to make coming home a bit more convenient. Your babies are in great shape—thriving and happy—but I suspect they're missing you a bit."

Sam turned off the ignition, stepped out of the car, and gave Marty a friendly hug.

"Oh, and I also cleaned up the boat a bit, started the outboard a few times, and made sure it's full of fuel for your return to the island."

"I'll be sure to write a glowing online review for you on the State Park website."

"Cool, thanks man." Marty grinned, looking pleased. "I'll walk you down to the boat and help you push off."

The two men made their way down a narrow trail toward the shore. Having reached a mid-point, Sam stopped suddenly, scanning up and down the trail for any onlookers. Assured they were alone, he motioned for Marty and they exited the main path between two tall fir trees and descended a barely discernable trail winding organically down the fall line to the water's edge.

Arriving at the place where he kept his aluminum boat in a tiny horsehead-shaped cove, Sam could just make out the silhouette of the craft concealed under a bent cedar blown partway over in a storm many years ago.

Sam climbed aboard and crouch-walked back to the outboard motor. He examined the fifty-year-old, green Mercury outboard he had carefully rebuilt two summers ago. Pushing the primer a few times, Sam pulled the start cord, and the small motor sprang to life. Waving at Marty to push off, he thrust the outboard tiller to the left to point the boat toward the outlet of the horsehead cove and into the Puget Sound, toward his island about a half-mile away.

Sam always studied the tide tables for the coming month, even while he was in the lockup, so he knew it was slack tide, and he could safely cross. The narrow channels of the South Puget Sound restricted the flow of massive amounts of water as the tides ebbed and flowed, making these seas deadly for the uninitiated.

Although his island was somewhat shrouded by a light morning fog, Sam could still make out its shape. He loved this little oasis. It was his fortress against the outside world; remote, yet right under everyone's nose. It had no ferry service, no landing strip, nothing except his home and a greenhouse.

Sam accelerated the small craft toward the only sandbar on the island and beached the boat solidly, cutting off the motor. Since he had no plans to leave for a while, Sam dragged the boat partially into the old growth forest covering the island. He swung his daypack over his shoulder and started up the path toward his house.

Climbing the steep trail reminded Sam he had done a lot of reading during his four-month hiatus in the lock-up and perhaps not enough exercising. He made note to remedy that imbalance over the next several weeks; he had much to do on the island in preparation for the coming spring.

Approaching the house, Sam paused to take in the late winter view of the structure from the trail below. He thought back to the time just after the eleven-acre island became his, through an odd twist of legacy. Sam came from an old Seattle family who had been among the city's founders. His great-grandfather, Samuel VanDerhout, had been a turn of the century logging baron and Sam's tiny island was part of Samuel's vast land holdings. Through the simple fact of its size and remoteness, the island had remained all but forgotten in the family trust. Sam had been delighted to acquire it as part of his inheritance.

At the time, he hadn't been sure what he was going to do with an eleven-acre island in the Puget Sound that had no access, other than by small boat. One day Sam had visited the island and noted a beautiful, massive hemlock obviously damaged several times during its existence. An idea formed in his mind to build a home in that very tree and move permanently to the island.

Sam continued on up the path, ascending the bleached white stairs cut from the huge driftwood logs that washed up on shore after the frequent winter storms. As he climbed, a strong feeling of satisfaction swept over him; the solid, long slabs of maple had the feel of concrete underfoot. Sam's motto of "anything worth doing is worth overdoing" was evident throughout the structure.

Arriving at the top of the steps, Sam started across the bridge/walkway, which crossed from the maple stairs to the first floor of the house. Sam had built the bridge on a sturdy branch that might have been the trunk of the tree at one time before it was knocked onto its side, probably by a storm. The tree had then started a second trunk growing skyward where it had been damaged. The massive tree gave the impression of being shaped like the number four, with the horizontal portion making up the foundation for the bridge, and the longer vertical section of the four making up the column to which the treehouse was attached. The massive trunk easily supported the weight of the house. Although in a strong wind, the house did complain somewhat as the structure moved with the hemlock, which served as its foundation.

Arriving at the antique, half-light entry door to the house, Sam turned the old glass knob and entered the first floor comprising the kitchen area. The remote nature of Sam's domain made locking the door unnecessary. In fact, the door didn't even have a lock.

It had been a long, eventful day and Sam was too exhausted to do anything but head directly to his bed. Fully clothed, he fell face first onto the soft mattress. He drifted off to sleep, grateful to be home at last.

4

Jolting awake, Sam wasn't sure where he was. His heart raced momentarily as he sat up in bed and attempted to get his bearings, glancing around his bedroom in the top level of the treehouse. After visually confirming he was no longer residing with the State, nor was he in Los Angeles, or any other place he considered hell, Sam slid his feet into his slippers and made his way down two levels, rubbing his eyes as he went.

Entering the kitchen, Sam realized the house was cold, so he started a fire in the small, wood-burning stove. That done, he began a brief walk-through of the treehouse, checking to make sure everything was in good order. Climbing back up the driftwood spiral staircase leading to the second floor, he emerged into the area that comprised the living room, as well as an ersatz library; descriptive of much of the house. The room was furnished with two antique, overstuffed chairs, and a couch for the occasional literarily induced slumber. There were three coffee tables crafted from solid slab cuts of maple driftwood, and walls lined with bookshelves, which were completely full, diverting Sam's unrelenting and eclectic literary diet to overflow onto every available surface in the room.

Assured the second floor was intact, Sam climbed the final driftwood stairs back to the top bedroom level. A quick scan of the room revealed all was intact here as well. He had been too tired earlier to note his bed sheets had been freshly washed, and the bed made; he knew that was the work of his thoughtful ranger friend, Marty.

Sam stripped off the jeans and flannel shirt he had been wearing now for about twenty-four hours and stepped into the shower. As the clean, warm water poured over him, he thought about Fields Pharmaceuticals. The size of the check Tim Mallory had slid across the table made it obvious how much his research was worth to them, and perhaps others as well. This sudden interest made Sam feel agitated, even here in his oasis. He had an uneasy feeling they were not done with him.

After drying off, Sam found his light green *Everweed State* tee-shirt and a pair of drawstring sweats from the dresser, donned the garments quickly, and hurried down two levels to the first-floor kitchen area.

Arriving in the kitchen, he opened the fridge and saw Marty had generously stocked it with the essentials: a half gallon of milk, a dozen eggs, a block of cheddar, a fresh bottle of ketchup, a loaf of whole wheat bread, bacon, and a half rack of Tree Top IPA, his favorite beer.

After devouring a breakfast of scrambled eggs and beer with the gusto of someone who had been eating reconstituted food for four months, Sam cleaned up the dishes, gazing peacefully out the kitchen window at the muted, late winter sunlight. He plugged in his phone charger and noted that a rash of voice mails had dammed up his iPhone over the past day; he took an hour or so to make obligatory phone calls to his family and several friends, who had all seemingly been informed of his early release.

Sam called Mickey Miller to let him know he had been pardoned.

"Dude, I can't tell you how much we all appreciate what you did for us." Mickey's voice sounded relieved. "I can finally stop worrying about you now."

He had been dreading this next call since leaving Mallory's office. He dialed the clinic's number. "Sheralyn? This is Sam VanDerhout."

"Sammy! I'm assuming you're a free man again since you're calling me from your cell." Sheralyn Finch was an energetic nurse practitioner at a low profile, alternative medicine clinic just north of Seattle. She and Sam had collaborated on using his tumor-inhibiting cannabis on several of her oncology patients.

"Yeah, free at last." Sam hesitated for a moment before asking, "Sheralyn, have you been contacted by anyone suspicious lately? I mean, has anyone tried to question you about our work together?"

"Not that I can think of, Sam. No way. I'd probably lose my license if I discussed our work together, you know that. Why are you asking?"

"Is there any way our patient list and raw data could have somehow gotten into the wrong hands?"

She was silent for a moment. "You know, we had a weird experience a few months back. We went to open up the clinic one morning and noticed the alarm had been completely disconnected—literally taken apart. But nothing was taken; we checked everything."

Sam shook his head. "I don't want you to worry about this. Really, it's nothing."

"Well, I hope so Sam. I may have a patient that I'd like to discuss with you once you get settled in." They spoke for a few more minutes before Sam ended the call.

"Shit," he said out loud, as he saw the time on his phone. "I'd better get moving."

Several minutes later he was walking quickly down the trail toward an old growth cedar stump with a well-crafted roof, which was set back in the thick woods covering the top of the island. He slid through a hidden opening in the back of the stump he had carefully cut out years ago. Inside, he had stowed his scuba gear wrapped in oil-soaked rags and thick waterproof canvas bags to protect the equipment from the salty elements. He pushed the gear ahead of himself as he worked his way back out of the thick, massive stump.

Once outside, he opened the bags and unwrapped the equipment, making sure everything was in good working order. He carried the scuba gear to the beach on the other side of the island and prepared to dive.

Sam walked backwards across the rocky beach and into the water. He tested the regulator one more time, put it into his mouth, and then slipped into the cold Puget Sound. He'd dove in this particular spot many times over the years and knew it well.

On the way down, Sam thought about when he first discovered the cave toward which he headed, shortly after he had built the treehouse on the island. The currents merging in this part of the Puget Sound had acted like powerful drills, burrowing into the island in some places, particularly where the geology was softer sandstone. The effect, probably over thousands of years, was the creation of several underwater caves beneath the island that could only be reached with scuba gear.

Maneuvering over the edge of an underwater cliff, he found the entrance to the cave he called, "the grotto" and easily swam through. After about forty feet, Sam surfaced inside the surprisingly dry, cool chamber.

He always liked coming here. The cathedral-like cave was quiet, peaceful, and because of the tall, angular, columnar basalt comprising the walls of the room, quite beautiful.

Sam chose this particular cavern to store his most precious seeds, and more important, plastic-wrapped records of his growing process and various sealed packages of genetic materials. The cave had a small, chimney-like opening to the surface that allowed fresh air and light to get in, but remained well disguised and nearly impossible to detect at the surface.

Sam pulled himself out of the water and onto the rock floor of the grotto. He removed his scuba mouthpiece, loosened his shoulder straps, and let the single tank slide gently onto the ground. He clicked on his lantern flashlight then peeled off the rest of his equipment, laying it beside the scuba tank, and walked swiftly over to the place in the grotto where years before he had carefully extracted an eighteen-inch chunk of rock, creating a small storage area inside the wall.

After carefully removing the chunk of rock, Sam could immediately see all was well. The sealed plastic bags of seeds from his best plants, and the plastic-covered sheets containing his fertilizer formulae, cannabis clippings, lighting and watering schedules, and genetic data, were all untouched. He reached to the very back of the space and pulled out a shoe-box-sized metal container. Flipping it open, he then lifted the flannel covering and gazed at the sparkling ampules neatly placed in rows. He carefully raised one of the small glass vessels and tilted it, moving the thick, brown liquid back and forth.

"Man, that's a relief." Sam said this aloud, his voice echoing inside the cave. He replaced the ampule, then inserted the heavy rock back into the opening of the wall. After having swiftly safety-checked his tank pressure and regulator and strapping the tank onto his back, he stretched the fins back onto his feet and slid into the water at the edge of the grotto floor.

As he surfaced and walked onto the beach, Sam realized he was tired and hungry. He pulled the scuba mouthpiece out, removed the fins, and made the short walk back to the house, where he temporarily placed the gear just inside the cedar stump-shed. Intending to return later and re-charge the tanks, he headed back to the house for lunch. As he crossed the kitchen, his laptop caught his eye.

Almost against his will, Sam was pulled into the chair in front of his computer. After several minutes locked in stalemate, he struck out in a search direction he was surprised he had never before considered. He fancied perhaps his subconscious mind had been chewing on the notion for some time, and the unexpected trip to L.A., and Fields Pharmaceuticals, had caused the thought to port over to his conscious mind.

Sam typed *History of Alcohol Prohibition* into the search engine box and gave a satisfying bang on the ENTER key. Up came the usual flood of articles, book references, and historical archive data and photos. He scanned the links, looking for the historical basis for alcohol prohibition, and studied several closely. As Sam read, he realized what his subconscious had been so tenaciously chewing: the parallel between alcohol prohibition and marijuana prohibition. Other than the clothes the people wore in the 1920s archive photos, and the rather stilted and unnecessarily grandiose language used in the parlance of the time, the parallel between alcohol prohibition and marijuana was immediately striking.

To Sam, the only difference between the two was the substance involved, and the groups of people wielding the power and profiting. Big pharmaceutical companies like Fields would be less than pleased to see cannabis legalized; an un-patentable, cheap, easy to grow, easy to dispense, wonder drug able to provide much-needed relief from dozens of conditions. Sam flipped his laptop shut. He felt out of sorts and needed to concentrate on re-booting his disrupted life. It had been a very exhausting end to a weird chapter. Tomorrow, he would start again.

Sam climbed the spiral staircase, running his hand over beloved pieces of driftwood as he ascended. He sat down on his bed for a moment, breathing deeply and releasing the uneasy feeling dogging him since his trip to L.A.

Sam didn't know where this was all leading, but he was fairly certain he'd find out soon enough, whether he wanted to or not.

5

Mackenzie Blake had to acknowledge how much she looked like her French mother as she neared thirty years of age. Managing to tame her dark curls into a twist at the back of her neck, Mackenzie leaned toward the mirror and dabbed a bit of concealer under her green, almond-shaped eyes. Lack of sleep had been creating dark smudges on her otherwise creamy skin and she wanted to appear as fresh and put together as possible. She straightened her shoulders and pulled her mid-thigh-length skirt down a bit, turning to admire the way her silk suit hugged her perfect curves. She walked the long hall toward a meeting with two executives overseeing her cannabis project, trying to appear calm.

Mackenzie knocked hesitantly on the open door and saw both Tim Mallory and Richard Aiken already seated on the comfortable chairs upper management always seemed to have in their offices.

"Ah! Mackenzie. Thank you for coming up on such short notice," Mallory said as the men stood.

Mackenzie sat down, crossing her shapely legs and tucking them under the table in one elegant movement. She was relieved to find them both smiling.

"Well, Mackenzie, we're all busy, so let me cut right to the chase." Mallory leaned back, lacing his fingers together. "As you may have heard, Washington State has apparently passed an initiative to legalize marijuana. While we of course appreciate and respect our neighbors to the north, and their right to determine what they want for their state, we also need to keep an eye on these developments as they may impact the future of Fields Pharmaceuticals." He glanced at Aiken. "Perhaps you should actually explain the details."

Aiken pulled a file from his briefcase. "As you may be able to discern when you read this dossier, we are very interested in a man named Samuel VanDerhout. Some vital stats may help." Aiken read from his portfolio. "Samuel Lawrence VanDerhout, the Third. Born at Swedish Hospital in Seattle, Washington, in 1972. Graduated with a doctorate in 1998 from the University of Washington. Majored in Botany, Biochemistry, Anthropology, and Mathematics."

"That's an interesting combination." Mackenzie tried to listen politely, in spite of her churning thoughts.

"He was a noted research scientist in ethno-botany for some of the best universities on the West Coast, doing research in the Amazon and in the Appalachian region of the United States. He authored a series of important papers until he suddenly dropped off the academic map about six or seven years ago. We think he may have the solution to our problems with TH-18."

Mackenzie felt a jolt of electricity run through her. "My team and I have been searching exhaustively for anything or anyone who can help us finish this project. There is no way we would have missed any reputable studies with applicability to TH-18." Mackenzie's first impulse was to defend her work. She looked quickly from Mallory to Aiken. "I want you to know we have worked very hard to stay on top of any cutting-edge research."

Aiken held up his hand. "We aren't saying that you or your team has dropped the ball in any way here." He looked at Mallory for support.

"No, Mackenzie. We are very happy with your work with TH-18. Richard, explain the situation, would you?"

"Apparently this Samuel VanDerhout published a paper called *Flora Sanitatum,* which describe certain results closely mapping the desired outcome for TH-18. We have reason to believe this gentleman may have actually developed a strain of cannabis that holds the cure for, at least, certain types of cancer."

Mackenzie still could not believe what she was hearing. "What makes you believe his findings are genuine?"

Aiken nodded toward the file in front of her. "Read that when you can. In the meantime, you'll have to trust us on this matter."

Mackenzie nodded, knowing she had been put in her place. "I assume you have spoken with…Samuel VanDerhout and offered to purchase his research?" She flipped open the folio on the table.

Aiken and Mallory shared a glance. "Unfortunately, VanDerhout is a bit of a character. He turned us down flat," Mallory said. "We have brought you here to talk about another approach to this situation. Richard?"

"We would like to transfer you, temporarily, to one of our subsidiaries in Seattle. We want you to gain an appreciation of the situation vis-à-vis Samuel VanDerhout, and the research he conducted. We need to know what was *not* in the academic paper he published. In a nutshell, Fields Pharmaceuticals needs you to obtain VanDerhout's knowledge and cooperation if possible, before he is able to provide that information to others, or worse, produce legal marijuana possessing these properties himself." Aiken paused for effect. "We need you, Mackenzie, to use whatever means at your disposal to get this information and hopefully secure a sample of this particular cannabis."

Mackenzie sat in stunned silence for a moment. While she understood the urgency of the situation, she was unclear as to how they expected her to accomplish this mission.

Mallory spoke softly: "Mackenzie, we are not asking you to do anything you find morally reprehensible here. We simply want you to carry out your job from Washington State for a time, and while you are there, find Samuel VanDerhout and…well, befriend him as best you can. Gain his trust. Try and convince him to cooperate with us."

Aiken added, "Actually, it is necessary to keep Fields' name out of this entirely, at least for the time being. Because you have been working on a top-secret program, your name is not easily identified with Fields. You may wish to rely upon the fact your next workplace is only a loose subsidiary and bears no reference to us. We'll issue you a new cell phone with a Washington number, for contacting VanDerhout. There will be no way for him to trace you to Fields."

Mackenzie nodded. Her head was spinning but she felt relatively calm.

"We also need for you to gain intelligence on Washington's progress with their marijuana implementation, since it does affect our business model. We will need regular reports." Both men waited patiently for Mackenzie to respond.

She stood, picking up the dossier Richard had given her. "Are you telling me to do this, or asking me?" She fixed her beautiful eyes on Aiken.

"We are asking, Mackenzie. Go read the dossier I gave you. I would like you to keep in mind, however, the fact our time is running out, as you well know. We are scheduled for trials in six months. If we are not ready, the FDA will make us wait another year, or more. With all that is taking place with cannabis legalization, our opportunity to solidify this market is on razor's edge."

Mackenzie shook hands with both men. "Let me take this back to my office. I'll contact you…as soon as I make my decision."

She walked the long hall to the elevator bank. Before pushing the button she turned back toward Mallory's office. Tapping at the door she said, "Yes. I'll do it."

Mallory stood, his face breaking into a broad smile.

"Stop and speak with my secretary. She will get you set up with everything you need for your temporary stay in Washington."

As soon as Mackenzie left the room again, Aiken shut the door.

"So, you think she can do it?" Mallory gazed at Aiken with uncertainty.

"I believe she can. Or at least I hope she can. Besides," he smiled humorlessly, "I'm taking the liberty of queuing up the third tier of our endeavor, just to be sure."

6

"The winter months in the Pacific Northwest are fit for neither man nor beast," Marty announced, after flicking the kill switch on the bright orange and white chainsaw, resting it on a section of windfall fir as the saw ticked itself cool.

"That's true." Sam gauged their progress as he surveyed the other downed trees and branches on his island. "Seems like our winters are pretty hard on the forest, as well."

"Yes, even trees face their hardships and risks, I suppose."

"I know I say this all the time, Marty, but I really appreciate your help."

During Sam's abbreviated stint with the State, Marty had maintained the island for his friend. Storms had blown down trees all over the Puget Sound region, from the state capitol of Olympia in the south to Orcas Island in the north, bringing snow all the way to sea level a couple of times during the winter.

Nothing had been spared, not even Sam's little island. There were two substantial fir trees that had crashed to the island's forest floor, one nearly striking the house, as well as countless branches littering the normally well-maintained island.

"Always a pleasure to help a good friend. Besides, if we hadn't slashed out some of this debris, your island might be fodder for a lightning fire."

Gulping down several mouthfuls of water from a scratched green and white camping thermos, Sam and Marty rested quietly, steaming away body heat and exhaling visible breath into the crisp air.

"Marty, we've been friends for quite a long time now. You're one of the most skilled people I know. In fact, I think there's not much you don't know how to do."

Marty laughed. "Coming from a modern-day renaissance man such as yourself, that's saying a lot."

"Thanks Marty, but I mention this because, although we have done plenty of work together over the years and smoked our share of weed, I don't know what you do when you want to do nothing."

"Well, as you know I revel in my work, and I love the Pacific Northwest. I enjoy the history of this place. So when I need a break, I try to find somewhere historic or remote to visit. Preferably a old town that's real, and relatively untouched by time. Not one of those 'theme town' places with painted-on European-looking façades and drunken tourists in lederhosen dancing around town slapping their heels."

"Sounds like we share that same interest. Frankly, I could use a short road trip. How's about I do a little research and find someplace new and interesting, and let's go check it out? I'll roll a few, and we'll see what kind of trouble we can get ourselves into"

"Sounds great, my friend. When do you want to hit the back roads of the Northwest?"

"I'll do some research and let you know. Let's head back to the treehouse, and I'll whip us up some grub."

"Well, I promised Vickie Jo a quiet evening at home playing Yahtzee. I'd better skip your offer of a fine meal and make haste in her direction. She doesn't like to be kept waiting—if you get my drift."

The two men gathered up the chainsaws, dropping them by the treehouse before heading down to the boat for the crossing back to Horsehead Cove.

"How are you and Vickie Jo doing, anyway?" Sam was at the tiller as he boated Marty back to Manchester. He knew Marty loved his girlfriend, and their often-stormy relationship made for entertaining stories.

"Well, Sam, love is a fickle mistress. As you know, Vickie Jo is a truly fine woman, by any measure."

Sam noted the use of the word "measure" with a degree of well-meaning amusement. Vickie Jo Mullen was a healthy, apple-cheeked woman of about 5'8", and roughly 210 pounds. Sam fancied she was the kind of woman who would be useful in a bar fight.

"I understand, Marty."

"I'm afraid my relationship with Vickie Jo might be in a period of hiatus." Marty sighed and grew thoughtful. "The vessel of our bliss has hit the doldrums of late."

Sam knew Marty and Vickie Jo frequently hit rough patches in their relationship, but they always seemed to work things out within a week or two.

"What happened, if I may ask?"

"Well, the other evening Vickie Jo wanted to clean her hunting rifle, and I was more inclined toward a round of horseshoes. Before I knew it, words were exchanged, and she put her firearm cleaning kit back in her overnight bag—which, I might add, also contained certain womanly garments. She left without a word." He looked at Sam with a frown. "I will never understand the female mind."

"I suppose, Marty. But you two seem to have lots of common interests, and you seem to mesh really well. She's amazingly capable." Sam was firmly on Team Vickie Jo and wanted the couple to remain together; she had drilled a new well for him and was generally handy to have around.

"True. The woman is certainly not without her charms. I'll vouch for that." Marty smiled affectionately.

"Have you two ever discussed moving in together, or getting married?"

"We have broached the subject of matrimony a time or two, yes. However, my chosen profession is indifferent to the demands of married life. The duties of the Park Ranger relent for no one." Marty sighed again.

"I see your point. Kind of a situation of not wanting to mess up a good thing."

"I suppose that's not far off the mark. While married life does seem to have much to recommend it, both Vickie Jo and I have a bit of the lone wolf spirit. We need our time alone, which also makes our time together that much more beneficial, if you get my read." He winked at Sam. "And the makeup sex, my friend, is amazing."

Marty jumped out of the boat when they reached the shore. "Better not keep her waiting."

Sam made the solo trip back to his island, enjoying the wind and the sharp smell of seawater. As he pulled his boat onto shore, he winced, noting the telltale stiffness in his body, largely a result of too much sitting in the last four months. Raising his strong arms above his head, he allowed the satisfying stretch to make its way down through his well-defined shoulders, into his upper back, and down his spine. He crouched, placed his hands flat on the sand, and performed a downward dog, cat's pose, and a few other yoga positions for several minutes. Noting how good the stretching made him feel, his mind turned to taking a quick row around his island.

Pushing the boat back into the water, he put the oarlocks in place and began rowing. He enjoyed not only the workout this gave his back and arms, but also the perspective of seeing his island from the water.

Sam suddenly realized he was halfway around the island, and the outgoing tidal flow was bringing his progress to a crawl. Now that his muscles were warmed up, and with the outgoing tide pressing against the small aluminum boat, he began pulling hard, leaning forward as he raised and pushed the oars, and then stroking back with all the force his fit body could give, leaning back as he pulled through, and raising the oars once again out of the water to push them forward quickly for another stroke, then another, and another.

After a time, Sam approached the south end of his island. As the tide pushed him close to the barnacle and rock-covered shore, he crabbed the bow of the boat into the flow, giving the impression the craft was sliding sideways against the strong current. He sweated and breathed hard now, but his body needed and wanted a good workout, so he didn't mind. Crabbing the boat several more strokes, he felt the tide beginning to work in his favor, pushing him back north, up-shore toward where he had started. He paused, allowing the boat to coast with the outgoing tide for a moment. After a few more oar strokes to allow his muscles to cool down gradually, Sam began navigating the boat to shore. As he pointed the nose of his boat toward the beach, he noted a lone fishing boat anchored near the southern, shallow part of his island. *Those two men in the boat must be from out of town*, he figured. That was not a good place to catch fish.

7

Mackenzie Blake had been unpacking all day. She had been given one week to hand off her projects and make her temporary move to Washington. She plopped down, exhausted, on the couch in the furnished apartment Fields had rented for her.

Mackenzie thought about the task that lay ahead. She picked up the dossier from the floor. She had studied this file until she knew it by heart, focusing on the fact this VanDerhout guy had walked away from a brilliant career and a future that would have brought him money, accolades, and perhaps the opportunity to "make lives better," as they were always saying at Fields. She had no respect for anyone who threw away their capabilities and talents, especially to do nothing better than get stoned all the time.

Photographs of VanDerhout in the Fields dossier showed him with a group of young, tough-looking men in a variety of adventurous locations: exploring a jungle, hiking a glacier, or climbing in the mountains. He looked like the kind of guys she knew from her home in Maine: strong, rough fishermen, *Gloucestermen types*. She shuddered at the thought and picked up her map of the Puget Sound.

"Why does this idiot have to live on some isolated, godforsaken island?" As the daughter of a fisherman, Mackenzie had been brought up to respect the sea and had spent a good deal of time researching marine maps since her arrival in Seattle. She had even called her father in Maine to get his take on boating on the Puget Sound, since this seemed her only access to Sam's island.

Mackenzie moved about the apartment, restless and feeling very much on her own with regard to this mission; her mind traveled to her project, TH-18, and the success that seemed to constantly elude her grasp. She gritted her teeth, feeling her frustration rise as it had done every day for the last six or seven months. It was like having a key that almost fit a lock— *almost* being completely useless in such a case. It was imperative Mackenzie find out if VanDerhout held the solution for the last molecules they needed to unlock the potential of this new drug, and make it the cancer cure of the century.

Having planned her assault on Sam's island for the following day, Mackenzie had called ahead to rent a small boat from across the channel and had set her time of arrival and departure per the tide tables. She knew she would need to rely heavily on her ability to engender a relationship with this man. As much as she had rehearsed her story, she knew this assignment would entail a great deal of improvisation, something with which she had little experience. Mackenzie was comfortable with her well-planned and heavily charted life. She did not like surprises.

Exhausted, she crawled into the large, unfamiliar bed and drifted off into an uneasy sleep.

Morning arrived, gray and drizzling rain. Mackenzie hurriedly showered and pulled on a pair of flattering jeans and a form-fitting sweater, trying to compose her roiling thoughts and prepare for what lay ahead. She paused in front of the mirror, shaking her dark waves of hair and letting them fall to her shoulders. Grabbing her coat and a small daypack, she drove quickly through the relatively light traffic to West Seattle, where she boarded a ferry for the town of Southworth.

Sitting in the warmth of her rental car, Mackenzie went through her plan again. She had decided to avoid calling ahead to introduce herself; VanDerhout might demur from meeting up with some woman he didn't know. Going straight to his island was the only way she could be assured he would actually see her, and give her a chance to initiate some sort of relationship with him.

Shit. I hope he's there when I arrive. Mackenzie sighed; it would be anticlimactic if she got to his island and found him out for the day.

The ferry eventually shuddered its way to Southworth. After a time, the huge steel vessel became silent, then vibrated and bounced gently into the dock.

Entering her destination into the car's GPS, Mackenzie made her way to the boat rental shop next to a marina near Manchester State Park. She was led to a small, sturdy aluminum boat, much like the kind she had grown up using in the waters off the coast of Maine. The outboard engine easily roared to life and she followed the shoreline north, eventually turning right across the inlet toward a tiny island.

The morning was waning late when she beached her boat onto a relatively sandy piece of shoreline. She grabbed her pack and started up the hill toward the center of the island, following a well-worn path she discovered leading through the overgrown forest.

Emerging into a clearing, Mackenzie saw what appeared to be a treehouse in the distance. As she neared, she shook her head in disbelief. "He lives in a tree?" She stopped for a moment to snap a few photos of the house and its surroundings.

As she took in the scene, Mackenzie thought she smelled food cooking. Noticing the steps leading up to a bridge that crossed a huge hemlock branch, she called out to herald her arrival.

"Samuel VanDerhout! Are you there?" Mackenzie's voice broke the profound silence, echoing off the surrounding trees.

Steeling herself, she ascended the rough, solid stairs to the door of the treehouse, her heart beating faster with each step.

As Mackenzie peered through the glass in the door, she saw a fit, broad-shouldered man, about six feet tall with wavy, mid-length dark blonde hair, plating what looked like breakfast.

"Good morning." She smiled. "Sorry to interrupt your meal."

The man—she presumed it was VanDerhout—turned to face her with a quizzical expression. She felt his eyes travel over her swiftly.

He opened the door and stretched a hand toward Mackenzie, his bright blue eyes settling on her face. "I'm Sam. Would you care to join me?"

Mackenzie offered her hand in return and he swept it up, holding it for a moment as he studied her in a friendly manner.

"I'm Mackenzie. Mackenzie Blake. And no thank you; actually, I've already eaten—although I have to say, that smells fantastic. But I would love a cup of coffee."

Releasing her hand with apparent reluctance, Sam pulled a chair from beneath a small table, gesturing her into it. Mackenzie sat down, watching Sam intently as he poured her coffee. She hadn't anticipated the possibility that VanDerhout might be this attractive. Cleaned up, he would be considered unusually handsome, even by Southern California's standards. She hoped it didn't complicate her assignment.

Sam's mouth edged up in a half smile as he sat across the table from Mackenzie. "So who, may I ask, *are* you?"

"Well, actually, I'm here on a kind of mission." She launched into her well-rehearsed story. "I saw an article about you in the *Tribune* a few months ago." She laughed. "I guess I'm curious about the guy who could grow that much high-quality marijuana in such a small area."

"Not my finest hour." Sam took a bite of his toast. "I prefer to avoid the subject."

"I apologize for bringing up what might be a sore subject for you, but it does relate to the reason I'm here." She lifted her eyes to Sam's face imploringly. "What I wanted to ask is if you could spare some time to let me hang out with you and perhaps give me a chance to get some hands-on cannabis growing experience?"

Sam knitted his brow. "Is this for you, personally? Or is this something else?"

"No. This is strictly a personal thing. I work in a lab all day." She sighed. "In all honesty, I'm desperate to find a way to change my life. With Washington heading in the direction it is, I guess I would love to somehow get in line for a grower's license or something. Getting some training and experience from you would do a lot for my chances." She prayed he would buy her story, but she could see from his expression that he was hesitant.

"I guess I just wanted to find the best teacher I could and kind of throw myself upon his mercy." She gave a short laugh and stood, turning to grab her pack. "I thought I would at least give it a try."

Sam seemed to visibly relax. "I'll tell you what, Mackenzie. I won't say I'm going to become your pot guru, but let's make a plan to meet again and discuss this further after I have a chance to think about it."

Sam got up to clear the table, giving Mackenzie another moment to study him. She noted that despite his overgrown, unruly hair, worn Levis and flannel shirt, Sam had an ineffable quality branding him as coming from a privileged background. He possessed an air of confidence and unselfconscious comfort in his own skin that Mackenzie had witnessed in some of her Ivy-League friends coming from generations of wealth. No wonder he had not been easily persuaded by money.

His sensual-looking mouth curled up into a smile. "I hate to sound like I'm trying to get rid of you, but you're going to have to leave in the next hour or wait until this evening."

"The tide!" Mackenzie exclaimed. She quickly pulled out her smartphone to check the table. "You're right. I'm losing the last slack tide of the day."

Sam stood. "Would you like a tour of the place before you go?"

Sam let his beautiful visitor take the lead up the driftwood staircase toward the second floor of the treehouse. He could not resist admiring her shapely behind as they ascended.

He was not inexperienced when it came to women, but this dark beauty, appearing out of nowhere at his door, had thrown him. Finding himself intrigued by her, some instinct told Sam she was hiding something. The mystery, however, merely deepened a profound attraction he felt the moment he laid eyes on her.

"This is my living room." He watched as Mackenzie surveyed the bright room, with its comfortable chairs and overflowing bookshelves.

"It's amazing, Sam." She reached out a slender hand to caress the spines as she glided across the room to a sophisticated-looking compound telescope positioned in one of the windows.

"Here, want to take a look?" Mackenzie stepped aside as he focused the scope. "It's my substitute for TV." He grinned, watching her closely as she leaned forward and peered through the telescope.

"Hah! I see a family of sea lions on your shore!" Mackenzie looked up at Sam with sparkling eyes. "Oh! They have a baby!"

"They hang out here quite often. The pup is new, I just noticed her for the first time a couple days ago." He tried not to stare as Mackenzie bent over the scope in obvious delight.

Shaking himself mentally, Sam led her to the third floor, his bedroom. "Sorry, I'm not one to jump out of bed and immediately re-make it in the morning." He was surprised when Mackenzie sat down on his bed. To him, it seemed an intimate gesture that both excited him and made him vaguely uncomfortable. Once again, he dismissed the feeling.

"We had better get you heading home. The tides wait for no one."

As Sam helped Mackenzie into her small boat, he assured her that he would call in the coming week with his decision.

Watching her small vessel disappear across the channel, he was left with a feeling of sailing into uncharted waters should he agree to work with her.

But somehow, he knew that course had already been set.

8

The small town of Lester is like a lot of Northwest logging towns: small, quaint, and when the economy is skidding on hard times, slightly depressing.

People all know one another, and the gas prices posted at the local station are actually twenty cents higher than what the locals really pay. Who knows what else works that way here.

As small towns go, Lester is neat, clean, and the lawns are generally cared for. Only the occasional house has a refrigerator on the porch, a rusted-out car in the yard, or occupants missing front teeth.

Having benefitted from the building boom in the 1980s and '90s, the Lester townspeople were now feeling the impact of the slowing economy as the demand for lumber tapered off.

As Greg Gunderson awoke on this February day, he could tell from the cold and muffled sounds coming from outside that it had snowed overnight. He rolled out of bed carefully, trying not to wake his wife, Becky, sliding his feet into his fluffy wool-lined slippers and pulling back the drapes covering the bedroom window.

Greg wiped the condensation off the glass with the edge of his hand and smiled at the heavily frosted morning outside. He and Becky shared a love of cold days inside their cozy, small home. He shuffled happily toward the kitchen to start coffee.

Greg pulled on a pair of Levis, his thick wool shirt, and the new boots he kept nice for the days he wasn't working up on the mountain setting choker cables on huge logs.

The coffee still brewing, Greg carefully poured off a cup into his *Loggers do it in the woods* mug, pulled on his blue goose down parka, and quietly went out the front door to enjoy the first rays of sun that had just begun to light the crests of the Olympic Mountains surrounding Lester on three sides.

Greg set the mug on the front porch rail and started walking toward the small convenience store near the center of town as he marveled at the shiny, jagged peaks above, still covered with a coat of white snow. He surveyed the town with a delighted smile. Greg considered Lester a picturesque little town on any day, but on a bright, late winter morning, it had the magical air of Disneyland or perhaps one of those perfect train set towns at a county fair. The rooftops were frosted white; the yards and streets sparkled with the early sun. As he walked, Greg listened to the squeaky sound of his new boots as the cold, pleasant sting of chilled air filled his lungs.

Greg entered the small convenience store; the quiescent silence was interrupted by the brash sound of a Korean radio station, played at full capacity by the storeowner, Mike Tran. Greg had often considered suggesting that Mike lower the volume, until he noticed the large, inexpensive hearing aids behind the old man's ears and understood.

"Good morning, Greg. Nice day!" Mike bellowed out in the cheery, alert voice of someone used to getting up before the roosters.

"Beautiful day, Mike!" Greg replied loudly, trying to make himself heard.

"You're lucky the paper guy made it up this morning, there's lots of black ice on the road coming up the valley into Lester!"

It pleased Greg that the logging operations were suspended, giving him the day off. He didn't have to wrangle his truck up to the logging site and risk sliding off the road into one of many steep valleys in the Olympic Mountains.

"Yes, I can certainly imagine it's pretty tough driving out there today." Greg picked up a copy of the *Seattle Times*, and a pint of cream for Becky's coffee.

After paying for the items, Greg wished Mike a good day and emerged from the din of the store into the muffled morning silence of Lester's frozen streets. He stood for a moment on the plank-covered sidewalk, considering going back the short route he had come. Instead, he decided to take the slower route past the edge of town, which would allow a bit longer to enjoy the sun breaking out over the mountains.

Pausing to gaze toward the now clear blue sky, Greg wondered if the sense of serenity and peace he felt was something like what a bear or a deer might feel in the forest. No work to worry about, no money problems; just eating, sleeping, and mating…well, and that survival thing. If, by some miracle, he didn't have to work, would he feel that same sense of freedom? Greg thought he'd certainly like to find out the answer to that question for himself, and for Becky.

Greg walked by the town library, located in the same small building as the Sheriff's Office and City Hall. Using the word "City" to describe Lester always struck him as somewhat optimistic for a town of about 1,200 people, nestled into a sparsely inhabited region.

As early as it was, Greg was not surprised to see the OPEN sign in the window of Lester's only florist shop. Leila and Lena Thorvaldsen had not closed their doors during working hours, 7 a.m. to 5 p.m., in all of forty years as far as he knew. On a whim, Greg stepped inside the warm, fragrant store, stopping to look at the explosion of colorful bouquets just inside the threshold. The gentle ring of the door chimes brought both sisters out from the back of the shop, smiling and gliding toward him.

"Good morning, ladies." Greg had the inclination to tip his hat or bow when he met up with the Thorvaldsen sisters. Both sisters, as usual, were dressed impeccably, with flowing scarves and brightly colored sweaters. At seventy-three years of age, the twin sisters retained their glow of Scandinavian beauty and were immensely proud of their figures.

"What can we do for you this lovely morning, Mr. Gunderson?" Leila held a bouquet of perfect pink roses that were an exact match to both her lipstick and the impossibly high-heeled shoes on her feet.

Greg couldn't resist a quick tease, "Leila, do you just walk around with those roses all day because they match your shoes?"

Leila raised her skirt and stuck her still shapely leg out for Greg to inspect the shade of her high heels. "Only if you want me to, Greg," she teased back.

In spite of being considered the cultural leaders amongst the ladies of Lester, the Thorvaldsen twins had obtained notoriety for favoring plunging necklines and short skirts. Most of the married women in Lester kept a "trust, but verify" attitude toward the twins when it came to their husbands.

Greg took a deep breath of the air in the shop, scented with flowers and rich earth. "I can't believe how you two keep growing all this year round. How do you manage it?"

"Magic." Leila said, smiling. "That and a good greenhouse with hydroponics."

"Hydro…what?"

"Hydroponics, Mr. Gunderson." Lena was busy arranging a colorful bouquet. She looked up at Greg and cocked her head slightly. "It's a fairly involved explanation. I'd be happy to give you a personal tour through our greenhouse sometime." She winked at Greg as her sister laughed.

"I'm sure you'd make it a *very* personal tour if you could." Leila's eyes twinkled as she goaded her sister affectionately.

"Well, at least *I'd* know what to do with him once I had him in there." Lena shot back to her sister, grinning.

"Implying that I wouldn't? I think I could give Mr. Gunderson a very enlightening outing in our greenhouse." Both sisters broke out in peals of laughter. Lena finished arranging the bouquet and held it out for Greg's inspection.

"I'll take it." Greg was glad to have an excuse to leave before these earthy septuagenarians notched up their sexual innuendo any further. "Becky will be thrilled."

Heading out the door of the shop, Greg now held the bouquet of bright summer flowers, wrapped and insulated for the cold.

Reaching the edge of town, he stopped to brush the frost off a bench in the town's small park and sat down, glancing at *The Seattle Times* now sitting in his lap. The headline of the paper exclaimed, "*An Early Spring Expected.*" An early spring meant a longer season for the logging operations still remaining in the region. Greg sighed, wondering how his body would hold up for another season of back-breaking, dangerous work.

Greg knew he needed to get back home since Becky would be awake soon, and he liked to give her coffee in bed. As he finished a quick scan of the headlines, he noted a story toward the bottom of the front page: "*State Exploring Way Forward for New Pot Law.*" He read the article with great interest: "*The State of Washington, following the passing of the Legal Marijuana initiative last November, is exploring options for the production, distribution, and sale of marijuana within the State. Unnamed sources in the State Capitol of Olympia are quoted as saying news regarding the specifics of implementing the voter's wishes will be decided in the coming few months. Ken Silver, the State's newly-appointed 'Marijuana Czar' has reportedly been working on defining a framework for making such decisions, but could not be reached for comment.*"

Realizing he was starting to get cold, Greg headed toward home. As he rounded a corner by the park, he noted the medium-sized warehouse that the local mill had used for general storage, before it went out of business. Now, all the logs coming off the hills outside Lester were immediately trucked off to the big mills closer to the shipping ports in Seattle or Portland. Greg had seen the warehouse, now boarded up and surrounded by a temporary chain-link fence, a thousand times but he had never considered the possibility of putting it to another use. The article he had just read in the *Seattle Times* made him look at the mill in a new way.

What was now an eyesore could be a business opportunity.

9

Sam awoke to the sound of his iPhone blaring the song, "Come as You Are." He rolled over, picked up the device and snoozed the alarm for ten minutes before lobbing it onto the old, overstuffed chair occupying a far corner of the room. Cozy mornings in bed were one of his delights in life; alarms, on the other hand, were definitely not on the short list of things he enjoyed.

As he tried to relax in bed for a few more pleasant minutes, his mind eagerly went to the day ahead. Last night he had done some research and happened upon a webpage from the University of Washington Suzallo Library archives showing pictures of a logging town called Lester located in a particularity beautiful setting, between the ocean to the west and the rugged Olympic Mountain range. The old photos of Lester were dated from 1895 to 1925 and showed old steam engines carrying improbably huge sections of old-growth trees to a river on their journey to a sawmill.

The men in the photos, frozen in time and standing next to the trains, and the trees cut into massive sections, seemed right out of his own heritage. The thought of visiting Lester immediately hooked him.

Sam sprang from bed and threw on a bright blue sweatshirt, khaki pants, and a pair of light hiking shoes. Grabbing his iPhone from the chair, he scampered downstairs two levels to the kitchen. He consumed a quick bowl of granola and milk while perusing a Benjamin Disraeli biography. Noting his iPhone showed 7 a.m., he stopped to roll a finger-sized joint and slid it into his pocket. He grabbed his daypack and added some trail mix, a couple apples, and a jacket for later.

After making the crossing to Horsehead Cove and parking his boat in its usual hiding place, Sam ran up the steep trail to the State Park lot, where he knew the always punctual Marty would be patiently awaiting his nearly always tardy arrival.

"Where's the fire?" Sam heard Marty's voice as he crested the steep trail at a run.

"Oh, shit! You startled me, Marty."

"Sorry, Sam. My stealth training at the State Park Academy tends to illicit that reaction in people."

"No worries. I'm just a bit out of shape; my heart's beating a little harder than usual."

The two men boarded the trusty Volvo. Sam rolled down his window and backed up the car as he enjoyed the cool morning' air filling his lungs.

"I think we'll both like Lester, Marty. It seems like the quintessential small Northwest logging town."

"I took the liberty of studying a map of Lester." Marty struggled to unfold an unruly map. "While there is only one main route into town evident on publicly available maps, we in The Service have access to certain cartographical information not available to John Q Public. I think I can accomplish rapid exit, should matters make that necessary."

Sam turned to look out the window to his left, feigning interest in something along the road, as he concealed his smile. This, Sam thought, was exactly why he liked Marty so much: there was nothing vanilla about the guy. Marty didn't know what the words *average* or *boring* meant; the guy only knew how to go full throttle at anything. In fact, if Marty ever ran into a brick wall, he was sure the wall would lose, and there would be a Marty-shaped hole in the bricks.

Sam pulled one of the substantial joints from his daypack and handed it to Marty. "Will you do the honors?"

"It would be my pleasure."

Marty extracted a shiny refillable lighter from one of the countless hand-made leather pouches and sheaths filling his belt, and lit the joint. Sam thought of asking Marty what all the belt pouches contained, but stopped short, knowing they'd be to Lester and back again before the detailed description of each was complete.

"Marty, why aren't you a cop or something?"

Marty thumped his chest with both hands. "I guess I just love the great outdoors too much. Plus, I really don't like most people. I think cops work with people all the time." He smiled proudly. "I would make a hell of a detective, though."

Marty cleared his throat. "You know, my friend, I'm not one to pry, but Vickie and I were talking about you last night. We both feel you should start thinking about finding the right woman for yourself."

"I'd not be truthful if I said I haven't been thinking along those lines as well, Marty." Sam had been unable to get the beautiful Mackenzie Blake out of his mind since her visit.

"Certainly, many women have attempted to breach the walls of fortress Sam, but to no avail. What happened to that heiress, or whatever, that made the beach assault with her seventy-five-foot twin-diesel Chris Craft, running it ashore right below your house so she would be forced to stay the night?"

"Wow. Yes, well, she was really a good person. Underneath the crazy."

"I would agree with the latter part of that assessment, my friend. That woman wore a thick layer of crazy, to be sure. Well what about that frumpy intellectual type, the one who ran the software company? While she seemed unfamiliar with the purpose of a comb, she appeared at least within earshot of your league in terms of savvy."

"Yep. A good mind, and a good soul, but not the type for me, I think."

"How about that gorgeous French gal? She was certainly easy on the eyes, spoke sexy French, and looked like she knew how to butter a croissant."

"Oh yeah. I forgot about her. Yes, very pretty, but didn't have much to say. I always felt I needed to keep her entertained, and my French wasn't that great."

"And then, of course, there was Marit…"

Sam sighed. "Yep. Marit. She'll always be the one that got away."

"Well, if I know you—" Marty suddenly punched Sam on the shoulder, causing the Volvo to lurch for a moment, "—when the right gal walks confidently into your life, you'll know she's the one. You're the kind of guy that will know her the second you see her, Sam."

"I hope so, Marty. As you know, I'm not what you'd call a vain guy. But I noticed my first gray hair recently. I'm not getting any younger." Sam glanced at himself in the rearview mirror, rubbing his chin and frowning slightly at his reflection.

"Take heart, my friend, the woman of your wishes and dreams is not far."

"I hope so. I love the solitude of my island, and I enjoy my research. But it would be nice to have someone special around to share it with." He couldn't shake the powerful sensation Mackenzie had evoked in him. He felt inexorably propelled toward her both sexually and intellectually in a way he didn't quite understand. Yet for some baffling reason he had not yet called her with his decision to take her on as a pupil. Sam rarely questioned his instincts, yet something was holding him back.

The two men settled into a companionable silence as they traveled south, taking the cutoff toward the coast and heading due west through the increasingly rural country of Washington's southwest interior. When they reached the city of Aberdeen, Sam pointed to the sign welcoming visitors. *Aberdeen: Come as you are.*

"Hey! I woke up to that song this morning." Sam looked thoughtful as they passed into the blue-collar, economically depressed city, the struggling downtown area speckled with faded signage and the occasional fast-food restaurant.

"This must have been a difficult town for an artist like Kurt Cobain to grow up in." Sam shook his head. "But I suppose art has to grow where it's planted."

"An artist can find beauty anywhere," Marty said, peering out the window at row upon row of ramshackle, military-looking housing.

Eventually they passed beyond Aberdeen and the neighboring town of Hoquiam and turned onto Highway 101, which led north toward the Olympic National Forest. The scenery grew dense with trees and the road steepened as they headed toward rainforest country and mountains. It was a rugged, sparsely inhabited region, pocketed with lakes and small logging outposts.

Sam's face suddenly brightened, "Hey Marty, look, that's the sign for the turnoff to Lester."

He let off the accelerator, allowing the Volvo's inertia to carry it toward the green sign marking the turnoff. Clicking the turn signal wand down he carefully executed the left turn onto the road, which immediately started winding its way up, seemingly on its way into the sky.

As they drove higher into the craggy, geologically new mountains, Sam marveled at the height of the distant, glacier-laden spires. There were frozen patches along the road where the late winter sun had yet to strive for the mid-day angle it needed to melt the snow into the thirsty roots of the giant trees that seemed to be everywhere. This was his world, and he had the rare capacity to be present with it, wholeheartedly.

Sam rolled down his window and stuck his head out. "I love this!" he yelled to the wind, grinning widely, his hair blowing around his face.

Marty suggested they pull off at the next opportunity and roll a few before they reached Lester. "Some of these little towns are like 'Pot Grand Central' but you never know if you're going to hit a zone with confused law enforcement. And I'm traveling incognito today so my official status won't help us if we get in trouble."

Sam laughed as he glanced over at Marty. "Incognito? As far as I can tell, you're wearing your usual ranger getup."

Marty patted the left front of his shirt. "No nametag. Hey, there's a good spot to pull off." Marty pointed toward a dirt road coming up on their right.

Seeing no traffic after checking ahead, and then in his rearview mirror, Sam guided the heavy Volvo off the pavement and onto the beginning of an old logging road. Satisfied they were safe from observation Sam kept the car running, pulled a mason jar full of his own-grown from his small daypack and rolled three rather generous joints.

Sam stuck one between his lips, and put the other two into his daypack. He lit the joint in his mouth, took a drag and handed it to Marty.

Marty suddenly froze. "There's a truck approaching from up the hill. Sit tight," Marty's voice had lowered to a whisper. "It'll seem too obvious if we move off suddenly."

As the pick-up truck approached, Sam could see it was an older, two-tone, green and white Ford F-150. "That's a nice truck." Sam cleared the smoke from his lungs out the open window. "*Real* nice truck."

The vehicle slowed and pulled alongside the Volvo. Sam hurriedly stuffed the Mason jar and rolling papers into his daypack and handed it to Marty, who shoved the pack under his feet.

"Hey strangers! Is that weed I smell?" The voice coming from the truck sounded vaguely muffled, and the driver himself was slightly shaded from view.

Marty leaned across Sam. "Unless you have legal jurisdiction here, we have the right to not incriminate ourselves."

Sam grimaced. "Pot? No pot here." As many times as he had been spotted with weed, he was always caught off guard; he could never lie with any grace.

The F-150 driver looked sternly at Sam and then suddenly broke into a wide smile. "Shit! That's too bad, I could use some weed right about now. I just got off work up the hill!"

The guy appeared to be in his late forties, with salt-and-pepper hair and a lean, intelligent face. He seemed friendly enough, but Sam's stint in jail had made him vow to be cagier when it came to pot—especially while people's attitudes caught up with legalization—so he smiled back. "Just taking a rest from a long drive. We're headed to Lester to check out the town." Marty continued to lean over Sam, glaring distrustfully at the man in the truck.

"Cool; well, have a nice day." The man gave a "thumbs up" and accelerated the old, but as Sam noticed, smoothly running truck toward the paved road.

Marty looked ruefully at Sam. "I think that guy asked too many questions; and me without my nametag and badge. I could have taught him a little something about respecting other people's privacy."

Sam laughed. "I think he might have been kidding us, actually." The two travelers waited a few minutes, backed the car onto the main road, and drove the last few miles into Lester.

10

As Sam pulled into Lester, he was delighted to see that the town looked, for the most part, like a time capsule. The buildings, the hardware store, the drugstore, the old school building, the library—almost everything looked to be late nineteenth century construction. Sam reached the center of the small town and spotted the tavern he had seen on his laptop the previous evening.

Pulling up to the front of the vintage 1910 structure, Sam was amazed. "This tavern looks almost *exactly* like it did in the old photographs!"

They sat for a moment in quiet satisfaction before Marty noted the green and white F-150 pickup parked beside them.

"You shouldn't have told him where we were going, Sam. He might be springing a trap." Marty looked suspicious as they exited the car.

Sam grinned and shook his head, gesturing for Marty to follow him across the ancient-looking wood plank sidewalk. They entered the tavern through a squeaky wooden door, the top of which slightly clipped and rang a small metal bell as the door opened, and again when it closed. Inside the Lester Tavern, he stopped to breathe in the wonderful scent that was a combination of old wood and beer all vintage taverns seemed to possess. He had often wished he could bottle that smell. Sam surveyed the interior of what looked to be an original structure, and marveled at the large beams spanning the entire width of the tavern.

"These beams have been holding up the roof of this structure for probably over a century," he said in awe.

Marty gazed warily about the bar. "We shouldn't stand here gawking. Good way to get our ass handed to us by some loggers."

The two approached the bar and sat down reverently on bar stools covered in ripped black vinyl.

"What can I get you?" asked Mary Malone, the pretty, middle-aged woman behind the bar. She looked directly at Sam, openly scanning his casual attire and his chin-length, wavy hair with the quick and practiced eye of a bartender. As she met his friendly gaze, a smile of appreciation slowly spread over her face. The fact women usually liked him was not lost on Sam; he bore lifelong gratitude for this gift.

Lifting his head slightly for a better look at the symbols on the tops of the beer tap handles he grinned at the bartender. "Tree-Top IPA, please."

Mary shifted her gaze to the smaller, ginger-haired man dressed in khaki. "And you?"

"For me, hmm." Marty studied the bar menu with furious concentration. "I will have a Fuzzy Navel." He looked up. "Hopefully you have real peach schnapps here? I can't abide imitation flavoring."

"Certainly, sir. We may be a small town, but we know our liquor." Mary expertly tilted the beer glass to minimize foam as the generous beer mug filled, setting it down in front of Sam with a broad smile.

The man next to them at the bar suddenly inquired, "First time to Lester, then?"

Sam turned to regard the man seated next to him and recognized him from the Ford pickup on the logging road earlier.

"Yes. This is quite the beautiful town you all have here." Sam gestured toward the man with his beer mug and took a satisfying drink.

"I see the old photos all around the bar, but is there an archive of photos somewhere in the town, from the early days?" Sam pointed at a particularly interesting picture of a sawmill with a group of wizened men lined up in front of it.

The man next to him seemed to warm to the out-of-towner. "Sure, Molly keeps up the old photo archive over at the library. But there's a lot of them on the walls in here, and over at the hardware store across the street."

"Cool." Sam took a drink from the heavy glass beer mug. The two men sat in relative silence for several minutes, while Mary continued to wipe down the already dry and pristinely clean bar top.

"Why do all bartenders, the world over, wipe down their bars incessantly?" Marty mused, sipping his cocktail. "I mean, you can be in Minneapolis or Moscow, and you all do that." He smiled and winked. "You make one mean Fuzzy Navel, my good woman."

As Marty and the bartender made small talk, Sam found himself humming along and mumbling the words to Johnny Cash's "Folsom Prison Blues" playing quietly on the bar jukebox.

"So, you like Johnny Cash?"

"Yeah, I like Johnny. He's the real thing." Sam stopped humming and turned to face the man next to him.

"Greg's the name. Greg Gunderson." He extended a strong, rough hand to Sam.

Sam smiled. "Nice to meet you, Greg. I'm Sam." They shook hands, then sipped their beers in silence for a while, both tapping their toes on the bar stools as Johnny Cash regaled them from the jukebox.

When the song ended, Mary pulled a large three-ring binder from behind the bar. "Check this out," she said, tucking her silvery blonde hair behind her ears and placing the binder in front of Sam.

Sam held the thick binder, on the cover of which was written in faded black felt pen simply, "Lester: 1885-1935." Opening it reverently, Sam immediately saw it was full of what appeared to be the original photographs taken of the town, and its environs, during that period. As his mind tingled with delight, he noticed that under each photograph, typed long ago on an old mechanical typewriter, were brief descriptions of the content: the place where the photo was taken, the names of as many of the loggers and other workers as could be identified, and an approximate date. Sam mentally immersed himself into the old photos, regarding each carefully as he slowly paged through the book.

"Wow…man…wow…." he said quietly as Mary and Greg looked on in appreciation of his obvious interest in their little town. "This is fucking amazing…" He glanced up quickly at the bartender. "Oh, sorry for my language. I get a little lost in my thoughts sometimes."

"No fucking problem," she said, laughing.

Sam continued examining the old photos, carefully reading the typewritten captions below each.

Greg reached across Sam, pointing at one of the photos. "That's my great-grandfather, Stein Gunderson."

"Wow. I can see genetics at work here." Sam studied the old picture of the middle-aged man in the photo, noticing a strong resemblance to Greg. As he continued thumbing through the binder, he came across one photo on which the typewritten caption said, *A rare photo of Samuel VanDerhout, logging pioneer, and logging claim owner—1915, Saunders Pass area.*

Sam paused in amazement. "That's my great-grandfather in this photo! Wow, look Marty, there are very few photos of Samuel. My dad always said his grandpa hated having his picture taken."

Greg looked stunned. At the same moment, the woman behind the bar stopped wiping the bar top and studied Sam with a surprised look.

"You're…a VanDerhout?"

"Yeah. But before seeing this picture, I didn't know my great-grandfather had a logging claim in this part of Washington. His claims were mostly in the Cascade Mountains across Puget Sound, not on the Olympic Peninsula." Sam looked at the pair from Lester. The thought flashed through his mind that most logging claim owners, back in the day, were about as popular with the loggers of the time as slave traders were with slaves.

But Sam knew the VanDerhouts were gifted with a charmed history. It was quite likely Samuel VanDerhout had made many more friends than enemies during his lifetime.

Greg said loudly, "I'll be goddamned."

The bartender picked up Sam's half empty beer mug, dumping it into the bar sink as she said, "Well, that first beer was free—and so is this one." She expertly filled another, this time in a pre-chilled and frosty beer mug, and placed it on the coaster in front of Sam. Wiping her hands briefly on her apron, she extended a strong brown hand to Sam, smiling as she said, "Mary's the name. Nice to make your acquaintance, Sam VanDerhout."

"Ahem." Marty looked a bit annoyed at being left out. "The name is Marty Stout." He shook hands with Greg as Mary slid another Fuzzy Navel in front of him.

Surprised and delighted by this turn of events, Sam said, "I can't believe you actually know about Samuel...that's totally mind-blowing."

"Your great-grandfather is a legend around here. Samuel actually helped Lester survive through the Great Depression by making sure the town always had work. To this day, nobody really knows how he did it, but when other places down around Portland and the like became ghost towns, Lester always had at least enough work to keep food on the table." Greg stared at Sam like he was some kind of apparition, or perhaps a reincarnated saint. "Man this is too cool, a real descendant of Samuel VanDerhout, sitting right here in the Lester tavern."

Sam looked thoughtful for a moment. "Hey, Greg, back on the logging road, you stopped and asked if that was weed you smelled, right? I mean that was you, and that's your F-150 pickup out front, right?" Greg nodded as Sam continued: "Well, that *was* my weed you smelled. Do you partake?"

"Does the Pope shit in the woods?" Greg replied without hesitation.

"Cool. I got a couple rolls." Sam patted his daypack, "Let's go outside and spark up!" Marty immediately rose from his barstool.

"Hey, Mary, mind if we spark one up in the Tavern?" Greg looked at Mary nonchalantly.

"Hell no, I don't mind," Mary replied. "But you know the Bar Rules. You gotta share any weed with the bartender, and if you burn the place down, you have to rebuild it."

Sam reached into his tee-shirt pocket and produced a thick joint.

"Wow," Greg said, "you certainly know how to roll one."

Sam retrieved a lighter and lit the joint, taking a long pull, holding his breath while he passed it to Mary.

"Bar Rules." Sam exhaled. For several minutes, the joint was wordlessly passed around between the four of them.

Greg pushed back from the bar, "Wow, man. I mean… WOW!"

Mary added, "Got that one right, Greg."

Sam, sensing it was safe, said proudly, "My own-grown. It's my own recipe."

Greg's eyes grew bright. "Man, we need to talk, my new friend Sam VanDerhout." He looked questioningly at Marty.

"Whatever you want to talk about, you can say in front of Marty. He's cool." Sam nodded at his friend, who lifted his cocktail in agreement.

"Well, I've been kind of thinking about the new legalization thing, you know, how the State's going to sanction the sale of marijuana." Greg paused and shook his head. "This is so synchronistic, meeting you here, it just blows me away. Anyway, Lester has an old sawmill and warehouse here in town. Leftovers from the logging boom days. What I've been thinking is that we are a perfect place to grow legal weed." He looked sharply at Sam, likely trying to gauge his reaction. "We have the manpower. And boy, we desperately need a new industry in this area."

Sam looked thoughtful. "There's quite a bit to this, Greg. You need cash up front to buy the growing equipment, good seed stock, and quite a bit of experience to make something like that work."

Marty leaned forward. "Not to mention the sanction of the State. You wouldn't want to run afoul of the law."

Greg sighed. "I realize I know nothing about this kind of thing. But I do know a shit-load about making things work." He looked Sam straight in the eyes. "Maybe it's just desperation talking here, but I know we could make a go of this."

Sam thought hard and fast. "You know, Greg. It might not be such a crazy idea. Let me do some research for you first, then let's make some more time to talk. Soon."

Greg grinned from ear to ear. "Really? You would do that, Sam?"

"Sure. Why not? It doesn't take a genius to grow pot."

Marty snorted from beside him. "*Right.* Like you'd know, Sam."

Sam smiled then penned his cell number and a quick description of where he lived on a napkin, handing it to Greg.

"Guard that napkin with your life," Marty said, "Sam doesn't hand out his information to just anyone."

Greg laughed and carefully folded and slid the napkin into his wallet. "I'm not going to lose this, that's for certain."

Later, before they left Lester, Sam went out to his car, retrieved an almost full mason jar of his best pot-craft from his daypack, and walked back into the tavern. He handed it to Greg. "For you and Mary."

"We will be in touch, Sam VanDerhout," Greg said, as the four smiling people shook hands heartily, and Greg and Mary bade the two men safe travels.

"This could get interesting, Marty." Sam's mind raced as they headed back home.

11

Sam drove away from the little town of Lester, his face smooth and peaceful. He had experienced a connection with the town, the people, and the way Lester was tucked into the mountains, seemingly carved from the surrounding forest. His conversation with Greg about producing legal weed there had definitely piqued his interest.

As he drove down the narrow road out of the small valley in which Lester stood, he thought for a moment about taking a left and continuing to explore. He glanced at Marty, sleeping in the seat beside him, and decided to head back to the island. Sam missed his little sanctuary, and the unique way it could insulate him from the world. He took a right toward home and accelerated down the road, letting the Volvo build speed in the same way he lived his life: as it wanted to. Cruising along toward home, he appreciated the forest that seemed to be slowly reclaiming the road as the huge fir, cedar, and hemlock trunks abutted and wrinkled the pavement.

With Marty in and out of sleep along the way—mostly out—Sam enjoyed the quiet ride back. Less than a mile from the State Park entrance, he spotted a State Trooper car a hundred yards ahead, parked off the road on the opposite side. He eyed the speedometer and thumped it with his fist. Convinced his speed was within limits, he drove on.

Passing the supercharged police interceptor a few seconds later, he saw in his rearview mirror that the vehicle had negotiated a quick U-turn and had fallen in behind him, though without its light-bars flashing. He eyed it all the way as it followed the Volvo into the parking lot of Manchester State Park.

"Wake up, Sleeping Beauty." He shook Marty's arm. "We're home, and I think we have company."

Sam drove past a black town car with tinted windows, the only other vehicle in the usually empty lot. The patrol car stayed on his tail. When he pulled into his spot, the other car came to a stop behind the Volvo, and an obese, leather-clad officer stepped out.

"Shit!" Sam glanced at his pack, glad he had left the Mason jar containing his pot with Greg and Mary at the Lester Tavern. He shut off the ignition and rolled down his window, preparing his license for compulsory deployment to the officer.

Marty grabbed Sam's arm. "Let me do the talking. We peace officers speak the same language, regardless which branch of service."

Sam could hear the squeak and crunch of polished cowhide approaching his car. "Marty, it might be best if I speak first. After all, I am the driver." The officer stepped up to his window and stood there. Sam looked up meekly. "Is there a problem, officer?"

"No problem." The officer shifted mirrored sunglasses while examining Sam's license carefully. "That's to say, there's no problem as long as you peacefully step out of the car and come with us." He flicked Sam's license back into his lap. Sam noted a second officer emerging from the passenger side of the patrol car.

Marty shook his head. "What a day for me to be traveling incognito."

"Where are we going?" Sam asked.

The patrolman indicated the nearby town car. "Someone wants to talk to you."

"Uh, okay," Sam replied, wondering what this was about, but almost certain he didn't really want to know.

Motioning for Marty to stay put, he accompanied the officers to the town car. A black-clad chauffeur scrambled out of the driver's side, opened the rear door and stood at attention. The two beefy patrolmen motioned for Sam to get in, and then started back toward their vehicle. The chauffeur gently closed the door after him.

"Dr. VanDerhout, welcome." The voice belonged to an expensively suited, silver-haired man sitting in the backseat. Sam vaguely recognized the guy as being someone he had once seen in the newspaper.

The man extended a well-manicured hand. "I'm Ken Silver, the acting head of Washington's new Implementation of Legalized Cannabis Task Force. My apologies for the waylay, Sam—may I call you Sam?" Silver smiled, not waiting for Sam's response. "We have actually been trying to get a hold of you since you were released." He lifted his cellphone. "You apparently don't answer your phone or check your messages."

"I know. I don't care for phones very much." Sam looked chagrined for a moment. "Still, you could have contacted me while I was still in the lockup. You certainly knew how to get a hold of me then."

"Well, we couldn't very well talk about the subject I wish to discuss today while you were in custody. And I did actually try to get you released early, myself." Silver looked disgusted. "Unfortunately, the Feds were involved in your sentencing, since the pot you were accused of growing was on Federal land. They tend to be rather strict about such things." Silver shrugged. "This is all beside the point. So now you know, I'm Washington's new Marijuana Czar." Silver laughed, seemingly pleased with his self-described title.

Sam merely nodded and looked casually about the car, biding his time until he could get this well-scented man out of his face.

"You should be aware that, as Marijuana Czar, I have certain authority, certain *responsibility*, to implement the voters' wishes."

"Yes, but what—" Sam began, but Silver interrupted.

"Here's where *you* may fit into this picture."

Sam sighed and sat back in the seat, quietly resigned to listening to the whole sales pitch. Silver continued: "I have learned, through certain sources, that you have unique capabilities in the areas of engineering, tending, fertilizing, and harvesting marijuana—would that be an accurate statement?" Silver stopped and waited for Sam's response.

Sam felt some anxiety, having spent the last four months in jail for doing just what Silver was describing. "Do I need to call an attorney or something, because I think—"

"Oh, no. Certainly not, Sam, there's no call for concern here. That kind of thing is ancient history. In fact, I believe we are very much on the same team here."

"I'm having a little trouble with the 'same team' part of that statement, Ken."

Silver waved his hand dismissively. "That's all in the past, Sam. What I am talking about here is the *future*."

Sam sighed. "Okay, I'm listening."

"Let me put my cards on the table: your reputation as adjunct professor and as a geneticist, botanist, and marijuana grower could help Washington State secure a smooth and profitable transition into this new industry. The State is prepared to offer you a very generous stipend, with profit-sharing, should you decide to join us as a consultant in this new enterprise."

Sam couldn't help but laugh. "So let me get this straight. You're telling me the State of Washington wants me to help them get into the business of growing and selling pot?"

"Well, you, of all people, know this is a very intriguing—and profitable—business."

"Whoa man, I have never sold weed, ever." It was a point of pride for Sam, the fact he had never made a dime from his weed-craft.

"Not to worry. We're among friends here. The whole complexion of marijuana in Washington, and perhaps the entire United States, is changing now. The tide is turning here and I am asking you to be part of that sea change."

"Why would the State want to do this? They didn't actually make the alcohol they sold at the State liquor stores, right? No State-owned brewing facilities or distilleries? They just required hard liquor to be sold in their stores, and taxed the shit out of it. Why not just buy weed from Washington farmers and sell it through…I don't know, State-owned pot stores?" Sam couldn't believe he was actually saying the words *State-owned pot stores*, much less to a government official.

"You're not actually that far off track. It would be kind of the same thing," Silver continued, "except more vertically integrated. We, the State of Washington, would not only profit from collecting taxes on the sale of marijuana, but we'd receive all of the profits. We, the State, would control and run the entire process, the entire business…*cradle to grave*, so to speak."

"But the recently passed marijuana initiative was legalizing it for the benefit of the people, not for the State."

"Listen, Sam, this money is for schools, fire stations, parks, better roads, bridges that don't collapse—the list is endless." The czar looked slightly annoyed. "If that's not benefiting the people of our State, I don't know what is."

Sam leaned back and thought for a moment. "Why me, Ken?" he finally said. "Why do you need me in this thing?"

"Do I look like I know anything about growing pot?" Silver smiled as he gestured toward his expensive suit. "Can you imagine any elected official knowing anything, or at least *admitting* to knowing anything, about the marijuana business?" He laughed. "You are from one of the oldest and most prestigious families in Seattle. Hell, they named a street after your family. You have a PhD in botany. We need your experience, scientific gravitas and your boots-on-the-ground knowledge of the business, or we may not get this started."

Sam let this enlightenment soak in. He imagined sterile, State-run farms with disinterested, drug-tested State workers. He was fine with taxing it heavily. *Hell, I drive on roads and use the parks too.* He even felt okay with funneling it through State-owned stores. What he couldn't stomach, either as a botanist or a person, was industrial farming—shutting out people like Greg, and towns like Lester, from the opportunity to grow good, organic pot and keep their towns alive and thriving.

"I think I'll pass, Ken." Sam stretched his legs in front of him. "Believe me, though. The fact Washington State has the balls to legalize pot is not lost on me. I think it's a brave act of sanity."

Silver looked pensive for a moment. "Is it a matter of money, Sam?"

"Why is everything about money?" he snapped.

"Because if it's about money, we're prepared to be very generous."

"What this is about for me is great quality weed grown by actual people on farms, city co-ops and in small towns; allowing real people to make a living from this, feed their families and keep their way of life. What it's not about is pot churned out by some industrial machine getting kickbacks from pesticide and fertilizer companies."

"So that's it? That's the way it's going to be?" Silver glared at Sam, his brow furrowed.

"Well," Sam replied, "I do have a proposition for you to contemplate." He thought about his discussion with Greg at the tavern in Lester. "I would be willing to offer up a beta test of sorts."

Silver nodded slightly. "I'm listening."

His mind was spinning. "Okay. I propose you let me set up and run a limited marijuana grow. I will select the people, the place and the growing methods. We grow it, you buy it. Actually, I have a place in mind already."

"What about security, packaging, and delivery? We'll have strict rules that must be followed in those arenas, or the Feds will shut it down in a heartbeat."

"That stuff is up to you guys. Tell us what to do, we'll do it." Sam was already miles ahead of Silver, coalescing a plan in his head. Lester seemed the perfect place.

"Let me sit on this for a while, Sam. I frankly don't know at this point. I'll admit I'm disappointed in your reluctance to accept my initial offer. But we'll be in touch. As a matter of fact, I'll have my secretary give you a call and we can set up a meeting. You can bring me more information about this place you have in mind."

Sam shook Silver's hand and made a quick exit out of the town car. As he neared the Volvo, he was amused to see Marty deep in conversation with both patrol officers. "If you don't keep your weapon completely clean, especially down here, around the firing pin, you're bound to jam—probably just when you need it most." Marty handed the gun back to the leather-clad patrolman. "Call me when you want to hit the range, Lonnie."

As the patrol vehicle pulled away, following the town car out of the lot, Marty asked about Sam's impromptu meeting.

"Do you believe in synchronicity, Marty?"

"Depends. If you mean in the Jungian sense, probably not."

As they gathered their things from the car, Sam tried to make sense of what had taken place. On one hand, he would love to see Greg and the town of Lester have a chance at growing weed for the State. On the other hand, he knew from experience that setting up an operation like this would be fraught with problems, perhaps even danger. In any case, he now knew he was meant to play a part in it.

Marty stretched and yawned loudly. "Well my good man, it's been quite the day." He slapped Sam on the back. "I'm off to my man cave. I don't know about you, but I could use a night on the couch."

Sam headed down the trail to his little aluminum boat, tucked under the branches of the cedar tree. He gave the Mercury a quick pull, and it came to life. Soon he found himself nosing it into the sandy area near his house.

He grabbed his pack and made the short walk up the narrow trail to the top of the hat-shaped island—to his treehouse. Once inside, he sat for several minutes in silence, contemplating how his normally sedate, isolated, academic life was now being dramatically affected by something as simple and logical as legalizing marijuana. His mind, fond of using analog to bridge the gap between the learner's mind and understanding, employed his recent ferry ride as the bridge.

It struck Sam that significant shifts in people's thinking were much like that massive ferry: not easy to turn in a new direction, but once the change has begun, nearly impossible to stop.

Sam had worked toward transforming attitudes about cannabis, and this change in the cultural trajectory had finally begun. He just wanted to ensure it reached the right ferry dock.

And avoid being crushed by it as it did so.

12

Mackenzie Blake had been waiting anxiously for Sam to call her with his decision to take her on as an apprentice grower. Unaccustomed to being ignored by men, Mackenzie was also growing angry at his apparent disregard.

Sam VanDerhout perplexed her. Mackenzie had found her visit with him a maddening experience. Men usually jumped when she even hinted at any interest; Sam had all but hustled her out the door.

"Who does he think he is?"

Cell phone in hand, she had made the practical decision to call him. Though an affront to her pride, she knew it was necessary. It was unfamiliar territory, once again.

"Hi Sam, this is Mackenzie Blake, you know, the uninvited guest from last week?" She kept her voice sunny.

"Mackenzie, yeah, I've been thinking about you. Sorry I haven't got back. I didn't forget. I just needed the time to think about what you proposed."

"I hope I didn't jump the gun, calling you like this." Mackenzie mentally kicked herself for her impatience. She quickly injected a casual note as to the outcome of his decision. "I guess I'm just curious to know if I should start looking elsewhere for my pot guru. It's perfectly okay for you to turn me down, Sam. I wouldn't blame you in the least, me being a stranger and all."

"No, actually, I think it will be fine. Yes, let's go ahead and try this out."

She pumped a fist. "Really, Sam? Thank you. You don't know what this means to me." She managed to infuse her response with genuine emotion.

Sam was not certain as to why he had finally decided on seeing Mackenzie again and agreeing to her request. The sound of her voice when she thanked him, though, was enough of an answer, as it spread a warm sensation through his body.

"How soon can we begin?" Mackenzie asked.

Sam surprised himself when he answered, "How about this afternoon? I have a meeting with a couple folks in Olympia. You might find it interesting."

"Really? That would be amazing. Where can I meet you?"

Sam experienced immediate remorse for having involved a complete stranger in his meeting with Greg Gunderson from Lester and Ken Silver, Washington's Marijuana Czar. They were going to discuss details with regard to a pot growing operation, the beta test Sam had suggested to Silver. In spite of his misgivings, Sam had always trusted his instincts. This invitation to Mackenzie Blake had come from that instinctual place all VanDerhouts had always trusted.

"Can you meet me at noon at Manchester State Park? We can drive together from there, if you'd like."

The meeting arranged, Sam hung up and pushed the doubts from his mind. He had made the decision, now he would see where it led.

He continued working on his plan for Lester, researching equipment and supplies, coming up with a quick monetary estimate. He knew money would be tight on this project and what they lacked in equipment would have to be compensated by creativity and sheer manpower. Virtually the whole town would be needed as volunteer labor. He sighed and closed his laptop, putting it into his daypack.

After showering he dressed in a pair of brown canvas pants and a white tee shirt sporting an oversized pot leaf with the admonition, *Don't tread on me.* He buttoned on a bright blue denim shirt, grabbed his pack and headed to the boat.

As he emerged from the trail and into the parking lot, Sam saw Mackenzie already waiting for him. Retrieving things from the trunk of her car, she turned in his direction at the sound of his footsteps. Her hair was pulled back in a twist, and dark spiral curls escaped in the wind. Sam's heart gave an odd leap in his chest when he looked at her.

Mackenzie approached him, extending her hand. "Thank you so much, Sam. You can't know how much this means to me." She shook his hand and gazed up at him.

She has green eyes, Sam noted.

"Glad I can help, Mackenzie—would it bother you if I called you Mac, by any chance? If we're going to hang out together, I prefer a monosyllabic name." Sam smiled down at the beautiful face in front of him.

"Of course, Mac is fine. All my friends call me that." Mackenzie resisted the urge to cross her fingers behind her back. No one who knew her, apart from her father, dared called her Mac.

"Great, let's get going." Sam took her daypack and led her to the Volvo.

"Umm, are you sure we shouldn't take my car?"

"You need to have more faith in your guru, Mac." He patted the roof of the old vehicle affectionately. "I have rebuilt nearly every piece of this car." He twisted his face into a mock-serious expression. "It only breaks down once or twice a week. I think it will get us there."

Mackenzie felt disorientated as she sat in the low, torn seat of Sam's car. She glanced at his serene expression as he scrounged for his keys, which apparently lay hidden in some deep recess inside his pack. She nearly jumped out of her skin when a *bang!* erupted from the outside of the car, causing it to rock back and forth.

"Marty!" Sam, laughing, rolled his window down as a strange, elf-like man dressed in a ranger costume stuck his head into the car. "This is Mac. She's hanging out with me today." Sam leaned back in order to let Marty see her.

Marty nodded. "Yes, I saw you when you arrived. Since you didn't leave your car, I was not called upon to check for your parking pass. Otherwise, we would have already been introduced."

Sam looked at Mackenzie and explained, "He's the Park Ranger around here."

Marty stepped back from the Volvo, removing his hat and sweeping it regally in front of him. "Have a wonderful time, Sam and Mac."

Mackenzie began to doubt her ability to accomplish this mission. She had worked her whole life to escape the "characters" and "local color" of her youth in Maine. In contrast, Los Angeles seemed somehow clean to her; its denizens' aspirations were not complex. Money, fame, sex and power—these were the motivations to which she had become accustomed. She felt lost here in Washington State, and especially in the company of this odd man.

She glanced over at Sam as he coaxed the car to life and pulled onto the highway. At least he was easy on the eyes. She liked the look of his square jaw and the muscular forearms emerging from his sleeves.

"So Sam, can you tell me a little bit about this meeting? I'm unsure what to expect." She pulled her mind back to the task at hand.

"It's actually quite a historical meeting. We're proposing the first State sanctioned marijuana grow targeted for sale in U.S. history, here in Washington State. It should be interesting. Although I'm concerned about Lester, the little town where this grow will be located, having enough monetary resources to pull this off. The folks in Lester really need this to happen."

Mackenzie noted the earnest tone of Sam's voice. "So this town, Lester, they are proposing to be a site to grow marijuana for the State? Is that how this is going to work?"

"That's what I hope we can decide today. My fear is this whole legalization thing will end up being an excuse for agribusiness or something."

During the drive, Mackenzie asked Sam questions about himself. He talked a bit about his past, being kicked out of several private schools, eventually ending up teaching English in Asia. Sam had discovered his love for plants in the humid jungles of Taiwan. "I never looked back," he said with satisfaction. "I've had my hands in the earth ever since."

Sam glanced at Mackenzie. "So let's hear a little about you. Were you born here in the State?"

"Actually, no. I grew up in Maine. My father is…well, he's a fisherman." Mackenzie had never talked about her father with anyone in LA. She wasn't certain why she told Sam.

"Really? Does he have his own boat? What kind of boat does he fish from?"

"Actually, yes, he owns his boat. It's a 125-foot, twin diesel Trawler. They go out mainly for swordfish. Dad is skipper, and he has a crew of guys who work for him."

Sam proceeded to pepper her with questions about her years in Maine and seemed fascinated by her experiences on her father's fishing boat.

"You must really miss being there," he said.

"I do? I mean, of course I do. I mean you can't really have a career there, unless you want to be a deckhand, or maybe a bartender."

"Sounds like a fine way to live, to me."

"Well to you, maybe," Mackenzie said defensively, "but I need to be challenged, to have real, concrete goals in my life to—"

"Make people's lives better?" Sam interrupted.

Mackenzie physically jumped at this use of Fields' favorite motto. She glanced sharply at Sam. "Yeah, I definitely want to help make people's lives better, if I can."

"How does learning to be a pot grower fit with your need for *concrete goals?*"

"It's a very concrete goal. It's a great way to have a home-based business, work with my hands and make some good money. I like the idea of being liberated from my nine-to-five job."

"What do you do exactly?"

She had already considered how to describe her job. She needed the ability to ask Sam some fairly sophisticated questions about his cannabis, but not appear so knowledgeable that she raised a red flag. She settled on telling him she was a lab tech—a chemist who worked with a variety of projects on a consulting basis.

"Huh. So you're kind of a chemist for hire?"

"I guess that's a fair description. It's dry work, for the most part. I'm exhausted with it, you know?" It pleased her that Sam seemed to accept this without question. "I'm hoping my chemistry background will help when it comes to growing pot."

"Well, a little science goes a long way when it comes to growing anything, in my opinion."

"I would think knowing something about the science of plant genetics would be important."

"I guess I was talking more about actually putting weed under a microscope and chemically changing it. You know, change a few molecules and call it 'Kannibas' or something." He spelled the variation out for emphasis.

Mackenzie could not keep herself from saying, "But there are so many areas for developing cannabis and pushing its therapeutic boundaries…" She stopped herself, horrified she had been led down this path.

"Right. But being a botanist, I have another theory. Cannabis has evolved for perhaps hundreds of thousands of years. It was there when we began to develop as a species, growing up with humans, a common weed, heavily utilized for hemp, seed and for its ability to heal. The whole plant is ingrained in our bodies. Hell, we are filled with cannabinoid receptors. Our bodies are tuned to use the whole plant; picking it apart might not only be less useful to humans, it might even be *dangerous*."

Mackenzie felt herself flush with anger. "You can't tell me you haven't played with genetics, putting the puzzle pieces together differently to make better uses of cannabinoid properties." Mackenzie had him there; she had read his research and knew he wasn't just a Rasta nature boy, but an active scientist himself. Perhaps he had genius, but apparently he had no desire to put it into practical use.

Sam appeared surprised. "Sounds like you may know something about my…former life as an academic." He paused and peered directly into Mackenzie's eyes. "Look, I'm basically a gardener. I do some grafting, try out different fertilizer formulae, and observe what happens. Sure, I may study plant genetics from time to time, but only to gauge the processes I accomplish in a very ordinary manner. I'm no mad plant scientist. I'm just a farmer with some book learning."

Mackenzie took a deep breath and exhaled. She had almost blown the whole deal right then and there. She composed herself and offered him a bright smile. "That is why I am so glad to be your acolyte in all this."

Sam pointed to the off-ramp just ahead. Mackenzie could see the state capitol building to her right, on its regal perch high above the city.

"I've always thought Olympia is beautiful," he said as they headed into a nondescript parking lot. He turned off the ignition. "Ready to go make history?"

13

S am and Mackenzie arrived at Ken Silver's Olympia office at the same time Greg Gunderson pulled up in his green and white pickup. Greg, dressed in his best Sunday suit, looked pale and very nervous.

"Sam! I'm so glad you got here at the same time. I have to admit, I'm scared shitless." He laughed and shook Sam's hand vigorously.

Mackenzie emerged from the car. Greg's eyes widened for a moment as he looked at her.

"This is my friend, Mackenzie Blake. She's going to be helping us on this project. Mac, this is Greg."

"Nice to meet you, Greg."

"And you."

"Let's get this show on the road." Sam motioned for them to follow him inside.

They entered the cold, bureaucratic-looking facility and Sam approached the reception desk sitting in the middle of the cavernous lobby. A woman quickly escorted them to a conference room, where Ken Silver sat at the head of a long table.

"Sam! I am so glad you agreed to this meeting on such short notice." Silver shook Sam's hand and motioned him into a nearby chair then looked at Greg. "And you must be our Lester representative, Mr. Gunderson?" Greg nodded and shook hands with the well-suited man.

"And who, may I ask, are you?" Silver eyed Mackenzie with obvious appreciation.

"I'm Sam's friend, Mackenzie Blake." She lowered herself into a chair. "I'm just here to listen and learn." She smiled brightly at Silver.

"Okay. As Sam knows, I'm Ken Silver." He took his place again at the head of the conference table and ceremoniously flipped open the binder in front of him as he continued to stare at Mackenzie. Turning toward Greg he said, "Just for the record, Mr. Gunderson, please state your full name and your interest in this meeting."

"My name is Greg Gunderson. I represent the town of Lester, Washington, and have been approved to speak on its behalf."

Silver seemed to let that information soak in for a moment. "As good fortune would have it, I am authorized to represent the interests of the people of the State of Washington, so I will proceed, if I may. As is the case with something new, a test is often the most prudent way to begin, before full implementation. I have been authorized to conduct just such a test."

"Is this about the beta test I proposed when last we spoke?" Sam tried to conceal a smile.

"Well, generally speaking—yes," Silver quickly retorted, "but there are certain Federal versus State law issues yet to be fully vetted, with regard to this particular initiative. In the interim, while those matters are being saucered and blown by the legal community, the State of Washington would like to propose the following to you, Sam, and to those you designate to take part in this test.

"The State will approve you, and a location you select, for this test," he continued. "You will be the sole and exclusive licensees for a period of up to one year, wherein you will either succeed in proof of concept with regard to the private cultivation, harvesting, and distribution of marijuana in our State...or you will fail."

Mackenzie gazed intensely at Silver. "So, what if this test fails?" She glanced at Sam; his eyebrows rose and she quickly smiled and shrugged. "It's a fair question."

"It is a good question; I don't know for certain." Silver looked serious. "If we fail, there exists a good chance the Feds will shut us down completely."

"What exactly constitutes *failure*?" Greg asked. "I mean, how will you be able to measure success or failure?"

Silver cleared his throat. "All of the details have yet to be worked out, but for starters, any transportation of anything exceeding one ounce of product from this test must be put in a special container, provided by Washington State for such transportation, and must be sealed with a State-provided and applied device ensuring the container has not been compromised during transport. Ultimately, though, if your marijuana should end up anywhere it is not supposed to be, we will have failed."

Sam seemed to consider all of this for a moment. "What about any startup money from the State for Lester to get going on this? I have a rough estimate as to how much they'll need to set up the grow."

"We're not exactly in a position to do a lot in that regard, Sam. We're laying off firemen and police officers as we speak." He glanced apologetically at Greg. "The best we can offer is a 50–50 funding match."

Sam nodded. "We can figure something out."

Silver began handing out documents to Sam and Greg. "I am due to get back to my superiors by 5 p.m. this afternoon with everything signed and sealed."

Greg looked at Sam for direction as Silver handed him a pen.

"Greg, I'm afraid we're just going to have to forge ahead on this if we're going to do it at all," Sam said, then looked at Silver. "I'm assuming you're winging all this just like we are, right?"

Silver nodded. "When one attempts something without precedent, 'winging it' is about all you can do."

Minutes later, Sam, Greg and Mackenzie emerged from the government office building. Greg held a binder of documents under his arm and looked like he needed a stiff drink.

"Don't worry too much." Sam put a hand on Greg's shoulder. "Honestly, I know it feels overwhelming, but I have your back on this."

"I can't thank you enough, Sam." Greg climbed into his truck, looking exhausted by the ordeal. "I'll be planning our town meeting in the next few days to discuss this with everyone. I'd really appreciate it if you were there. You too, Mac, if you'd like."

Sam and Mackenzie watched Greg's truck as it left the parking lot. "Well, Miss Blake. Pretty interesting stuff for your first day of training." Sam grinned and opened the car door for her.

Mackenzie shook her head in disbelief; she couldn't quite believe how much raw data she had been gifted with in one day. As Sam climbed into the driver's seat, she knew that she would be funneling all this information to Fields within hours.

"Thanks, Sam. Thanks for including me in this." She stared out the window for several miles, not feeling energetic enough to maintain her façade. She glanced at Sam. As he met her eyes for an instant, Mackenzie looked away.

"Are you interested in coming to the Lester town meeting when it happens? I'd be happy to pick you up in Seattle, and we could ferry back to the peninsula."

"That would be great, Sam. I would love that."

At this point, Mackenzie just wanted to get back to her apartment, call Richard Aiken with the information, and put all this out of her mind for the night.

When they arrived at Manchester, Sam helped Mackenzie out of the low-seated car. Standing, she lost her balance, and Sam's arm quickly wrapped around her for a moment, steadying her. It surprised her how solid he felt as she leaned into him for a split second.

Sam stepped back, grinning. "Good night, Mac. Drive safely."

Ears burning with embarrassment, Mackenzie pulled out of the parking lot. She'd have her status call to Aiken completed by the time she arrived back in Seattle.

14

"I hope you're bringing Mac, too. Wow, Sam, where did you meet such a beautiful woman?"

"She just showed up on my doorstep, Greg." Sam laughed. "Yeah, I definitely think she'll want to tag along and see the town."

Sam received a call from Greg the next day. A town meeting had been planned for the following Saturday night. Greg suggested Sam come to Lester on Saturday morning for a tour of the town.

Sam hung up the phone. He couldn't shake the feeling Mackenzie was holding something back from him, but by this time he thought about her constantly. Dialing her number, he found himself anxious to hear her voice again.

Mackenzie was running late. For the first time in many years, she had no tight schedule and was not completely focused on her work. Fields had temporarily pulled her access to the TH-18 project and she had no actual assignments at Allied Laboratories, the subsidiary where Fields had placed her while in Washington.

At first, Mackenzie felt as though she had been exiled into an unknown land with no map or compass. In an effort to quell her anxiety, she had shopped and walked all over downtown Seattle, finding a taste for leisure she had not known existed for her. She'd even begun sleeping in a bit longer every morning.

This newly discovered attitude had led to her waking up late on the morning Sam was coming to take her to Lester. She had just finished her shower when Sam called to inform her that he had arrived and was on the way up. She started to dress quickly, but instead decided to relax and meet him at the door in her robe. Moments later, she heard a knock. It annoyed her to feel a nervous jump in her stomach as she padded barefoot to open the door.

"Hey Sam." Mackenzie moved aside to allow him in. "Sorry I'm running late. It's not something I do very often." She suddenly felt shy, standing in her short robe, hair damp and curling around her face.

Sam eyed her up and down. "You look great. Just throw on some jeans and a sweater and we can make the ferry." Sam wore a pair of Levi 501s and a blue and green plaid flannel shirt. Mackenzie noted grudgingly that he looked good, in spite of his apparent disregard for fashion.

She hurriedly dressed in a pair of corduroy pants and a white silk shirt. Pulling on a thick, oatmeal colored sweater and a pair of boots, she re-checked her overnight bag, making certain she had packed everything for the evening, and emerged from her bedroom. "Ready to go, boss."

"You might want to bring a windbreaker. It can get breezy on the ferry."

"It's okay, I run hot." She smiled as they headed out the door.

Half an hour later, Mackenzie stood on the deck of the ferry, shivering and wishing she had brought a coat. Sam excused himself for a moment and returned with a thick jacket. He wrapped it around her and stepped back. "You should wear polar gear more often, it really suits you."

He then stood in front of her, blocking the wind that was picking up speed as the ferry made its way across the Sound toward the town of Bremerton. "You're going to get cold yourself." Mackenzie huddled by Sam, appreciating his efforts to shield her.

"I love the Puget Sound." Sam leaned into the spiraling air and salty mist thrown upward from the emerald green water as the fast-moving vessel powered through a light headwind, his hair whipping loosely around his face. He looked over his shoulder at Mackenzie. "Sorry, you look miserable. Let's go back in."

Making their way into the seating area of the ferry, they sat facing each other on the hard orange benches.

"Greg wanted us to have lunch in Lester, but I think we may need sustenance before then. Can I grab you something from the food concession? The breakfast burrito is actually pretty good."

"No thanks, I'm not much of a breakfast person." Mackenzie found herself growing warm and sleepy. Feeling the boat's gentle rock and comforting hum, she removed Sam's coat from her shoulders and tucked it under her head as she curled up, then drifted off.

As the call for passengers to return to their vehicles crackled over the ship's PA system, Sam gently woke Mackenzie, letting her sit up and mentally reboot for a moment.

"Wow, I really nodded off. Did you get something to eat?"

"No, I stayed here beside you. I enjoyed watching you sleep, actually."

They made their way back to the car and sat waiting for the telltale bump of arrival. Sam started the car and negotiated their way off the ferry.

"Bremerton's a bit rough around the edges." Sam guided the Volvo through the streets of the blue-collar Navy town.

"Hey, are those aircraft carriers over there?" Mackenzie pointed toward the enormous vessels packed together on the waterfront like massive steel sardines.

"Those are inactive ships kept here and maintained until it's decided what their fate will be. Those huge ones are aircraft carriers. The battleship *USS Missouri* was here for a few years; it was the ship on which Japan signed their surrender in WWII. I took a tour of it before it was towed to Hawaii for permanent display at Pearl."

"The 'Mighty Mo' was here?" Mackenzie smiled. "My dad's a naval history freak. He would love this place."

They drove in companionable silence. Mackenzie had decided the best way for her to build a relationship of trust with Sam was to match his relaxed rhythms and go with the flow. She had tried asking him direct questions about his growing techniques but he had been elusive on the subject, merely promising she would learn what she needed to know from her participation in the

Lester experiment. All in all, she felt optimistic about her progress with Sam, and it had proven amazingly easy to blend into his life. She stole a glance at him as they drove; she believed it was only a matter of time before he trusted her enough to talk about his research, and about the cannabis she had been sent to find.

Sam and Mackenzie pulled into Lester just after 1 p.m. and parked in front of the tavern. The trusty old squeaky door announced their arrival. Mary the bartender shouted, "Sam VanDerhout! How nice to see you back in Lester!" Her eyes shone as she looked at Sam.

Sam replied with equal enthusiasm as they approached the bar, "Mary! Nice to see you again as well. This is my friend, Mackenzie Blake."

Mackenzie shook Mary's outstretched hand as she slid onto the barstool.

"Greg's on his way," Mary said. "Sam, a Tree-Top IPA for you. Mackenzie, what can I get you?"

"I'm actually more of a wine person. Do you have any Chardonnay?"

Mary reached into a small refrigerator under the bar and produced bottles of nice premium Washington State wines, describing each at least as thoroughly as any well-versed sommelier.

"I'll take the Columbia Valley." Mackenzie gestured toward the bottle in Mary's right hand.

Mary placed coasters on the bar, giving Sam his brew dispensed from the tap into a frosted mug. She deftly opened the chardonnay with a Swiss Army knife and provided Mackenzie with a generous pour.

"I'm not one to parse words, Sam, but everyone in town wants to meet you. I can't tell you how excited Lester is to be getting this opportunity." Mary gazed at Sam like she wanted to jump over the bar and kiss him.

"Sam!" Greg erupted through the tavern door, a huge grin pasted across his face. With him was an attractive, middle-aged lady with tousled hair. He shook Sam's hand and hugged Mackenzie.

Greg placed him arm around the smiling woman at his side. "This is my wife, Becky."

Becky Gunderson hugged Sam and Mackenzie. "Sam, I feel like I already know you. Mackenzie, when Greg said you were pretty, he wasn't kidding."

Mackenzie found herself responding authentically to the cordiality exuding from these people. "Thank you for the compliment, I may have to move here soon." She laughed and glanced at Sam, who eyed her with an unreadable expression.

"Are you both ready for a spin through town?" Greg asked. "We're planning to feed you at the Bakery. It's not fancy, but the bread is great."

The Gundersons led Sam and Mackenzie down the street to a brightly painted storefront with a round, gold leaf sign that read, *Lester Bakery*. The windows revealed a warmly lit interior and glass cases brimming with golden pastries and a variety of breads.

"Here we are at the Lester Bakery. Small town or not, everyone loves fresh baked bread," Becky said, looking through the window. "The pastries here are to die for."

Sam and Mackenzie followed the Gundersons into the Bakery. The delicious smell of freshly baked bread, just discernable in the outside air, now hit them full-on with its irresistible warming scent. A handsome older man was pulling a flat wooden paddle covered with golden brown loaves out of the hot, wood-fired brick oven.

"Morning Jeffrey."

"Greg, a fine morning to you as well. I see you've brought some new customers to my humble establishment."

The baker stopped working, dusted off his flour-covered hands on his white apron, and shook everyone's hands.

"Nice to meet you, I'm Jeffrey Floyd." He stared at Sam. "You must be Samuel VanDerhout."

"My friends call me Sam. Nice to meet you, Jeffrey."

Mackenzie took in a deep breath. "This place smells fantastic."

"Would you all like a fresh slice of bread, hot from the oven, before I serve your lunch?"

Sam nodded. "Absolutely."

Jeffrey pulled a serrated knife from a block that had been set into the marble working surface and swiftly knifed off four slices of steaming bread. He quickly slathered on a generous coating of butter, which began melting into the small bubbles in the bread. Jeffrey watched in silence as they all sampled his work.

"This is wonderful," Mackenzie said, licking the butter off her thumb.

The two couples sat at one of the brightly covered tables as they were served steaming bowls of homemade soup and several plates of various pastries stuffed with meats, cheeses and vegetables. The food kept coming until Sam held up his hand in protest. "Jeffrey, I don't think we can handle any more. This was delicious."

Jeffrey carried out a French press full of coffee and a glass pitcher with fresh cream. He sat down beside Greg and poured them all tall, steaming cups.

"This is certainly a lovely town," Mackenzie told Jeffrey.

"We sure think so. My grandfather moved here in 1909 to work in the old mill, which was shut down some time ago. That's how I eventually ended up in the bakery business."

"Thank god you did," Becky said, wiping her lips with a napkin.

"We don't want to keep you, Jeffrey. I just wanted to make sure you had a chance to feed our new friends before the town meeting."

"It was my pleasure. Have a great time in Lester. I'll see you later at the meeting."

They exited the sweet smell of the bakery as Greg's nickel tour of Lester continued. He led them into a barbershop with an entry door built into the corner of a structure that also housed a small shop with an artistically painted sign, *Simon's Treasure Trove*, as well as another storefront touting, *Mystics, Monks and Magic: Palm Reading and Fortune Telling*.

"Sam, Mackenzie, this is Wallace Hammond, Lester's tonsorial technician."

"At last we meet. I've heard so much about you. Feels like I've known you for years. I think our mayor, Roxanne Martin, has called just about the entire town by now, letting everyone know you're here."

As greetings were exchanged, Sam gave a quick look around the shop. There were two barber chairs, but only one appeared to have been stocked with the requisite equipment. The other, while appearing equally worn, gave the impression it wasn't used for cutting hair, but rather served as a place for someone to sit and chew the fat while a friend, cousin, or child was getting their hair cut. The interior of the barbershop looked like it had been carefully frozen in time from the 1920s.

"I like your shop, Wallace. It looks like something from an old *Life* magazine."

Mackenzie added, "Yes, it's perfect."

"Well, thanks for the compliments. I'm a bit of a collector of barbershop memorabilia."

Greg glanced at his wristwatch. "We'd better be moving along. I'm sure everyone else in town has heard from Roxanne by now, so they'll all be awaiting our arrival."

Greg led them into the next shop, Simon's Treasure Trove. Entering the small, cozy establishment, Sam was somewhat surprised to see a large man of about 6'5" and at least 300 pounds standing behind the counter. The man appeared uncommonly blessed with size and strength.

The enormous man spoke in an almost delicate tone that seemed to be a voiceover from someone else. "Finally! What took you so long, Greg? I've been waiting patiently all morning for your arrival with our new friends. Oh, it's so nice to meet you both! I'm Simon, what a joy to have you in Lester. I trust your stay thus far has been enjoyable?"

"Yes, it's been wonderful," Mackenzie said as she shook his massive but gentle hand. "Your town and the people here are so pleasant and accommodating."

The shop was an explosion of antiques, memorabilia, and knick-knacks of every shape and color, all artfully arranged in an impossibly small space.

Sam immediately headed toward the part of the store with shelves of antique tools and bins of old hardware. "This is amazing, Simon. I'll definitely be back to spend some time here."

"Oh, you just have to meet Carmen, next door. She's the town mystic, and she's wonderful."

Taking Mackenzie's arm, Simon carefully led her to the shop next door, the others following.

"Carmen! I'd like you to meet Mackenzie. Isn't she adorable?" Simon said excitedly. "And Sam too."

"Nice to meet you both. I'm Carmen Alford. I'm sure you know by now Roxanne has let everyone know you're here. No crystal ball needed to figure that one out."

Simon laughed politely, adding, "Carmen is a wonderful fortune teller and palm reader. When my partner and I need some guidance, we always seek her help. She's never steered us wrong."

As Sam looked around the interesting shop, he said, "I wish I had known you a few weeks ago, Carmen. You could have saved me a trip to LA."

"I'd be happy to give you both a complimentary palm reading sometime. Just let me know."

Greg again moved them along. Outside, he said, "Kind of an interesting story about Simon. A few years ago, his partner Dennis's car broke down while visiting Seattle. Of course, Seattle is a progressive place for the most part, but there are thugs in every city. Dennis is a small guy and was being harassed by some idiots on the street. About that time, Simon showed up. The thugs all ran, except this one guy, who hadn't seen Simon coming up behind him. Simon lifted the guy by his armpits, completely off the ground, and gave him a stern talking-to until the cops arrived. Dennis snapped a couple pictures with his phone and the story was on the five o'clock news that night. Pretty hilarious pictures."

Sam laughed. "I'm surprised all crime didn't stop permanently after something like that. There are times when you could really use a guy like that on your side."

"One last stop before we head over to City Hall." Greg led the group around the block to the door of a small, white church with a classic steeple and bell. Stepping inside, they noticed the figure of a man just visible in the far right front row of pews, head bowed in in prayer.

"Excuse me, Father Donneghy," Greg said as the group quietly approached the pious-looking figure, who looked up.

"Ah. Yes, Greg. How are you today?"

Mackenzie noted that the pastor appeared to be in his late fifties, with gray hair tied back in a ponytail, a carefree face, and sparkling gray eyes.

"Fine, Father. I'm sorry to bother you in your time of prayer."

"Hah! No worries, there. I'm watching the Mariners play San Diego in a Cactus League game. Never too early for baseball season." Winking, he held up an iPad, which had been sitting in his lap.

"Ah. Carpe Baseball."

"Indeed."

"Father, allow me to introduce Mackenzie Blake and Sam VanDerhout. I'm sure you've heard about their visit today."

Standing, Father Donneghy turned toward the couple. "Nice to meet you, Sam and Mackenzie." He wore a black, short-sleeved shirt and white collar, with a pair of bright red suspenders. "Yes, I've heard all about your mission here in Lester."

Sam looked uncomfortable. "Father, I hope this isn't too much of a problem with the church here. I realize it would be a stretch to ask for your blessing in this…endeavor."

Father Donneghy held up his hand in a gesture of benediction, a wide grin breaking out on his face. "Although I can't speak for the Episcopal Church as a whole, you have my personal blessing." He looked around the small, clean interior of the church and sighed. "Quite honestly, when our parishioners fall on hard economic times, so does the church. I'm ready to bless anything within reason that helps Lester survive both materially and spiritually."

They left the church with Father Donneghy promising to attend the town meeting and give his support.

"I suppose it's time for us to think about heading over to City Hall. Sam, I'd like to go over what I'm going to say with you before I start." Greg looked stressed. "I'm not one to enjoy public speaking."

15

A few miles outside of Lester, on the shore of the largest and most impressive of the lakes dotting the region abutting the southern end of the Olympic rainforest, stands Lake Kiutan Lodge—"The Lodge", as it is known in Lester. Originally built in the late 1800s as a hotel for travelers making their way on horseback to the lake and surrounding rainforest, the original structure burned down in 1924. In 1926, a quorum of lumber tycoons with names like Mercer, Denny and VanDerhout, hired prominent Seattle architect Nick Bevanda to design a great lodge along the lines of Old Faithful Inn at Yellowstone Park. On August 18, 1926 Lake Kiutan Lodge was born.

For the townspeople of Lester, The Lodge was the place where all events of gravitas, celebration or import occurred. A few of Lester's more aged residents even remembered when Franklin D. Roosevelt visited The Lodge in 1937.

On this particular evening, the majority of Lester's adult citizens gathered in the grand lobby, with its huge river rock fireplace, and an air of nascent festivity spilled out into the cool darkness and surrounding forest.

Lester's mayor, Roxanne Martin, addressed the audience: "Welcome, everyone. If you all will take your seats, we can begin."

Now in her fifth term as mayor, Roxanne had presided over Lester so long she had begun to lose her enthusiasm for local government. This new turn of events had given her a fresh and animated interest in her mayoral duties and she positively beamed with excitement.

"Thanks all. Before we begin, please stand for the Pledge of Allegiance."

Papers rustled and chairs creaked as people stood and men removed their hats, placing them over their hearts.

The solemn ritual complete, Roxanne continued: "Thank you, please take your seats. As you all know, we have dedicated the entirety of this month's Town Meeting to the subject of leasing the old mill warehouse and accepting the State's offer to allow Lester to be the first town in the United States sanctioned to legally grow marijuana for sale in State dispensaries. Being the first in the country to do this, the eyes of the country, and in fact the world, will be upon us. Tonight we will begin with a briefing from our own Greg Gunderson."

Greg stood and replaced Roxanne in front of the fireplace. The townspeople gave Greg a hearty round of applause.

"Greetings folks. Please feel free to interrupt with questions as I go along. It's just too hard to hold all questions until the end." Greg cleared his throat and straightened the notes in his hand.

"As Roxanne just pointed out, you all know most of this proposal already. However, in the interest of making sure we're all level-set, here's a quick recap: Last November, Washington State passed an initiative to legalize the cultivation and sale of recreational marijuana within its borders. Since this has never been done before, by Washington State or any other state, the Governor and her newly appointed Marijuana Czar have agreed to license Lester as the sole location for a test grow, what they refer to as a beta test. This test will be conducted for a period of up to one year, but can be terminated anytime at the State's discretion, should the State see a need to do so."

Simon raised his hand. "Greg? I have a quick question about this test."

The huge man stood and straightened his tie before speaking. "What if we put all this time and money into this test, this beta test, and the State does shut us down. Do we lose all the time and money we put into it?"

"That's a very good question. The State has agreed that, should we proceed with this test under their oversight, they will provide fifty percent of the start-up funds. We will need to come up with the remaining half. If this test should be terminated, for any reason, we would lose the half we invested. However, we would not be required to repay the State's half."

"I see. Okay Greg, thank you."

Greg added, "We will have oversight by the State, but otherwise have complete control and responsibility for the production facility. Meaning we do all the work, or hire someone to do the work necessary to make this test a success."

Carmen Alford raised her hand. "I realize as the town's only psychic, I should already know the answer to this question." She smiled as several chuckles arose from crowd. "What kind of oversight will the State have in place? I mean, will they be all over us every time we go to the bathroom? Or will the oversight be less intrusive?"

"The exact nature of the State's oversight has yet to be determined. But in our discussions with Ken Silver, he has assured us the State will be as unobtrusive as possible. Ken has given us his assurance they want this test to be successful as much as we do. The State stands to generate windfall tax revenues from the sale of marijuana in Washington. It needs and wants this all to succeed just as much as we do, believe me."

"Has Ken given you any specifics on what the oversight might look like?"

"Yes. Ken thinks, at this point, there will only need to be one, or perhaps two State oversight employees from his office here, on sight at the pot plant, from time to time to oversee things. Also, to ensure the shipment of our marijuana doesn't breach state boundaries, his office is having special State of Washington shipment bags manufactured, to their specification and at their cost, to be used exclusively in any and all shipments made to the dispensaries across the State. The bags will have some sort of security lock system the State will also oversee."

Carmen thanked Greg and took her seat.

"Hey Greg." Mike Tran stood. "Why are those bags necessary?"

"Well, to answer that question, we almost need the framers of the United States Constitution here, from what I understand. But, with Thomas Jefferson otherwise indisposed, I'll do my best. Individual states have certain powers to decide for themselves how they conduct their business and what they want to do, generally, within state boundaries. However, the U.S. as a whole, at the Federal Government level, reserves the ability to override the states where there is a conflict, or where the good of the country as a whole is better served by overriding state's rights. I'm not an attorney—and seldom does a day go by that I'm not thankful for that fact—but that's the nutshell of the problem. We can decide the matter of legal marijuana for our State, but if the marijuana we produce should cross state boundaries into states that have not passed similar laws, it becomes a Federal Government matter, and the Feds then have jurisdiction. They could and likely would shut our State marijuana production down. So the need to control this entire process is critical to our success."

Greg paused, then went on: "The State wants this test to commence as soon as possible. There will, no doubt, be questions that arise as we move ahead with this process. As a result, Roxanne and I have discussed a motion to have herself, Leila and Lena Thorvaldsen, and me, form a temporary oversight body. This is simply to have someone to go to with questions as they arise, and to have someone to represent Lester to the State of Washington, if or when that becomes necessary."

Mike Tran raised his hand again. "What about Sam? Will he be part of this oversight body also?"

"Sam has generously agreed to be the technical advisor to help with the cultivation and harvesting process. He has also agreed to perform this duty for us at no cost, and has adamantly declined any profit sharing. He is doing this simply because he wants it to succeed."

The Lester townspeople broke into applause. As they all scanned the room for Sam, Greg spotted him standing against the back wall.

"Sam's back there. Another round of applause for our favorite genius!"

Sam looked visibly embarrassed as he waved off the applause. "Thanks, all. Back to business, please."

"Thank you, from us all, Sam."

Greg covered several other points, fielded a few more questions, and put the oversight body, funding proposals, and other matters to a vote. All passed unanimously, and Roxanne closed the Town Meeting with a happy, "Let's all go to the dining room for a celebration!"

Sam had lost sight of Mackenzie at some point before the meeting started. He gazed over the heads of people making their way into the huge dining room, trying to find her.

Greg and Becky approached Sam just before he entered the dining hall. "How'd I do, Sam?" His grin ran from ear to ear.

Becky hugged Sam. "You will never know what this has done for Greg," she whispered in his ear. Pulling back from Sam, Becky hastily retreated, wiping her eyes as she went. As Sam and Greg stood waiting for their drinks, Sam said, "Who are those two guys over near the door? I saw them during the meeting as well and was fairly certain I hadn't met them yet."

Greg turned just in time to see two men quickly exit the dining room. "I have no idea who they are, Sam. Maybe just visitors to the Lodge?"

"Yeah, that's probably it." Sam's brows were knit for just a moment. He felt he had seen the shorter, more muscular looking man before, but just couldn't quite remember where.

16

Mackenzie was happy to be staying the night at the lodge. She could not even imagine making the long trip back to Seattle, and the strain of playing a role was beginning to exhaust her. She had spent time visiting with various townspeople, enjoying the wine and conversation—the former rather more than she had expected.

Taking a break from the festivities, she had retreated to her room for a while to regroup and change her clothes for dinner. She smoothed the silky green of her dress; it had been too long since she'd dressed up for anything. She slipped on a pair of matching high heels and swept her thick hair into a French roll at the base of her neck.

Sam had displayed an unusual restraint with her so far. She had given him several opportunities to move their relationship into a more physical arena, something she thought necessary to building trust with him. She had to admit a growing curiosity about Sam as a man, which reached beyond her mission. She had never met anyone like him; his open and easy manner seemed to belie a deeply enigmatic nature—something she found strangely attractive. Mackenzie felt Sam was someone who kept much to himself, and she was bound and determined to break down his defenses.

She moved down the long hall from her room to the giant wooden staircase that took her into the dining area, aglow with lamps and sparkling chandeliers. Heading quickly to the turn-of-the-century bar sitting at the far side of the room, she leaned over the gleaming mahogany and ordered another white wine, catching sight of her flushed cheeks in the beveled mirror behind the bartender. She smoothed the loose tendrils of her hair into place and began scanning the room for Sam, finally locating him surrounded by a group of women. He saw her and immediately waved her over.

"Where've you been? I need a rescue," Sam whispered into Mackenzie's ear as she slipped her arm around his.

"Mackenzie?" A huge man in a pinstriped suit approached. "I love your dress! It looks like a vintage piece."

"Hi Simon, you look quite dapper yourself." Mackenzie smiled and spun around for him to see the whole dress.

"This is Dennis. Dennis, this is Mackenzie." She shook hands with the much smaller man standing next to Simon.

Mackenzie was amused to see she was not the only woman in the room who had dressed for the occasion. Sam introduced her to two older ladies dressed in flowing, low-cut gowns and dangerously spiked heels.

"Mac, this is Leila and Lena Thorvaldsen; they are amazing florists and will be my go-to girls for the whole project." Both ladies moved to Sam's side, effectively nudging out Mackenzie.

"We're looking forward to being Sam's right and left hands." Lena gave Sam a quick kiss on his cheek.

Mackenzie could see Sam was becoming increasingly uncomfortable with all this attention. "Ladies," she said with a conspiratorial smile, "I know you will understand if I ask for a bit of 'alone time' with Sam?"

The Thorvaldsen twins burst into laughter. "When you're done, let us know."

Mackenzie laughed as she steered Sam toward the door and led him out into the silent hallway. "Are you surviving, Sam?"

"God, I need a break." Sam looked her over and gave a low whistle. "You look beautiful."

"Thanks. I found a room you need to see; come on." Mackenzie grabbed his hand and pointed down the dimly lit hallway.

"Hmm, okay." Sam raised his eyebrows and allowed himself to be led down a flight of narrow stairs, stopping at a heavy wooden double door.

"Wait until you see this." Mackenzie's eyes were fixed on Sam's face as she swung open the doors.

"Wow! Mac, this is awesome!" A huge room filled with shelves of books and scattered plush chairs appeared as Mackenzie flicked on the chandelier.

Sam roamed to each shelf, pulling out books and blowing off dust, a look of delight on his face. He turned to Mackenzie, his eyes glowing. "How did you find this?"

"I read the hotel history, it's in every room." She felt uncommonly pleased by his reaction.

"Here's one." Sam flipped open a book titled, *A History of Healing Plants*. "Let's have a seat and I'll give you a tutorial."

Sam turned on the gas fireplace and the two sat side by side in a red velvet loveseat. Flipping to a chapter, "6000 Years of Cannabis," he began reading out loud while Mackenzie leaned into him, shoulder to shoulder.

"'Marijuana was first cultivated in approximately 4000 BCE in China, close to the Hindu Kush region and declared to be, "'The Supreme Elixir of Immortality'"'…" Sam stopped and looked at Mackenzie. "Sounds like somebody enjoyed being stoned."

He continued reading, his calm voice describing the ancient use of cannabis for food, fuel, medicine, and sacrament. Mackenzie was quite familiar with much of what Sam read, but it didn't matter. She found herself feeling warm and peaceful, her head eventually resting on Sam's shoulder. She was not accustomed to drinking more than one glass of wine and found herself drifting off to sleep…

Mackenzie awoke in her room at the lodge early the next morning.

She had a vague memory of Sam picking her up and carrying her to the room. Looking at herself, she wondered how she ended up fully clothed in her pajamas, with her green silk dress hung neatly over a chair, her shoes placed together near the bed.

She quickly showered and placed her things into her overnight case. Heading out into the hall she knocked briskly on Sam's door, but he did not answer. Mackenzie walked downstairs to the dining room and saw him eating breakfast with Greg and a number of Lester citizens, looking fresh and happy.

Mackenzie sported a pounding headache and was in no mood to put on her happy face. She stealthily poured a cup of coffee and sat alone in the lobby, going over the events of the previous evening. She had never known a man, aside from her own father, who behaved like Sam. Though certain he was physically attracted to her, he had carried her to bed, helped her change clothes, tucked her in and left. *He has way too much integrity to take advantage of a situation like that.* She felt vaguely ashamed by this thought.

"How are you this morning? You were out cold last night." Sam was suddenly standing over her, smiling benevolently.

"I'm good, Sam," she replied sheepishly. "I really appreciate you tucking me in."

Sam laughed. "It was a pleasure, I assure you. We should probably get going soon; I need to get back to my greenhouse."

Mackenzie perked up. "Are you working on anything special?" She figured Sam would answer ambiguously, as he always did when she tried to ask specific questions about his work.

He looked at her for a moment, then appeared to make a decision. "Yes, Mac. I'm actually preparing the seeds and cuttings for Lester. Would you like to come to the island and get some hands-on experience?"

Mackenzie scrambled out of her chair. "I'm ready to go anytime you are, Sam."

After making their goodbyes they took the inland drive back to Manchester. Mackenzie's spirits soared; this was the chance she had been looking for. She glanced at Sam as he drove, feeling a momentary prick of conscience. He was definitely growing on her. Even though pushing such thoughts from her mind grew increasingly difficult, she had five years of her life and a career riding on the success of TH-18. She could not afford to let anything stand in her way.

Arriving back at the State Park, Mackenzie told Sam she wanted to take a separate rental boat to the island, so she wouldn't have to impose on him for a return trip. After some arguing on his part, Sam relented and the two made their separate ways to the island.

When they had finished eating lunch, Sam finally led her to the greenhouse, Mackenzie could feel her heart beating as she took her first steps into Sam's organic sanctuary. It seemed ordinary enough to her on first inspection, with long trays of marijuana plants arranged in various, increasingly tall stages of growth. There were drip and mist watering systems, and piles of what seemed to be common gardening manure but smelled much different, somehow richer and very clean. There were also a few more mature plants toward the back of the greenhouse in larger pots.

They sat down at one of the well-lit metal tables and Sam pulled one of the plants in front of them.

"Okay, Mackenzie. Cannabis 101." Sam smiled and touched the leaves on the plant lovingly. "First thing to know is that cannabis is *dioecious*, meaning male and female flowers grow on separate plants. Only the female plant produces THC."

For the next three hours Sam went through some of the mechanics of growing pot with Mackenzie: his high-pressure sodium and metal halide lighting system ("it's the 'gold standard' for growing weed"), his recipe for fertilizer and the importance of root PH.

Mackenzie listened with fascination to the tutorial, impressed with his exhaustive knowledge. When he turned to the subject of creating feminized seeds, she found herself straining to note every word.

"I know this sounds strange, but what I do is create a 'mother plant' with genetic characteristics I find useful and force her to grow male pollen sacs." She noted that Sam sounded quite professorial as he spoke. "It involves isolating the female plant from male plants and allowing her to flower too long, forcing her to create her own means of self-pollination. Once she has produced her own pollen, I use it to fertilize other females and obtain seeds that are 99% female and contain the correct genetic features."

The afternoon passed quickly and Sam finished by showing Mackenzie his favorite "mother plants" from which he would derive the seeds for Lester.

"I've bred these plants specially; when grown with the right light and then forced into darkness for a time, they will have an incredibly fast and productive growing cycle. They're hearty plants and produce a beautiful, rich bud, with a variety of different qualities for each strain."

Mackenzie lifted her eyes to the far corner of the greenhouse, where she could see several plants partially hidden from view. "Are those more mother plants?"

Sam quickly replied, "Uh, I'm working on those at the moment. Just some…creative type research." He stood and stretched. "Let's go back in and have some dinner, what do you say?"

"Sounds good, Sam. I have to be back out on the water by 10 p.m. at the latest to catch a slack tide."

"You are more than welcome to stay, Mac. I have a comfortable couch. I'm not certain I like the idea of you boating in the dark." Sam held open the door to the greenhouse for her, closing it firmly—like his treehouse, it had no lock—and leading the way up the stairs to his house.

"I'm not afraid of boating at night." Mackenzie had formed a plan and needed the dark to cover her actions. "Besides, I'm going out of town on work for a couple weeks."

Sam looked surprised. "Where are you going?"

"I'm working a job in Nevada. Nothing earth shattering, just something to pay the bills." Mackenzie affected a casual note.

"Well, hurry back." Sam smiled. "You've got a lot more to learn."

They ate dinner together and Mackenzie helped Sam clean up. Completely focused on her mission now, she subtly avoided any physical contact with him and closed her mind to everything but her goal.

As she rose to leave, Sam offered to walk her down to her boat. "No, please don't bother. I like the solitude here; I enjoy a walk in the dark occasionally." She clicked on her flashlight. "It's a strong light. I'll be fine."

She stood at the door, looking at Sam as he moved toward her and enveloped her in a quick embrace. For a moment, she felt herself molding into him, her body finding his solid, warm and exciting. His face moved from her hair and his lips brushed hers ever so gently. "Goodnight, Mac. Call me from Nevada if you get a chance." He stepped back and opened the door.

Mackenzie entered the night, flashlight in hand, and quietly made her way back to Sam's greenhouse. She would not return to L.A. empty-handed.

17

After much negotiation with the bank, Greg was finally able to close the lease on the abandoned mill warehouse near the edge of town. Fortunately, he and a group of other Lester townspeople were able to get the cash together to secure a five-year lease—but only just. Greg knew, as he unlocked the padlocked and chained gate of the modest facility, they would have to make this work, otherwise there was no way to cover the lease after the first year.

He made his way across the overgrown grass- and weed-riddled gravel parking area to the entrance bearing a sign, *Eye Protection Required In This Area.* Unlocking the door, he pushed it open against the creak of the rusty hinges and entered the facility.

Inside, Greg was immediately struck by the musty smell and the dust, dirt, and debris left behind after the mill owners had beat a hasty retreat. Before closing the deal on the warehouse, he and Sam had made a quick walk-through of the property; they noted a number of large steel tables that would come in handy later in setting up the production process, as well as several bundles of plastic pipe, a stack of plywood and three old yellow Schwinn bicycles with front baskets.

Heading into the back area of the building, Greg passed through a pair of dirty canvas swinging doors with clear plastic windows in the upper half. Sam had mentioned the rooms seemed well suited for storing their harvested product for shipment later.

He knew that others from town would be there soon, so he made a quick assessment of the extent of cleanup needed. In the silence of the abandoned building he could hear the faint, but recognizable voices of several people coming through the walls and echoing slightly inside the thin metal-shelled building. Hurrying back to the entrance, Greg reached for the doorknob just as a group of about twenty Lester folks approached. As he opened the squeaky door, his mental state suddenly shifted from stressed and worried to relieved and confident; there stood his friends in work clothes, carrying brooms, shovels, garbage cans, and other tools for cleanup.

The mayor was dressed from head to toe in canvas Dickies work clothes. "Well, don't stand there with your mouth open, young man. Put us to work!" she exclaimed.

Greg hastily made assignments for sweeping, moving debris out back to the loading dock, window washing, and other tasks.

As mid-day approached, Greg stopped cleaning in one of the back rooms and walked around to gauge the progress. To his pleasant surprise, the floor of the entire facility had been swept and thoroughly mopped, the debris removed.

Standing in the middle of the facility, Greg powered out a shrill whistle. As everyone paused he yelled, "Lunch break. See y'all at the Tavern. Mary has sandwiches and pitchers set out for us."

The hungry group propped brooms and shovels against the walls and steel columns of the structure and hurried the few blocks to the Lester Tavern. Inside, Mary had set out generous plates of thick ham and turkey sandwiches with pitchers of cold beer on each table.

As they ate, Sam VanDerhout entered the Tavern and the din of conversation broke momentarily as Greg shouted over the heads of the others, "Sam! Great to see you. Sorry Mac couldn't make it."

Sam made his way through the maze of handshakes and back pounding to the table where Greg sat with Becky.

"Hey Greg! Yeah, Mac had to work. So how did things go over at the plant this morning?"

"I can't wait until you see what we've done with the inside of the Pot Plant, Sam. It's looking great. I think you'll be impressed." Greg appeared happy, basking in the glow of a successful morning of work, augmented by a few beers.

"I knew you folks would get the place whipped into shape quickly."

"Yep, we're on it. I wanted to ask you about the growing process, and how that might affect the way the place is laid out. I took some rough measurements of the facility. Would you mind us tossing around some ideas now?"

"No sweat. Got some paper?" Sam pulled up a chair and sat down.

Greg produced a legal pad and sketched a rough footprint of the facility. Sam studied the dimensions for a few moments and started making a series of rough sketches, one after another, with descriptions of the dimensions, materials, and purpose of each. He drew the tables, removable hydroponic germination drip trays, the mechanisms that would need to be built using gears, sprockets, bearings and other materials left in the facility, as well as a list of other materials that would need to be procured.

Greg watched Sam sketch in a speedy, almost unconscious manner. Page after page, Sam described each component, each weld, rivet, screw and bolt. As he drew, Greg absorbed the information as rapidly as Sam could talk and sketch it out.

Sam requested that the Thorvaldsen sisters come to the Tavern for a quick discussion. "I need their involvement with this last part of designing the process."

Greg called the florist shop and soon both of the girls entered the tavern, looking bright and full of mischief. Leila headed straight for Sam.

"My, what a pleasure!" She bent down and planted a kiss on Sam's cheek.

"Don't hog him, let me in there." Lena wrapped an arm around Sam's shoulder and kissed the other cheek.

"Girls, we have work to do." Greg laughed at Sam's expression.

The twins pulled up chairs and settled into a more professional demeanor. "We're ready to listen."

"What I propose," Sam said, "is a cultivation method known as 'sea of green'. We will use cuttings taken from mother plants that are rooted and grown under continuous artificial light until they're about a foot tall, then we need a method for putting the whole grow into darkness. The light deprivation will throw the plants into their budding cycle and speed the maturation of the flowers."

Lena nodded. "We use that method for encouraging our flowers to bloom."

"I thought you two would know something about that."

"I think we will also need some kind of breathable blackout material." Leila pulled her glasses out of her purse and began writing in her day planner.

"We may need to build a series of knee walls to allow air exchange while the plants are blacked out." Lena pointed to Leila's busy pen. "Write that down too."

Sam shook his head in amazement as the two discussed the merits of porous metal screens and exhaust/intake fans.

An hour or so later, the ladies gathered up their things and headed back to their shop to create a list of materials.

As they finished eating lunch, Greg studied Sam's sketches in silence before carefully sliding them into an accordion-like folder of documents he had taken with him to the facility that morning. "Sam, sometimes I think you VanDerhouts aren't actually real. It's almost like you and your family are the patron saints of our little town of Lester; you're always on hand when we need you."

Sam laughed. "Well, Greg, as one of my favorite sayings from the Tao goes: 'Wander where there is no path'."

The two men walked together over to the old mill and completed an inspection of the building. Greg's progress impressed Sam.

"In another week, I'll be bringing you the first seeds and clippings for the grow. At that point, this thing will start to feel real."

"I have so much to do, Sam, but I really feel like the whole town is pitching in, each in their own way." Greg's eyes misted over for a moment.

Sam slapped him on the back. "Greg, this is happening. And it's going to exceed all our expectations."

18

As the aircraft leveled off after takeoff from Sea-Tac airport, Mackenzie had the opportunity to reflect on the frenetic events that had taken place over the past few weeks. Yesterday, she had stopped at a Fed Ex store and furtively mailed to herself the carefully packed parcel containing samples of Sam's cannabis. It would be waiting for her when she arrived back at Fields Pharmaceuticals.

Leaving Sam's house on her last visit, she had crept inside the greenhouse and clipped small, discreet samples from each mother plant, including the ones partially hidden from view.

Richard Aiken had called the previous evening confirming her return to L.A. "Don't lose sight of your assignment, Mackenzie," he'd said—unnecessarily, she thought. "We've entrusted you with a task that could potentially take our company to a new level, and we're counting on you to get this job done."

After landing at LAX, Mackenzie quickly caught a cab to the sprawling Fields Pharmaceuticals research complex. Walking through the labyrinth of offices and labs as she had done hundreds of times before, she felt the familiarity of life in L.A. flooding back to her.

Entering the executive complex, she made her way to Tim Mallory's office. As she walked in, she observed that Mallory and Aiken were engaged in some sort of intense discussion. Both looked up quickly.

"Ah, Mackenzie! Good to see you back from the Great Northwest, and right on time, too." Mallory pointed to a comfortable-looking chair between the two men.

"I want you to know I've spoken to the president of Fields Pharmaceuticals about you," he went on, looking pleased. "We've decided you will be promoted to the position of Senior Manager and will lead the implementation of this project going forward."

This surprised Mackenzie. She felt a strange tightening in her stomach at the implication her assignment might be over. "Well, thank you, but there's still much to be done in Washington and—"

"Maybe," Mallory interrupted, "but I am sure, after we hear about your progress in Seattle, we'll be prepared to get the ball rolling on your promotion."

"Thank you, I appreciate your faith in me." Mackenzie's mind raced uncomfortably as they all sat.

Aiken said, "We know this project status meeting, and your travel back to L.A. for that matter, was somewhat rushed, so we don't expect cute charts and graphs. We just want your impressions and an unvarnished assessment of what you've learned during your stay in Washington. We're hoping you can give us information on the potential for marijuana production, distribution, and sale in Washington State." He glanced quickly at Mallory. "We'll also want to know how your mission is progressing with VanDerhout."

Mackenzie considered what to say, and how much. Her professional, logical side was rapidly gaining the upper hand again, now that she was back on her home turf. "Actually, I've learned a great deal about what is taking place in Washington State. As you know, I had the good fortune of attending a meeting with Washington's leading politico on that very subject, and I have been quite involved in the initial plans for a beta test implementation.

"I have been able to spend a goodly amount of time with Sam VanDerhout. Yes, I can tell you quite a bit about him, as a matter of fact, as well as what the State is planning to do, going forward. Furthermore…" She paused for a moment, taking a deep breath, "I have a sample of the marijuana VanDerhout has been developing. I was only able to obtain a few, small samples, but it should be enough for our lab to derive its chemical composition in detail."

"Where are the samples?" Aiken asked, excitement in his voice.

"I mailed them overnight delivery; the package should be here by now."

Mallory looked ecstatic. "I can't believe you were able to get this done so quickly, Mackenzie. This is very exciting news."

"Mr. Mallory—Tim, I can't guarantee this is the cannabis we're looking for; it has to be thoroughly examined in the lab first. I hope to be able to tell you one way or the other in a few days." She tried to lower their expectations, as well as her own.

Knowing how cagey Sam had been with regard to his research, she was far from certain she had obtained what they were all looking for.

"It's still an excellent stride forward, in any case, Mackenzie," Aiken said. "We'll just have to wait and see the outcome." He indicated Mallory. "Why don't you quickly recap the rest of your intelligence for Tim?"

"Yes. Washington State intends to have a very secure process to control the cultivation, distribution, and sale of legal marijuana within their State. But first, their plan is to conduct a beta test of the process and security measures to ensure a successful outcome."

"Do you know any of the particulars of these processes and security measures, at this point?" Tim asked.

"I know most of the details, but not everything." She looked sharply at Aiken. "I've kept Richard informed of my findings on an ongoing basis."

Mallory frowned at Aiken. "I haven't been debriefed in any detail, as of yet."

"Let me fill in some details for you then." For a moment Mackenzie basked in the power of knowing things both these men found incredibly important. "The beta test will be conducted utilizing only one licensed growing location. That location is going to be a town called Lester on the Olympic Peninsula. It's a rather remote, forested location near the Washington coast, an old logging town that has somehow survived."

Mallory considered this for a moment. "How do they intend to control this test?"

"For security, they intend to use specially produced satchels to transport the marijuana to its retail locations. Richard knows the details on this."

As Mackenzie concluded her summary of what she had learned in Washington, Mallory beamed.

"Outstanding work, Mackenzie…truly outstanding. Fields Pharmaceuticals is grateful to you for your work on this project. We won't soon forget what you've done for the team here."

"Thank you, Tim. It's nice to be recognized for my hard work, now and again."

"Excellent. Well, Mackenzie, we are going to release you back to your lab. We will expect a full report on the cannabis samples as soon as you know the outcome." Mallory stood and extended his hand. Mackenzie shook it.

"Thanks again for the recognition."

As the door clicked shut behind her, she could hear the two executives already talking in excited voices.

She wound her way through a series of key-carded entrances until she arrived at her research complex. After a few quick greetings with her co-workers she entered her spacious, contemporary office, where a package with her own neat writing on it awaited. She quickly opened the box; it emitted a now familiar scent, slightly skunky and earthen. Mackenzie felt tears suddenly rise. She shook herself mentally. "I must be tired." Still, the tears came.

The box smelled of green, of Washington State, and of Sam.

19

Richard Aiken was finishing his meal when Tim Mallory arrived.

"Good timing," Aiken said.

Mallory pulled up a chair in the outdoor, cabana styled restaurant, waving away the waiter who immediately approached him. The luncheon crowd had dispersed, leaving the men in relative solitude.

"We've completed the lab tests on the plant samples Mackenzie—uh, acquired. There is absolutely nothing remarkable about them; they're strong but common marijuana."

"God damn it, Richard!" Mallory took a deep breath and blew it out slowly. "We can't seem to catch a break with this thing."

"As I told you, we have a three-pronged plan. We just need to move forward with that plan, and as you know, we are already doing exactly that. Look, if you want this to succeed we have to expect the occasional setback and keep pressing forward."

"What do you recommend?"

"I recommend we give Mackenzie more time. She has already brought us important information and she's making headway with VanDerhout."

"I suppose you're right, but I'm starting to get nervous about leaving this whole thing up to her."

"I thought you didn't want to know about the third part of my plan."

"No. Actually, I don't. Just make it work. We can't afford to fuck around with this anymore."

"My thoughts exactly, Tim."

After Mallory left, Aiken headed to Long Beach to meet with his old friend Doug Delaney. He soon arrived at a graffiti-riddled aluminum warehouse in a run-down part of the city and parked near the entrance.

Aiken had called ahead so his friend could give the armed and badly tailored pile of muscle that served as the security guard some warning he would be coming. He disliked having guns brandished in his face. He gave the guy a quick nod and slid the aluminum carriage door aside, entering the dimly lit facility.

"Richard. Good to see you."

Aiken scanned in the dim light for Delaney as his eyes adjusted.

"I'm over here."

"Jesus, Doug, can't you spring for some lights in here?"

"I've been making other upgrades. I had a closed-circuit security system installed a few days ago. See, the camera images are on my computer screen here. I've been watching your car for several blocks. The idiots down the street don't even know I put cameras on their warehouse roof." He let out a coughing laugh.

"Matter of fact, meat sack out there doesn't know he's being replaced by this system. Don't tell him that, by the way."

"Sounds like an appropriate overhead cost reduction to me."

Doug Delaney rose from behind a green metal desk. Of medium height, he was nevertheless powerfully built with a thick, muscular neck and a broad, ape-like back.

The two had met in their tough, South Central L.A. high school; Aiken knew Delaney was a cash and carry guy who could generally be relied upon to produce results. Their friendship veiled an uneasy, mutual distrust born of long association.

Finding an ancient office chair that squealed in protest as he sat down on it, Aiken said, "So. You know why I'm here."

"Yeah, I suppose. You want to know if my guys have anything to report."

"That would be a fair guess."

Aiken watched as Delaney poured himself a tall whiskey, neat, from the desk drawer. He nodded toward the bottle and looked at Aiken.

"No thanks."

"Okay, here's the report so far: fucking nothing. My men have been following this VanDerhout guy for weeks now, watching his every move like you wanted, but—and here's the problem—they don't know what the fuck they are supposed to be looking for." Delaney thumped his glass down for effect.

Aiken shrugged. "I realize I haven't been forthcoming with details so far." Delaney snorted loudly at this.

"Forthcoming? You haven't told me shit about this job. Just… you know, go follow this pothead around and report when he takes a dump, or whatever. What is it you want from this? If I had some idea, maybe I could actually give you quality intelligence. As it is…well, here, I'll read you some of the reports I get." Delaney turned to his laptop and thumped on the keys for a moment. "Okay, here's an example:

"*10 a.m., subject is seen leaving his house and walking to what appears to be an outbuilding of some kind. Noon, subject walks out of building and back into his treehouse.*"

Delaney stopped reading, "The guy lives in a treehouse. His house is in a fucking tree." He glared at Aiken for a moment. "Anyway…

"*4 p.m., subject walks to boat and crosses channel toward where we are currently watching him. Subject speaks with Park Ranger and gets in his car…blah, blah, blah.*"

"Has VanDerhout done anything out of the ordinary? Have your guys seen him, say, go anywhere on the island, or on any trips that seem odd?"

"Jesus, I don't know." Delaney scanned his laptop for a minute. "Okay, here. The guy goes scuba diving around his island, he chainsaws a bunch of shit, he dates some hot-looking chick, and he likes to visit a shithole town called Lester and hang out with the yokels. Oh, and he smokes a shit-ton of weed." Delaney looked up from the laptop. "Anything in there worth what you're paying me?"

"Did you say he scuba dives around his island?" This interested Aiken.

"That's what my boys say. Are you wanting to continue having him watched or should we step things up like we talked about?"

Aiken shook his head. "I just want you to watch him for the time being."

"Okay. But my employees are getting lazy just hanging out, fishing and following this asshole around. I think I'm gonna have to fire the whole crew up there once we're done."

Aiken smiled. "I have another job in mind—nothing too complicated, but very important. It's too soon to flesh out the details at this point, but I want you to be ready to move when I ask."

Delaney nodded, his eyes brightening.

"We need this job to be done perfectly. No mistakes. We're willing to double the usual fee."

"Richard, this is exactly why I've loved you all these years," Delaney said, grinning.

Aiken stood. "I'll be in touch with the specifics. As always, I rely on your ability to keep quiet."

Delaney listened until he heard Aiken depart through the back door. He was trying to put the pieces together. He would take Aiken up on this lucrative business deal, whatever it was, but he believed there might be a much bigger payoff in this venture. He didn't know exactly what it was VanDerhout had, but he knew it must be worth a hell of a lot, otherwise Aiken wouldn't be willing to take such risks, and pay so much money, to get at it.

Delaney watched his security camera as Aiken navigated the big BMW out of the parking lot and then reached for his cell phone.

"Hey. Yeah, it's me. We might need to make a few adjustments in your assignment."

20

As Sam awoke, he realized he had been dreaming about the very thing on which he had spent every waking hour recently: the Lester beta test. Rolling out of his comfortable bed, he reoriented himself with his surroundings back on the island. The last three weeks had been spent in Lester, working on the initial setup and putting in the first starts of marijuana. He was immensely glad to be home for a while.

It particularly pleased Sam that it was Saturday; everyone had been delighted with the progress they made at the Lester grow-op, and a weekend to rest and recharge was most welcome.

Earlier in the week, Sam was enjoying a home-cooked meal at Greg and Becky's house when the topic of an impending meteor shower came up. He had shared a story of a high school trip to New York and a tour of the Museum of Modern Art, where he had been fortunate enough to see Van Gogh's *Starry Night*. He recalled having been mesmerized by the unearthly swirls of yellow on blue that so perfectly captured the feeling and raw emotion of a late summer night under the stars.

After dinner, Greg had brought out a map of hiking trails. Before long they found a path that followed an abandoned railway spur near Stampede Pass, which led up to a small plateau in the foothills of the Cascade Mountains. Sam had decided to take this trek at the peak of the meteor activity.

The next day, Mackenzie had called to let Sam know she had arrived home safely. She had phoned him regularly during her extended absence and Sam had found himself looking forward to her calls. While delighted with the fact she was back in town, he had a sense something was bothering her, and in his opinion, no better cure existed for a troubled mind than getting out in nature, especially under a star-filled sky. He had suggested she accompany him on his hike to see the meteor shower.

"You'll have to dress warm, Mac. But I promise it won't be a forced march or anything; I found a pretty gentle hike that should get us in a perfect spot for stargazing."

He filled his pack with blankets, flashlights and a variety of snacks. He dressed in layers and brought a warm jacket for Mackenzie, who would likely dress too lightly.

Later, Sam knocked on the door of Mackenzie's apartment. She opened it and stood smiling for a moment before Sam encircled her with his arms, bringing her close and breathing in her lovely scent. Stepping back, Sam gazed down at the beautiful face looking up at him.

Mackenzie had returned with a renewed goal of getting her assignment done as quickly as possible. She tried to ignore the fact her heart was beating faster. "Hey Sam."

"I've missed you, Mac. I'm glad you're going on this hike with me. I realize you haven't been home that long, but this particular celestial event isn't to be missed."

"I'm totally up for this," Mackenzie lied, as Sam helped her with her coat.

"Hold on. I need to see what you're wearing on your feet."

Mackenzie stuck out one foot and turned it from side to side. "See? I went to REI and bought some actual hiking boots."

Sam grinned. "Good girl."

As they made their way out of Seattle and onto East I-90, they spoke about the progress being made in Lester. Sam had kept Mackenzie up to date during her absence, recounting stories about various characters in the town and how well everyone seemed to be working together.

"I still can't believe that Lester is actually going to be harvesting their first grow so soon." Mackenzie shook her head in disbelief. "You still haven't told me how the hell you got things moving so fast!"

"It's…uh, a special strain of cannabis I developed, plus the use of some standard techniques and growing methods taken to a creative edge." Sam nodded. "In the end, I think it's also the sheer determination of the Lester folks to make this a success."

"How many different strains of cannabis do you think you've created that are utterly unique?" Mackenzie tried to sound casual.

"Oh, maybe a dozen or so actual strains—in a purely botanical sense, perhaps slightly less. Believe it or not, I take my cannabis research very seriously. It's an amazing plant, with so much potential for healing." He grew silent.

Mackenzie tried to keep Sam from shutting down, like he usually did when discussing his work. "Have you come up with anything miraculous yet?"

"I'm working on it, believe me. But until there is a true shift in people's perception, getting some miraculous marijuana cure out there for public use is nearly impossible. Most folks want their medicine to come from a bottle, acquired by a prescription."

"What's so bad about that? They've already developed Marinol and other prescription drugs based on cannabis. If that's the way people want to use it, why deprive them?" Mackenzie knew she was treading on thin ice with Sam, but she needed to keep the conversation going.

"I...haven't had the best experiences along those lines." He gave Mackenzie a curious glance. She sensed he was on the verge of telling her something, but she also felt his reluctance.

"I think you have to follow your gut instincts on things, Sam. But I'm curious to know what kind of experience would make you so...intransigent on the subject of marijuana being used as the basis for prescription medications."

Sam appeared thoughtful as he watched the road ahead, with its natural beauty and massive two hundred-foot-tall evergreens crushing inwards toward the road.

Finally he said, "While on the last of the many trips I made as a graduate student in Botany, I was working with the native curator of a botanical garden in the rainforest outside Iquitos, Peru. It was an amazing place, a clinic, conservancy—and a place of healing. At any rate, among the many medicinal plants in use there, I discovered one from some of the tribal shamans used for occasional demonic exorcism. The local doctor told me this particular plant seemed to have an almost immediate curative effect on seizures. I took a sample back with me to the University and was able to clone it and conduct some rudimentary experiments. We tested the whole, unaltered plant and simply ground it into a paste and fed it to lab rats that were genetically altered to exhibit the symptoms of epilepsy. This plant eliminated seizures completely with no discernable side effects. It was miraculous."

Sam's grip tightened on the steering wheel. "One morning, I was walking across campus. As I neared our research building, I sensed something was wrong; I didn't know why. When I arrived at the lab our research documentation, all of the samples, and everything we had accomplished was gone…"

"What happened to it? Do you know?" Mackenzie's quiet voice broke his silence.

Sam looked grim. "The University claimed all research done under their auspices was their property. They took it and sold it to some unnamed pharmaceutical company."

"Do you know if it was ever developed into a treatment for epilepsy?" Mackenzie was hesitant to ask this question. She recalled a list of 'orphaned' drugs that Fields kept. It seemed to her that an epilepsy drug something like what Sam was describing had been on the list.

"It took years, but I finally learned it had been purchased, then shelved. Between the cost of reproducing it synthetically and the fact its anti-seizure properties were so effective it didn't require frequent dosing, the drug was deemed an *unprofitable investment*." Sam shook his head.

Mackenzie grew very still. She felt acutely uncomfortable with herself at that moment.

"So, you see how I might be a little gun-shy when it comes to big pharma." Sam smiled and shrugged. "Sorry, I didn't mean to depress you, Mac. But you did ask."

Mackenzie leaned over and quickly kissed Sam on the cheek.

21

An hour or so had passed since leaving Seattle when Sam and Mackenzie arrived at a trailhead situated high in the Cascade Mountains near Stampede Pass.

"That was a fast trip." Mackenzie peered out the car window at the mountains rising above them.

"There's lots of recreation within an easy drive of Seattle."

They climbed out, grabbed their packs and walked to a set of abandoned railroad tracks winding along the edge of the forest. A sign marked the path: *Depot Ridge 1.5 miles.*

"Are we walking the train tracks?" Mackenzie glanced nervously at the late rays of the sun dipping behind the mountain ridges.

Sam, testing his flashlight, looked up at Mackenzie, seeming to note the hesitancy in her voice. "This whole area was used by the Northern Pacific Railroad." He searched in his pack for a moment. "It's not too far, Mac, but if you want to skip this hike,

I'll completely understand." He slipped a knit hat on her head and grinned as he stepped back to look at her. "I promise I'm a great guide, though."

Mackenzie adjusted the hat, annoyed she had shown any fear. "I'm sure you're a regular Sacajawea, but I do have some concerns about hiking back in the dead of night." She picked up her pack. "Let's go."

They walked in silence as the rusted rails became helter-skelter, no longer bound by the spikes that had long since been released by the rotting wooden ties. A few minutes farther along and there remained little to indicate a railroad had ever been there at all, with the exception of the crushed rock bed demarking the route it had taken, and the notch in the horizon that gave away its path through the trees. As they walked, the forest almost completely reclaimed the crushed rock path. Up ahead, they could make out a train tunnel carved through a granite ridge.

Sam flicked on his light and shone it toward the entrance marked by a thick concrete archway, his beam illuminating the date, *1902,* still cast neatly into the concrete.

"Wow, we get to walk through an old train tunnel!" Sam exclaimed, but the thought of it troubled Mackenzie.

"Is this safe, Sam?" She peered into the inky darkness ahead and turned to face him, a look of apprehension on her face.

Sam grabbed her hand and smiled. "Just stay close if you're nervous."

As they walked through the tunnel, cold water dripped from the ceiling and ran down the mossy walls as it emerged from deep inside the ridge above them. Mackenzie stayed close to Sam as they moved in near total darkness. Rounding a curve, she was relieved to see a dim light shining through the other end. Emerging into the dusky daylight, they came upon what appeared to be remnants of a small railroad and logging town set into a bowl-shaped valley, about two miles long, and wide. Another matching train tunnel appeared in the distance as the track bed wound higher into the mountains.

"Did you know this was here, Sam?"

He shook his head, pointing in the rapidly dimming light. "That looks like it was a house, and that's probably a coal shack or something." He walked to what appeared to be a small warehouse, moss-covered, rotted, and collapsing. Peering through the window he said, "There's still stuff in these buildings. Almost like people just picked up and left in a hurry."

Mackenzie hugged herself, looking at the gloomy structures nervously. "Yeah, well. I don't blame them."

"It's a real ghost town, all right!" Sam appeared beside himself. He stopped to study what looked like part of a heavy iron gear. "This place must have been a train depot a hundred years ago."

Mackenzie dreaded walking back through this desolate spot in total darkness. "Are we close to our destination?" She no longer cared if he knew she was uneasy.

Sam pointed to the final golden glow on the peaks ahead of them. "We're in the home stretch, Mac."

Negotiating this last portion of the steeply sloped trail, Mackenzie was grateful Sam walked a few steps ahead of her, keeping a watchful eye on her progress. Minutes later they emerged into a broad meadow, just as twilight turned to darkness.

Sam suggested placing their blanket on a section of the meadow through which pillow basalt had protruded, since it would retain warmth for a time. They spread the first blanket, leaving the second for a cover in the cooling evening.

Mackenzie had suddenly become inexplicably shy with Sam. In all her former experience with men, she had maintained total control. Men pursued her and occasionally she would allow one to catch her, if only for a time—and only on her terms. This man was breaking the rules.

Stretching his lean body out on the blanket and rolling to his side, Sam pulled out a flask and two metal cups. He looked up at Mackenzie, who stood to one side, shivering and surveying the meadow while attempting to regain her composure.

"I brought some hundred-year-old scotch. It seemed apropos somehow." He patted the blanket. "Sit and have a drink. I find scotch to be a perfect way to warm up."

She sat down, cross-legged next to him. "I figured you'd be bringing pot along, not hard liquor."

"I'm not much of a drinker, true. But there is something about grain alcohol and a cold night that just seem to go together." He raised his cup to Mackenzie and they both took a drink.

The warming sensation from the scotch moved through Mackenzie's insides. *No wonder they call this liquid courage,* she thought.

Sam pulled a variety of snacks from his pack and shared them with Mackenzie, who now discovered she was quite hungry.

He suddenly pointed over Mackenzie's shoulder. "I just saw the first shooting star!"

"Really?" Mackenzie twisted around and looked up; the sky had already begun to fill with stars. "Oh my god! It's beautiful."

Sam leaned back and reclined fully, hands behind his head. Mackenzie lay down carefully alongside him, leaving room between their bodies.

Together, they watched the cosmos unfold above them as their eyes adjusted ever more acutely to the night. The longer they looked toward the sky, the more stars came into focus.

Mackenzie gasped as the first meteors shot through the night sky. "Look over there, did you see that? There were two or three in a row!" Presently, the shower filled the night sky with streaks and bursts appearing in regular intervals.

"Could we use that extra blanket? It's freezing."

Sam sat up and spread the blanket over them. Reaching toward Mackenzie, he pulled her closer to him.

Mackenzie was grateful for Sam's warmth as she rested her head on his firm chest and huddled into him, still looking up at the tiny streaks of light blazing across the sky. She found herself becoming acutely aware of the way his body felt next to her. Sam, on the other hand, seemed content to immerse himself in the meteor shower, appearing meditative as he watched the heavens.

This was becoming a source of frustration for Mackenzie, who was not used to being overlooked when this close to a man, especially a man to whom she felt sexually attracted. She drifted into a mild sulk as Sam continued to watch the stars, seemingly lost in his own world.

"We don't need to stay much longer Mac, I don't want you to completely freeze." Sam had suddenly become sentient again and turned his body toward Mackenzie, still huddled into his side. He pulled her tightly to him with both arms, his face close to hers. "Thank you for sharing this with me, Mac."

Mackenzie went still as she felt Sam's warm lips on hers. She responded to him by opening her mouth slightly and allowing his kiss to deepen. She wrapped her leg around Sam's and the two were drawn closer. Mackenzie shivered as Sam's cool hand slipped under her sweater and moved against her bare skin.

Suddenly, the two broke apart and sat bolt upright.

"Did you hear that?" Mackenzie's heart pounded.

"Sounded like a tree snapping and falling." Sam rummaged in his pack for the flashlight. Shining it around the perimeter of the meadow, he saw nothing out of the ordinary.

Mackenzie jumped to her feet, "Perhaps we had better be heading back."

Sam hid his concern as he and Mackenzie gathered the blankets and other items into their packs and started back down the trail, both with flashlights on to guide their steps.

"What do you think that was?" Mackenzie looked frightened as they carefully made their way down the steep trail.

"It was probably a deer, or an elk. Or an old tree that had rotted enough, or an ant took that last bite, and down it went." Sam reached forward to steady Mackenzie as she stumbled. "Slow down, Mac. Everything is fine."

Sam, though, remained uneasy. He could hear a faint cracking of branches behind them. He knew this area was home to black bears and the thunderous snap they heard earlier had sounded like a tree being broken in half. He was anxious to get out of the thick part of the woods and into a more open area as quickly as possible.

Having negotiated the trail leading from the high alpine meadow, the steepest portion of their hike back to the car was over. Sam stood on the rocky abandoned railroad bed for a moment to ensure they were heading in the right direction. "We're making good time, Mac. You'll be tucked into your bed before you know it." He took her hand and they proceeded down the gradient, cut through the wilderness well over a century ago.

Passing the abandoned town they had briefly explored earlier, Sam paused for a moment, surprised at the level of detail reaching their eyes on the clear, moonless night. He moved his flashlight around the ghostly landscape as Mackenzie stopped to drink from his canteen. From the corner of his eye, he saw movement— something seemed to duck out of sight when he turned his head. Sam looked at Mackenzie and decided to say nothing.

"Almost to the train tunnel, and then it's just a short walk to the car." He put his arm around Mackenzie as they threaded through the old town, flashlights beaming before them. The tunnel entrance loomed ahead and he felt Mac's arms wrap around his waist, her face almost buried in his coat.

"I don't like this, Sam."

"It's an adventure, Mac. Another life experience." Sam stopped and faced her, pulling her hat low over her ears. "Just stay close and we'll hurry right through."

Silently, they turned and took the first steps into the tunnel, moving quickly through the palpable darkness, their footsteps echoing as they walked.

Sam could hear sounds echoing dimly around them. Black rivulets of water trickled down the tunnel walls sounding like the barely perceptible whispers of conversation. He couldn't shake the sense they weren't alone. Feeling spooked, he glanced at Mackenzie, who didn't seem to hear anything. He suddenly noticed movement above their heads. He aimed the flashlight beam toward the ceiling of the roughly cut passageway.

"Mac, I'm considering whether or not to tell you this."

"What is it?"

"Do you like being happy?"

"Sam, what kind of question is that?"

"Okay. Don't look up at the ceiling, and you'll remain happy."

Mackenzie did what any intelligent, well-educated person would do: she cast the beam of her flashlight upward, and screamed.

On the ceiling of the dripping tunnel were thousands of bats, hanging upside down while they relaxed from having completed their nightly foraging. The bats had been resting quietly until Mackenzie's scream, and now thousands took wing and made haste for the tunnel opening as they flew just above their heads.

Ducking down, they both ran; Mackenzie shrieked as they exited the other side of the passage.

Catching their breath, Mackenzie insisted Sam check her hair for bats, steadfastly ignoring his explanation that bats don't actually get in people's hair. "Holy shit! That was terrifying!"

Sam squinted toward the entrance behind them. "We're not far from the car now. Why don't we pick up the pace and jog a bit; it might warm us up."

He trotted behind Mackenzie, glancing around as they went, his ears attuned to the sounds coming from the surrounding forest.

"There's the car, I'll race you."

The two broke into a sprint, Mackenzie taking the lead. Breathing hard, she dropped her pack by the Volvo and turned to face Sam. "You really know how to show a girl a good time." They broke out in relieved laughter.

"Well, you know what they say: blind terror is the elixir of love."

As he pulled out onto the highway, Sam finally let himself relax, exhaling deeply. A seasoned explorer, he was surprised at how jumpy he was during what should have been an easy hike. Some intuition or sixth sense had awakened in him during the last few weeks causing him to feel on high alert. If only he knew what he was afraid of.

22

Arriving at the mill warehouse-cum-marijuana production facility—dubbed the Pot Plant—Sam and Mackenzie drove across the gravel parking lot and pulled in front of the building.

"Sam and Mac," Greg said as they emerged from the car, "good to see you two this morning."

"Greg, you're looking younger every time I see you." Sam gave him a quick hug, and then stood aside for Mackenzie.

"I can't wait to see what's been happening here." Mackenzie planted a kiss on Greg's whisker-stubbled cheek.

Red-faced, Greg led them through the double doors of the warehouse. "Sam's already seen all this; he's been with us every step of the way." He beamed at the sight of the clean, industrious scene before him. "Most of the town is in the warehouse getting the last row of growing bins set up. We're about ready to put the next batch of seeds in the ground."

"Great," Sam said, "let's get to work."

As they walked farther into the main building, Mackenzie was shocked at how much progress had already been made.

"Check this out." Greg pointed toward waterfall-like hydroponic seed germination troughs rotating on a chain drive system attached to a timer. "This system allows each trough to be soaked in the nutrient-rich soup, which Sam concocted, at the correct amount of time each day."

"I can't believe you guys did all this." Mackenzie was genuinely in awe that these people had created such a professional operation in so short a time. She looked at Sam's handsome, intelligent face, beaming with pride. *He's deriving so much pleasure from this*, Mackenzie thought, a*nd he gets absolutely no money at all.* For a moment it reminded her of her own father, and the delight he took in his humble profession. It made her ashamed for a moment.

Greg continued: "You know that idea you had, about making the troughs removable from the nutrient dip-tank, so that each eight-foot section can be easily detached? We're using that design to transfer the sprouts in the hydroponic germination gutters to the soil growth bins. I'll let Lena and Leila explain how they do this. Girls, got a sec?"

Lena Thorvaldsen sashayed in their direction, while Leila disengaged from Jeffrey, the town baker.

"Would you mind demonstrating for Mackenzie how these germination trays are transferred to the soil growing bins?"

"Sure, this way, Mackenzie," Leila said, as Lena took Sam's arm. "See how easy this is?" Leila pushed a green button, putting the system in motion.

Mackenzie studied the system, noting how an electric motor turned bicycle gears driving a chain, which in turn rotated the perforated gutter sections into the hydroponic nutrient mix in the tank below for a specified period of time. It also was designed to stop so an entire section could be easily lifted out of the rotisserie-like machine.

"Did you design all this, Sam?" Mackenzie asked.

"He most certainly did. With some input from us, of course." Lena reluctantly relinquished her grip on Sam, carried the gutter section over to the soil mixture bins, and slid the starts directly from the gutter, *en masse*, into the awaiting nutrient-rich soil composition.

"How easy was that?" Lena said proudly. "Thanks to you, our beloved mastermind."

Mackenzie knew quite a bit about manufacturing; it amazed her how the entire process had been laid out, as though an industrial engineer had spent months designing it all. She looked at Sam and Greg; both were happily discussing improvements to the system. The realization hit her, on a visceral level: Sam VanDerhout was a genius.

"You do know Greg is a mechanical whiz trapped in a logger's body," Sam told her.

"Yes, I can see that from my surroundings." Mackenzie could not tear her eyes from Sam. She had never fully appreciated the depth of his prodigy.

Greg then led them to where the growing bins, all on wheels, were rolled into the lighting/growing section, which comprised rows of bins full of plants of increasing maturities. There were about fifty bins across for each row, which were lined up as they progressed through the maturity sections. The rows were separated by black drapes so the perfect amount of light and nutrients could be applied in the way Sam had predetermined were optimal for that phase of the plants' life.

As they walked farther down the production line, Mackenzie could just make out the last row of the growing process.

"Check it out, Mac, it's beautiful," Sam said. "The budding room."

They continued on toward the end of the production line to where the seasoning and drying process was located. "This is where we really went to town. See those flat iron-plate tables?" Greg indicated a row of heavy metal tables.

"Yes. Curing, right?"

Greg nodded. "We used the thick steel plates the mill left behind in the machine shop to fabricate curing tables that distribute the heat evenly. I got to thinking about the curing table design you sketched. I put that together with the small geothermal hot spring just about half a mile from here. I realized for the cost of some insulated pipe, we could heat the curing table with geothermal water and *go green*, so to speak. After the hot spring water heats the curing table, I hope to design a cascading set of hot tubs just outside the building, right over there." Greg pointed to the back of the warehouse.

"Oh, one more thing, guys. Let's go to the packing room, over this way."

Greg led them through swinging double doors. As they pushed the surprisingly heavy canvas doors aside, Mackenzie noted a number of pallet boards lining the room, each with stacks of heavy, rubber-coated satchels bearing the seal of the State of Washington on their sides.

As Sam and Greg talked in the doorway, Mackenzie slipped her phone surreptitiously from her pocket and snapped a few pictures of the satchels and security systems. She listened from a distance as Greg addressed Sam in a low tone.

"One more thing, Sam: as you know, we were still about $50k short on Lester's share of the operating capital for the first year. The state escrowed their funds in full, and we need to do the same before the deadline in two weeks. We're hoping to make some cash from our little festival next week, but it's going to be tight."

"Listen, Greg. I don't want you to worry. Get what you can and I'll make certain you have the rest."

Mackenzie looked at her phone, thinking of the pictures she had just taken, and her reason for doing so. She watched Sam and as he continued to talk, his hands elegantly tracing some new idea in the air for Greg to visualize.

With a few swift moves of her fingers, Mackenzie deleted the photos.

23

Mayor Roxanne Martin stood beneath a banner that read, *Lester's First Annual Hemp Daze,* ironing out the last details of the day's events. Sitting at the back of the meeting, Sam shook his head. He had tried to "edit" the festival's name to *Lester's Inaugural Hemp Daze* but had failed to convince anyone it was impossible to have a "First Annual" anything. He was fairly certain today would be a big, entertaining mess.

"Leila and Lena, you two have your floral booth and are helping Jeffery at the baked goods, correct?"

"Oh, yes. We're quite ready," Leila replied, giving Jeffrey a wink over her shoulder.

Roxanne went through every booth and event, checking each off her list. "Okay, important stuff here: Wallace and Carmen, do you have the cash box and tickets in place?" Carmen gave a wordless thumbs up.

Roxanne sighed and adjusted her glasses. "Whose idea was adding the 'Pin the Joint on the Stoner' game back onto the festival list?"

Simon tentatively raised his huge hand.

"Simon, I thought we had decided to defer that in favor of our chainsaw bong sculpture event."

Sam leaned over and whispered to Mackenzie, "You should have seen the list of events before I edited them." She laughed quietly and slid her hand into his.

"Speaking of our chainsaw sculpture event, are we ready to go with that?"

Sam winced as this and several more questionable "events" were discussed. In his opinion, the whole concept of "There's no such thing as a bad idea" had unfortunately prevailed long past the brainstorming phase.

"Are all of the security and traffic management contingencies covered?"

Marty Stout had graciously volunteered to handle security for the event. "Every 't' crossed, and 'i' dotted, my good mayor. Should a riot or any other form of civil disobedience come to pass, I have a couple off-duty Park Rangers on standby, ready with tranquilizer darts should the need arise." He indicated two slightly overweight men in ranger khakis and sunglasses, who nodded back at him.

"Let's hope it doesn't come to that, Marty." The mayor shook her head. "Thank you, though."

"Greg and Sam, you'll be running interference, ready to jump in if needed, in the event something unexpected should arise. Are you ready to go?"

"Yep. Ready to go, Roxanne," Greg replied. "The security team has walkie-talkies to contact each other, but we'll have our cell phones on too, so feel free to call any of us for whatever you need."

"Great! Well, that was the last of the details I had on our checklist. Let's go make some money for our Pot Plant and everyone remember—have fun!"

By the time Lester's Hemp Daze festival opened, cars were lined up for several miles. Sam, Marty and Greg found themselves on parking control duty, attempting to keep the endless stream of cars parked in some semblance of order.

Marty's voice crackled over the walkie-talkie: "Eagle Two to Eagles One and Three; come in Eagles."

Sam quickly replied, "Marty, what the hell's with the Eagle stuff?"

"I thought we agreed that you'd be Eagle One, I'd be Eagle Two, and Greg would be Eagle Three."

"I don't recall discussing that, Marty; let's just stick with names, if that's okay. I mean, *this is a pot festival.*"

"A good point. In any case, *Sam and Greg*, I am noting an alarming number of dreadlocked attendees taking over the field area by the Pot Plant with their hacky-sacks. My Park Ranger backup units are asking if they can cuff-'n-carry these guys. May I signal my approval as Security Chief?"

Sam sighed. "Marty, tell Barry and Keith those are paying customers. It might put a wet blanket on next year's, or for that matter, this year's attendance if we start apprehending folks as

REBECCA BAUMGARTNER

they enter. Besides, if we turned away everyone with Rasta locks, Jamaican colors, or Birkenstocks, we'd be left sitting here all by ourselves."

As lunchtime approached, the Hemp Daze grounds and the town filled with sedate revelers. The smell of pizza, baked goods, and marijuana hung sweet and thick in the air. Over the loudspeaker, Mayor Roxanne's voice announced, "The Lester Hemp Daze bong chainsaw carving competition will begin at noon. That's in fifteen minutes, folks, over in the field by the Pot Plant. Don't miss it!"

The din coming from the crowd rose slightly after Roxanne's announcement and the enthusiastic, but slightly anesthetized crowd seemed to be migrating in that direction as Greg came across the walkie-talkie. "Marty, from what I understand, your girlfriend, Vicki Jo, has entered the bong sculpture chainsaw carving competition. Is that correct?" Greg's voice sounded muffled.

"Why, yes. She's quite an artist with the chainsaw. In fact, if you look closely at the lapel of the hunting jacket she wore to today's festivities, you'll note a twenty-year pin commemorating her membership in the Peninsula Chainsaw Carving League."

Greg laughed. "Wow. Why don't you and Sam go watch the competition? The traffic has really dropped off, and I can handle it."

"Superb," Marty replied. "We'll keep checking the walkies. Let us know if you need any help."

"Will do. Enjoy the show, guys. Let me know how it goes."

"We will," Sam replied, as he hurried to see Mackenzie, who worked the ticket booth.

170

"Are you doing okay?" Sam leaned over the counter for a moment, appreciating the sight of Mac laughing and enjoying herself.

"This is a total hoot, Sam." Mackenzie's eyes were particularly shiny; she leaned forward and kissed him full on the lips.

Sam pulled back for a moment, an amused look on his face. "Mac, are you stoned by any chance?"

"No way! Well, maybe. These peanut butter cookies have quite a kick." She smiled a bit absently. "Let's have some alone time a little later, what do you say?"

Sam left her for the time being, promising to return shortly. He had never witnessed her stoned and was slightly surprised at how much it affected her.

As the carving competition began, the scream of chainsaws being used to their very limits filled the air, and sawdust flew in all directions. Although Vicki Jo's turn wasn't for a few more rounds, Sam watched with amazement as the highly skilled artists transformed three-foot-high sections of Douglas fir into various interpretations of bong shapes. Sam found Marty and noted he was smiling broadly as he ate chocolate brownies.

"Those brownies look great, Marty."

"How rude of me. I'm sorry, here, have a few." Marty handed a plastic-wrapped pack of three to Sam.

Biting into a brownie, Sam noted what seemed to be an alarmingly high marijuana content. "Wow. Did Vicki Jo make these for you?"

"No. Vicki Jo has many enviable skills, but making pot brownies is not one of them."

"Where'd you get them?"

Marty pointed over his shoulder with a half-eaten brownie. "At the baked goods booth, over there."

"Oh, shit." Sam surveyed the people around him, noting that almost everyone in the crowd looked sleepy and seemed to be carrying a bag or paper plate heaped with baked goods.

"Excuse me for a second, Marty." Sam started to make his way through the crowd toward Greg.

"We may have a problem," he said.

"What's up?" Greg replied.

"It seems that someone may have accidentally augmented the pot content of the brownies, and probably other baked goods, more than suggested in the recipe."

Greg pondered this. "Well, it's an adults only festival, and certainly a bit of extra weed won't be a big deal. Might even improve bakery sales today, and attendance a year from now." He laughed.

"I think they boosted the recipe more than a little."

"Like how much more?" Greg asked, as the smile on his face altered to a look of concern.

"Let me put it this way, Greg. I have been enjoying marijuana since college. That's a very long time, and in that time I've never had brownies like this." Sam held up the remaining two delights Marty had given him.

Greg asked, "May I?"

"Of course. You'll see what I mean."

Greg took a bite. Then another. "Holy shit."

"That's what I said, too."

"Vicki Jo is probably up soon in the competition. I better stay here and keep an eye on things. Why don't you go get Marty after she's done, and we'll talk this through." Greg pocketed the rest of his brownie.

Sam made it back to his seat in the temporary bleachers set up for the event and sat next to Marty, just as Vicki Jo's turn at the competition began. He watched in awe as she summarily trounced everyone, modeling an astounding unicorn-shaped bong, with the single horn functioning as the mouthpiece, and the bowl forming the tail of the mythical creature.

As this round of the competition concluded, and knowing the winners would not be determined until the final sculpture was complete, Sam leaned over to Marty as the crowd gave a round of applause for Vicki Jo's flawless performance. "Marty, we better get back to Greg. I think there's a matter that demands our attention."

"Very good, Sam. Back to our official responsibilities here at Hemp Daze."

They exited the bleachers and started toward the vendor booths as Sam explained the apparent issue at hand. "Marty, it seems the Thorvaldsen twins helped Jeffery last night, and many of the baked goods have somehow wound up with more marijuana content than prescribed."

"So that's why Vicki Jo's bong appeared to be a unicorn! I wondered about that; she's never carved a unicorn before. Sam, you're a bright guy—what in the hell is a unicorn, anyway?"

Sam put his hand on Marty's shoulder, stopping him for a moment as he looked into his eyes. Seeing Marty was in need of a nap, Sam suggested, "Marty, I think we need to get to the bottom of this. Then I'm going to take you back to the Volvo. When the back seats are down, it makes for a pretty comfy place for you to nap."

Marty yawned. "Sounds great, Sam. Forty winks don't sound half bad."

Sam led Marty through the crowded vendor booth area, which included the usual hemp-related items: indoor plant growing equipment, Bob Marley paraphernalia, pipes and bongs of every imaginable shape, size, and description, and woven hemp clothing.

Sam slowed momentarily in front of a simply decorated booth of mostly black, with a large white square glued to the wall at the back of it.

"A priest's collar."

"What did you say, Marty?"

Sam scanned the area around them, looking for Father Chris Donneghy.

"No, Sam. Right there."

Sam turned to look in the direction Marty now pointed.

"I don't see him."

"That white square, glued to the back wall of the pastor's booth. There. It's supposed to make the booth look like a huge priest's collar. You know, that black-and-white thing they wear around their necks? Hell, you're the one that went to a private Catholic school."

Examining the booth's décor, Sam noted the black-and-white collar motif with colored letters in an arched rainbow shape announcing, *Blessings From On High*. Father Donneghy stood just outside the booth, engaged in lively conversation with a group of earnest-looking people dressed in Jamaican colors.

Sam shook his head and smiled as he heard Father Donneghy say, "But isn't Rastafarianism more a way of life than an actual spiritual ideology?"

The pair moved on, approaching a stand with a sign saying, *Jeff's Totally Baked Goods*, where Lena Thorvaldsen attended to the booth alone.

"Hi, Lena." Sam tried to be nonchalant as he and Marty stepped to the front of the long and rapidly growing line of customers. "Are Leila and Jeffery around?"

Lena looked up from incorrectly counting out change for a customer. "Oh! Sam and Marty. How are you today?"

Sam noted that Lena looked more mellow than usual. "Have you eaten any of the baked goods, by chance?"

"I'm sorry, Sam. Did you ask something?" She stood and cradled Sam's face in her hands admiringly, adding, "*My god,* you're a handsome man."

"Thanks, Lena. Have you seen Jeffrey or Leila?"

"Oh, yes. You asked that, didn't you?"

"Yes, I did. Have you seen Jeffrey, or Leila?" Sam tried to be patient.

"I think they went back to the bakery to get more goods to sell…but that's been a while." Lena wore a puzzled expression on her face.

"Okay. Thanks, Lena."

Sam pointed Marty in the direction of the bakery, and they wound their way through the throng of attendees.

As he entered the bakery, Sam noted Leila in the front, near the counter, looking into a small compact mirror and putting on lipstick. Jeffrey entered from the back room, tying his apron strings behind him.

"Sorry to disturb you guys, but I need to ask an urgent question," Sam said, slightly embarrassed.

Jeffrey looked surprised. "What's up?"

"It seems the brownies, and perhaps other goods at the bakery booth, have rather a large amount of pot in them. Any idea what happened?"

Jeffrey thought for a moment, a confused look on his face. "What? I carefully measured all the ingredients, including the marijuana, myself. How can that…hold on a minute."

Sam waited while Jeffrey collected his thoughts.

"Well, it was getting late last night, and we had several batches of brownies, cookies and the like almost mixed and ready to go in the oven. All we had left to do was to fold in the marijuana. Leila and I, well, we took a quick break to go down the block to my place to…uh, get some things. On our way out the back door, I pointed to the big bag of ground up pot and asked Lena to add the marijuana."

"How large was this bag?"

"Maybe…say, Leila, how big was that bag?"

"A Hefty kitchen bag, the kind you line a tall trash can with." Leila snapped her compact shut and smiled brightly at Sam.

"Good lord. Did the entire bag get used up?"

"I'm afraid so." Jeffrey looked chagrined. "Was that too much?"

Sam shook his head and laughed. "It's not going to kill anyone, Jeffrey, so don't worry about that; but Lester's pot is quite strong, and that was a shit-load of it."

Sam turned to Leila. "Please start a *very* strong pot of coffee, and get as much as you can into Marty. Then see if you can find a couple of those huge coffee makers they use at church gatherings or whatever, and you and Marty can set up a free-coffee booth near the parking lot exit. By the time the festivities are over, the effects of the brownies and cookies will have worn off anyway—but just in case, we'll pour coffee into anyone who needs it before they leave."

Sam left Marty with Leila and headed out the back door to check on Mackenzie. After asking around, he located her inside the tavern, sound asleep in one of the booths. He gazed at her for a few moments, reaching out to smooth her silky dark hair and cover her with his jacket.

As the late afternoon began casting tree- and mountain-shaped shadows over the Hemp Daze festivities, Sam and the now revived Marty scanned the attendees heading to the parking area, while Greg and Lena handed out cup after cup of hot coffee to the people exiting.

It pleased Sam to see the happy, smiling, slightly sunburned faces of the attendees as they left. All and all, the day had been a huge success.

As the crowd continued to dwindle, Sam's suddenly noticed two men standing just slightly outside the festival grounds. He squinted as he turned to face them, the sun making it difficult to focus on their faces. He began moving in their direction, quickening his pace as he saw them starting to move away.

"Sam!" Greg stepped in front of him pulling an overly full, red wagon. "It looks like we need to announce a 'Lost and Found' area right away. People are leaving all kinds of shit here."

Momentarily side-tracked, Sam spoke with Greg for a moment or two, examining the wagon's contents. When he looked up, the men were gone.

Sam shrugged and returned to the tavern to wake Mackenzie. "God, how long have I been sleeping?" She yawned and pushed the hair from her face. Indentations from the wooden bench on which she had been sleeping were etched in her cheek.

"Not too long, Mac." Sam smiled down at her.

"Did I miss anything good?" She took his hand, and he helped her up from the booth.

"Only if your idea of 'good' is watching someone chainsaw a giant sculpture of a unicorn bong from a log." The two exited the tavern together, laughing.

24

Sam had originally planned to stay in Lester after the conclusion of the Hemp Daze festivities and help with the cleanup.

"Go home and get some rest." Greg relaxed in Mary's tavern with Sam, enjoying a well-earned beer. He looked at Mackenzie. "She's out again." Mackenzie, curled up next to Sam, had her head on his lap.

Sam rubbed his eyes. "Yeah, I think I will head back, if that's okay." He had been thinking of his island off and on all day and felt a strong urge to be home. Rousing Mackenzie, he guided her back to his car.

"If it's all right, I'll just tag along with you back to the island. It'll save you some time." Mackenzie appeared to wake up a bit more. "I'm feeling really good, actually. Can I drive and let you rest for a while?"

Sam smiled and shook his head. "I'm wide awake, but thanks. And yes, it would be great, if you don't mind spending the night on the island."

They rode on in silence. Ten minutes later Mackenzie fell asleep again.

As they approached Manchester, Sam's sixth sense began to kick in. He had a feeling something was wrong at home.

He awakened Mackenzie, and they made their way with the aid of flashlights to his boat and proceeded north up the shoreline toward the island.

In his haste to return home, Sam quickly realized he had not checked for the time of the slack tide. A convergence of streams from several directions had created confused seas, and he had trouble controlling the small boat. Keeping the craft steady on the way to the island was in fact becoming very difficult, as the tidal flows grew more swift and dangerous by the second.

As the eleven-acre island came into sight around a bend in the shoreline, Sam saw a whirlpool spinning toward them caused by the tide, which was split by the north end of the island, and then rejoined at the south end. The vortex attempted to seize and spin the small craft like some huge, powerful, unseen hand.

"I haven't seen a whirlpool that big for a long time," Sam said, sharpening his mind while simultaneously shifting his feet further apart, lowering his body's center of gravity.

"Watch out!" Mackenzie yelled, leaning forward and clutching either side of the boat with her hands.

The vortex made a dogleg turn directly into the small boat's path, grabbing and pulling them toward the center of the dark, spinning abyss. Sam gunned the mercury engine for all it was worth.

He suddenly turned the outboard tiller around, pointing the craft into the center of the whirlpool. The small motor, which had been fighting the current, suddenly revved as the boat gained a burst of speed, now using the momentum of the swirling water.

Trusting his instincts, Sam knew that *the only way out was through.*

The boat, seeming to skate across the swirling water, set into a slightly nose-down pitch as it rapidly gained speed. Looking up, he realized they were now starting toward the mouth of the turbulence.

Sam brought his intense focus immediately back to the center of the whirlpool, carefully gauging their speed, as Mackenzie continued to grip the edges of the boat. He thrust the outboard tiller to the left, causing the aluminum boat to make a sudden, but increasingly laborious attempt to carry them from harm.

"Are we all right?" Mackenzie looked frightened. She watched Sam struggle with the tiller, the frigid Puget Sound waters roiling around the boat.

Even during the summer months, anyone who fell into the Puget Sound unprotected had about the same amount of survival time as someone dumped into the open Pacific Ocean: about fifteen minutes. Any time spent in the water after that would result in hypothermia, muscle cramps and eventually—death.

"We're okay now." Sam expertly guided the small craft into the island's harbor and quickly jumped out, giving Mackenzie a hand. "I should never be in a hurry like that. Sorry Mac, I screwed up by not timing the tides."

"You are one amazing sailor, Sam. Not many people could handle dangerous waters like that." She looked at him with an expression of awe.

They made their way across the hat-shaped island along a well-worn trail leading through towering hemlock, cedar, and fir trees. As they reached a gap in the foliage, the treehouse came into view. "I need to check something really quick," Sam said, moving toward the small, multi-windowed building that served as his greenhouse.

Mackenzie followed him into the hothouse warmth as he flicked on an overhead light. He went from plant to plant, counting them out loud.

"Is something wrong, Sam?"

He shrugged. "I saw marks in the sand on the beach when we arrived. I think someone's been on the island." He returned his attention to opening drawers and flipping through stacks of binders.

"Is anything missing?" Mackenzie peered through a window. "Could anyone be here now?"

"No. Well, at least I doubt it. The boat is obviously gone." Sam walked toward the door. "Better stick close, just in case."

They made their way to the treehouse, Sam in the lead. He pushed open the door and clicked on the light. The room appeared untouched.

"It looks fine in here." Sam motioned for Mackenzie to follow him up to the second floor. As she watched, he went to the bookshelves and ran his hand along the spines, moving throughout the room, his eyes alert for any change in the familiar details surrounding him. "One more level to check and we can relax." A quick look in the bedroom revealed no obvious intrusion.

"Mac, I'm trying to decide if I want you to make a quick check of the island with me, or stay here." Sam pulled on a dark, hooded sweatshirt.

"I'm not staying here alone." She followed him back downstairs.

"Here," Sam tossed her a jacket, "put this on." He grabbed two flashlights and handed one to her.

"This feels like déjà vu." Mackenzie snapped on the light. "Let's go."

They made their way down the driftwood stairs and out onto the trail. A wind was picking up and the trees swung and groaned as they walked the perimeter of the island. Sam knew every inch of his property and was able to lead Mackenzie quickly along the trails. They stopped by a ledge overlooking a small stretch of beach and watched the twinkle of lights in the distance.

"We're good, Mac. No one is here." He reached for her hand. "You're freezing; let's head back."

The pair made their way back to the treehouse. Appearing wide-awake, Sam started a fire and then whipped up a couple of omelets. While eating, Mackenzie looked at him curiously.

"Tell me what is going on here, Sam. There's obviously something you're not telling me." She reached across the table and took his hand. Something told her that Fields may have been involved with this intrusion, and she felt extremely uncomfortable.

Sam took a deep breath and told her about his encounter with Fields Pharmaceuticals. "I've been worrying for a long time about what might happen if big pharma started focusing on this cannabis strain I developed. I wrote a paper with an oncologist that has Fields Pharmaceuticals pissing their pants. I have a strain of cannabis that may significantly slow, or perhaps even arrest, the progression of certain cancer cells." Sam talked freely now, seeming to derive relief from telling someone of his worries.

Mackenzie's eyes grew wide as she listened. This was the moment she had been working toward for some time. But now, as she listened to Sam, she realized for the first time the full implications of Fields' goals.

Mackenzie shuddered. "So you think…Fields has something to do with this?"

Sam shrugged. "The timing is just too coincidental; I've never had anything like this happen before. They wanted my research, and my samples—you should have seen the size of the check they offered me."

Mackenzie sat in silence as Sam fed the fire. She felt confused and sick to her stomach.

"So you are absolutely certain you can't…work with them?" Mackenzie asked this question hesitantly; already so angry and disgusted with herself and with Fields, she would have immediately discouraged any positive response from Sam.

"Not a chance in hell. That's why it's so important now to make this legalization work, so we can get this kind of medicine into the hands of the people, not a pharmaceutical company. Otherwise it could take decades to get this to those who might benefit from it, and it will cost hundreds of times as much to those who need it."

"You may right about that." Mackenzie recalled the predatory look in Richard Aiken's eyes as he spoke of Sam's cannabis secrets. *These guys are desperate and greedy*, she mused. It suddenly occurred to her they could be dangerous as well. This thought had never entered her mind until now, and she quickly tamped it down. What they had done up to now was not illegal...perhaps unethical, but not against the law. They were business executives and white-collar professionals; they wouldn't take a chance with theft or violence. At least, she hoped...

"I read your paper, *Flora Sanitatum*...it was in a stack of academic papers I found on the second floor," Mackenzie said. "I hope that's okay."

"Sure, Mac, you're welcome to read anything you want that's around the house." Sam smiled. "I want you to think of this place as home."

Her curiosity was getting the best of her. "You've written several pieces of breakthrough work and by all accounts you were developing a brilliant and prolific career. What made you drop out of academia? Did it have anything to do with the university selling your epilepsy research?"

Sam nodded. "Listen Mac, let's talk about this tomorrow. I want you to sleep in my bed tonight. I don't think I'll be able to sleep, so I'll just stay down here and keep an eye out." He rose and pulled Mackenzie up from her chair, enveloping her in his strong arms.

She relaxed against him, her head resting on his warm, broad chest. He raised her chin and kissed her slowly, his breath coming faster as she wound herself around him. He gazed deeply into her eyes. "I would love to follow you upstairs, but I think I'd better keep watch tonight."

Mackenzie stepped away, feeling the coolness of the night as he released her. "Are you that concerned? I mean, maybe someone just mistakenly landed on the island." She wanted Sam in bed with her, more than she ever wanted any man.

"I'm really anal about my research and where I keep everything." He had returned to the fireplace, throwing in another piece of wood and peering into the flames. "I know for a fact that my binders had been moved."

"God, Sam. Why didn't you say anything?"

"Go to bed, Mac. You'll be safe." He gestured toward the stairs.

Mackenzie headed upstairs, washing up quickly and pulling on one of Sam's tee-shirts. She crawled in between his sheets, enjoying the scent of his bed. She was exhausted, mentally and physically, but sleep was elusive. A thought she had never considered until now disturbed her: Sam would hate her when he found out who and what she really was.

25

Sam awoke with a start. He stretched and pulled himself up into a sitting position on the couch. The events of the previous evening came flooding back to him: his greenhouse had been broken into and searched.

A shiver ran through him as he made his way upstairs to check on Mackenzie. She slept peacefully, and Sam stopped to watch her for a moment. *She's so beautiful*, he thought, watching her dark eyelashes flutter against her cheek. She seemed so small to him, and vulnerable in her sleep. He reached out and gently smoothed her hair.

Sighing, and wanting very much to climb into bed with her, Sam instead quietly pulled a change of clothes from his dresser and gently closed the bathroom door. Starting the shower, he climbed in and closed his eyes, wishing he could wash away the entire previous year of events and just be here in peace—with Mac.

When Sam emerged from the bathroom, Mackenzie was sitting up in bed. He walked over and sat down next to her, reaching out to take her extended hand in his.

"Are you okay, Sam?"

He nodded. "I'll get over it." He stood and pulled her up, enfolding her in his arms. "We have somewhere to go today, if you're up for it."

"Couldn't we just have a day to hang out here?" she asked as she started for the bathroom.

"God, I wish." His eyes traveled down her body. "You really know how to wear a tee-shirt. I—or we—have an appointment in three hours. I'm supposed to meet with the woman running the retail end of the State pot sales."

Mackenzie looked surprised, "So soon? Wow, this thing is really happening, isn't it?"

"It's happening, but there's a lot left to do." He kissed her. "No time to…" His arms drew her closer, and the two stood in a deepening embrace. He finally pulled away, his breathing rapid. "I'm two seconds away from carrying you to that bed over there." He touched her face. "Maybe I'm crazy, but when we finally make love, which I hope we do soon, I want all the time in the world."

Mackenzie nodded, her voice husky. "I understand, Sam." She smiled as she closed the door. "I'll take a cold shower."

After a quick breakfast, the two made their way to the ferry dock at Southworth just as the ferry arrived.

"Let's go up top and enjoy the view. It's perfectly clear today, and unless I miss my guess, we'll be able to see Mount Rainier."

Climbing to the steel- and glass-enclosed area on the top deck of the ferry, Sam noted it was one of those rare days in the

Pacific Northwest: warm, with perfectly clear, dark blue skies. Spring had arrived, for at least a day—a glorious thing.

They walked outside, and Sam lifted his face to the strong breeze caused by the surprisingly fast-moving ship, struck by the beauty that lay before him.

"Wow, Sam. That's amazing." Mackenzie indicated Mt. Rainier, to the southeast.

"Yep. Mt. Rainier is beautiful, isn't it? It's 14,411 feet of glacial ice and volcanic rock."

"It's still a live volcano, right?"

"Alive, but thankfully for now, it's dormant."

Enjoying their east-facing view of the geologically older and relatively smooth Cascade Mountains across the Sound ahead of them, they saw the ferry had already started its deceleration into the West Seattle Fauntleroy dock.

They returned to the Volvo and drove off the ferry. After making their way through West Seattle and across the bridge, they merged onto North I-5.

"What made you select the store we're visiting?" Mackenzie asked. "Won't there eventually be a couple hundred around the State?"

"Yep, Ken said there are ultimately going to be at least a few hundred stores. But this one was the closest to being completed and will be ready to receive the first shipment from Lester.

"There's the University of Washington, my alma mater." Sam pointed out the campus as they crossed the ship canal bridge and exited toward 45th St., just north of Seattle.

They soon reached Stone Way and parked on the street. "Where is it?" Mackenzie glanced up and down the colorful avenue, bustling with vegan eateries, coffeehouses, galleries, bars and vintage boutiques.

"Not sure, Mac. It's supposed to be near the corner…oh, there it is. The windows are papered over. It's next to the Goddess Spirit Gift Shop." Sam grinned and shook his head. He loved the creative explosion of this particular university neighborhood, but as he had gotten older, he could only take the assault on his senses in small increments.

"Excellent, I could use a coffee." Mackenzie walked toward the Starbucks already positioned next to the pot store.

Minutes later, Sam knocked on the paper-covered door of the shop. Expecting to see an officious-looking State employee, he was surprised to be greeted by a young, tattooed and Rasta-locked woman of about twenty-five. She wore a men's commando-cut tee-shirt sporting a gravestone with a pot leaf and *Illegal* and *RIP* written on the stone, as well as some green drawstring scrub pants, and stout-looking construction boots covered with sheetrock dust. Shaking her hand, Sam noted callouses and surprising strength, given her petite frame.

He smiled at the burst of quasar-like energy and intelligence emanating from the young woman. "I'm Sam VanDerhout, and this is Mackenzie Blake."

"Everyone knows who you are, Sam. You're even cuter than the Internet pictures I found." The young woman spoke quickly, a no-nonsense cadence to her voice. "Hi Mackenzie," she added with a quick smile.

Closing the paper-covered door behind her, she said, "I'm Jillian Lovell, the Seattle District Manager, but just call me Jill. I oversee all of the development and sustaining activities of the Washington State marijuana retail stores in the greater Seattle area, which will eventually comprise twenty-three stores in all, to start. Please excuse the mess; we're further along than it might appear." She glanced around the small space disapprovingly.

"Looks like things are progressing pretty well," Sam noted as he scanned the interior of the facility. "The wiring and plumbing look complete, sheetrock seems almost done—just paint, cabinets and you're there."

"Yep. We'd be further along, but we've been harassed with press and curiosity seekers. Thus the paper over the windows. We got tired of all the interruptions." Jill moved around the room, picking up empty boxes as she went. "Not much to see yet, but Ken said you'd be stopping by, and I wanted to finally meet you, Sam. So it seemed like a good chance to accomplish that."

"How did you find your way into this position?" Mackenzie asked.

"I get that question a lot. I received my Masters in Botany and an MBA a couple years back, and have been doing a lot of traveling and some post-graduate work abroad. I came back to the States last year, and have been watching this legal pot thing from Bellingham. I saw an Internet ad for this job, and here I am."

Jill waved them toward the rear of the store. "The back office is actually finished, so if you don't mind the smell of wet, environmentally friendly paint, I can show you an artist's rendering of the interior design for the stores. Just so you can get a better idea of what this mess will look like when it's ready to open."

Passing through an unmarked door in the back, Sam noted there were three offices and a medium-sized conference room.

"Not all of the stores will have offices like this one," Jill explained. "This is the main office for the region, so it'll be where I, and a couple support staff, will manage day-to-day operations."

Jill explained the details of the product distribution and retail sales process. "We'll use secure State trucks and drivers to begin, in order to ensure delivery and initial success of this endeavor. We're projecting overhead cost reductions in years three and four when we will be switching over to commercial carriers like UPS, Fed Ex, etc. Eventually product transport satchels will be bar-code scanned into, and then back out of every stage in the distribution process, and each satchel can be tracked, much like you'd track the shipment of any product to your house."

Concluding with an artist's rendering of the interior design, Jill added, "It's going to be bumpy with the first few shipments, though. We are pushing this really fast." She looked at Sam, her eyes softening. "You guys in Lester geared up faster than we could have predicted. You must have one hell of a fast-growing strain of cannabis."

"Yeah, we were anxious to get this started up before the State could change its mind." Sam grinned at the young woman, impressed with her intelligence and obvious organizational talents.

After a few more questions, Sam and Mackenzie made their way back to the car. "Say, Mac, since it's such a nice day, would you mind if we drove by my mom's place? She lives on Queen Anne Hill, just a few miles from here. I haven't seen her since I was released, so I'll get a real dressing down. If you're there, she might be nicer about my belated visit."

"Sure, I'd like that…but shouldn't you call first?"

Sam shook his head. "She's always there."

Mackenzie found herself greatly interested in meeting Sam's family. Her research into his life had been lacking with regard to his familial background.

They made their way through the Fremont neighborhood, up the steep slopes of the north side of Queen Anne Hill, then through the business district at the top, and wound their way to the south slope of one of the hills overlooking downtown Seattle. Sam pulled the car into the crescent-shaped brick drive and parked under the porte-cochère.

"Aren't you worried they'll tow you away?" Mackenzie looked at the large, impressive building in front of them.

"No, I'm pretty sure I'm fine here."

Walking to the door they passed a man hard at work mowing the already perfect lawns. "Hi Sam!" he exclaimed as he shut off the mower.

"Hey Chuck! How's the family doing?" Sam stopped to chat with the middle-aged man while Mackenzie examined the imposing structure before them: a huge, brick, federal-revival building, with solid marble columns and white accents, set into the side of the hill with a southern exposure.

At that moment, the front door opened and a gray-haired woman emerged. "Sam! How nice to have you back."

Sam hugged the woman. "Cheryl, this is Mackenzie."

They shook hands. "I'm so glad to meet you, Mrs. VanDerhout."

Cheryl laughed, "I haven't the pleasure of calling Sam my son. His mother is having tea on the patio. Shall I let her know you're here?"

"That's okay. I'll surprise her."

As they walked through the foyer, through the expansive dining room, and across the kitchen on their way to the patio, Mackenzie said, "Wow, most apartment conversions like this ruin the structure of the building."

Exiting the large commercial grade kitchen and stepping out on the patio, Mackenzie was struck by the view. They seemed to be perched right above the Seattle Center area, about equal with the top of the Space Needle, with the bulk of the city spreading out behind and below.

"Oh my god! This isn't an apartment building, is it?" Mackenzie put her hand to her mouth.

"No. This is my parents' home. I grew up here. You can probably imagine how great the sledding was when they closed down the steep roads."

"Samuel. At last, the prodigal son returns." A sophisticated-looking woman of indeterminate age rose from her seat. Mackenzie immediately saw a resemblance to Sam as she turned bright blue eyes in their direction. She looked as though she had been very beautiful in her youth but was still slender and comely, despite the encroachment of age.

"Hi Mom." Sam enveloped her in a hug. "Mom, allow me to introduce Mackenzie Blake. Mackenzie, this is my mother, Nina VanDerhout."

"How nice to meet you," Nina said, holding Mackenzie's hands as she regarded her with obvious appreciation. "She's a stunner, Sam. I think you should keep this one."

Sam glanced at Mackenzie and laughed. "Mom, Mackenzie is a friend. And yes, I'd like to keep her if I can."

"Sam, women aren't just *friends* with tall handsome men like you."

Mackenzie winked at Sam as they sat, and the housekeeper brought out tea and sandwiches.

"Well son, as usual, I have no idea what you're up to these days." Nina stirred her tea, looking at Sam with an amused expression. She turned and smiled at Mackenzie. "He was our youngest. He emerged from the womb like a little Sphinx; his father and I learned to keep him on a very long leash." She reached across the table and put a hand on Mackenzie's. "So tell me about yourself, Ms. Blake."

Mackenzie took a deep breath. She wanted to tell this beautiful, elegant woman she had a PhD and was a senior manager at a Fortune 500 pharmaceutical company. Instead she said, "I work for a laboratory in Seattle. Nothing too exciting."

Nina's blue eyes twinkled. "You seem like a very accomplished young woman. I know quality when I see it."

Cheryl approached the table and Nina whispered something quickly to her. Moments later, she returned with an elaborate photo album in her hands and set it before Sam's mother.

Nina flipped open the album, smiling indulgently, and slid it to Mackenzie. "You might like to see a few pictures of my son when he was young."

Sam put his face in his hands. "Mom. Really?"

"She needs to know you weren't necessarily raised to live like an indigent." Nina laughed, sounding genuinely amused.

Mackenzie sifted through the pages, enjoying the photos of Sam dressed like a young man of wealth, holding up tennis trophies, always smiling and laughing. He was a beautiful child and young man, his intrinsic good nature shining through the pictures. There was a series of photos taken sailing, on holiday, and hiking in the mountains, Sam posing with a stunning blond woman.

"Who's this?" She found herself more curious than she had a right to be about his romantic past.

"That was Marit Nichols." Nina VanDerhout answered for Sam. "They were engaged for a number of years."

Sam shook his head. "Thanks for that, Mom." He looked apologetically at Mackenzie. "I think everyone has a past. I haven't seen Marit for a long time."

"Marit wasn't right for you, Sam." Nina looked at Mackenzie. "She isn't half as lovely as you, dear."

Mackenzie closed the photo album, laughing. "Thank you, Mrs. VanDerhout. I do appreciate knowing Sam didn't start life as a hobo."

They visited for another hour, Sam's face turning red on more than one occasion from the plaudits of Nina VanDerhout. Finally excusing themselves, they made their way down Queen Anne and through downtown Seattle, toward Mackenzie's apartment. Sam apologized a few times for his mother.

"She means well, but she and my father weren't quite prepared to have a son like me. I can't blame her for trying to show you the part of my life she takes pride in."

Mackenzie was emerging from shock, having been completely taken off guard by Sam's familial home and obvious wealth. She reached over and took his hand. "You certainly don't have to apologize, Sam. I really enjoyed meeting your mom." She looked at him with sincere awe. His humility and complete lack of pretense had once again surprised her.

Sam dropped her at her apartment building in downtown Seattle. He held her briefly. "I'm so grateful you came into my life, Mac." They kissed in the car, Mackenzie feeling heat spreading from the pit of her stomach.

That evening she dreamed she was swimming at night in an unfamiliar sea. She started to panic until she felt the caressing buoyancy of the water propelling her forward, toward flickering lights on the shoreline. *I'll just let the tide take me home*, she had thought in the dream, seeing Sam standing near the water, his arms outstretched, waiting for her.

26

The invasion of his island home had thrown Sam into a pensive mood. He had spent the last few days alone, contemplating the direction his life was taking. Today, he awoke feeling as though he had made peace with his path. He could move forward now.

He called Mackenzie and apologized for his preoccupation. "I've just been sorting out some things this week, mentally. But I think I've come to some good decisions." Hearing her voice made him ache to see her. "Can you come for dinner tonight? Marty and Vicki Jo are coming too."

"I'd love to," Mackenzie replied. "Tell me what I can bring."

Sam took a deep breath before asking, "Mac, how long has it been since you've gone scuba diving?"

The question surprised her. "Let me think. I was in Hawaii last Christmas and did some diving there. Why?"

"Good. I wanted to show you some of the Puget Sound from a unique perspective today. Would you be up for a dive this afternoon?"

"Sure. That sounds...interesting. Is there somewhere close where I can get some equipment? My diving stuff's in Maine."

"If you can get here by noon, we'll pick up some gear."

Sam met up with Mackenzie in the Manchester parking lot. "I have something special in mind, Mac." He pulled her into his arms, kissing her quickly. "Don't ask any more questions for now. I'll fill in the details soon enough."

They drove to the Manchester Dive Shop, renting a tank and regulator, fins, mask and snorkel, weight belt, and other equipment. Sam loaded it all into the back of the Volvo.

Mackenzie gazed at him intently as they drove back to the park, a look of concern on her face.

Sam noted Mackenzie's unease. "I've been thinking a lot about what's developing between us." Sam parked the car and turned to look at her. "I've been holding you at arm's length for a lot of reasons, none of which are important now. If I want to bring you closer, I need to trust you. One of the ways I can act on that trust is to show you where I keep things important to me."

Mackenzie's eyes widened. "Sam, you know I've never asked you to divulge anything to me you're uncomfortable sharing. I...I don't want you to have any regrets."

Sam shook his head and smiled. "I've decided I can't let fear run my life. If I have any regrets, I'd prefer the kind that comes from taking too many leaps of faith."

They loaded up Sam's boat with equipment and groceries and made their way to the island.

"Joseph Campbell once wrote, 'The cave you fear to enter holds the treasure you seek.' That seems fitting in light of the fact I'm taking you to a place I call the grotto. It's a bit risky to get there; it's at the end of an underwater cave."

"That's okay, I learned to scuba back in Maine. My dad and I would have to do underwater maintenance on his boat, sometimes even in open seas if something broke. It wasn't the easiest diving. I think I can handle diving through a cave." Mackenzie appeared unconcerned.

"I'm sure you can too. The dive itself isn't where the danger lies; it's the *timing* of the dive that poses the risk."

"I've watched you navigate some pretty rough water. I'm sure it'll be fine."

"It does get pretty dicey with all the whirlpools that can be seen from the surface. But it's even more of a challenge beneath the surface." The shoreline of Sam's island came into view. "I just want you to respect the risks involved. There are places near the island where the currents and whirlpools can pull you over an underwater cliff and down hundreds of feet to a lung-crushing depth."

Arriving near the shore, Sam directed the boat near to where he knew the grotto cave entrance lay below in the dark, rippling water.

"Let's unload the equipment we rented for you, here. I can go and grab my stuff while you're getting prepped."

"Sounds good, Sam."

Mackenzie jumped from the bow of the aluminum craft onto the rocky, shell-covered beach. Dropping the concrete-filled coffee can anchor above normal high-tide line on the island, she strode back to the boat, steadying it briefly as Sam got out and set off to retrieve his equipment.

Several minutes later, Sam emerged from the trees. He saw that Mackenzie had already tightened her tank straps and now tested the regulator, preparing to transition from the beach into the water.

Sam pulled on his gear quickly and turned to double-check her equipment. "So this is what you have to look out for when diving here; this side of the island has a vertical cliff about thirty feet offshore. I think it goes down about three hundred feet, and then levels off. That's what most of the navigation charts I've found over the years seem to indicate, anyway. I've pushed my depth limits a few times, but I've never been able to see the bottom, so I have no idea whether that depth is accurate."

"I understand, Sam. I'll stick close to you."

"Please do. We're at a slack tide right now, so we'll have maybe fifteen or twenty minutes of relatively calm water before the momentum of the outward tide really starts to build. So the plan is to dive quickly to the cave entrance, where you'll follow me through and into the grotto. We'll have only a few minutes to be there safely before the currents get too strong, so we'll have to take a quick look and get back out."

Sam surveyed the water's surface, noting a small, aluminum boat floating about 300 yards from shore. He strained his eyes for a moment, attempting to make out the two figures fishing from the boat. He momentarily considered postponing the dive.

"Is everything okay, Sam?" Mackenzie looked at him with a quizzical expression.

"Yeah." He pulled his gaze from the small boat and smiled at Mackenzie. "Let's get going."

Mackenzie pulled the mask over her face and inserted the regulator into her mouth. Sam did the same, and the two disappeared beneath the gentle waves lapping the rocky shore.

Pausing briefly to ensure Mackenzie's proximity, Sam pulled himself over the cliff's edge and descended toward where he knew the murky depths concealed the opening to the cave leading to the grotto. As he swam, he could feel the all-too-familiar nudge of the salty currents as the powerful forces of moving water acted upon his body.

Just ahead and below, Sam caught the first glimpse of a much bigger whirlpool as it moved in their direction with the now rapidly accelerating outward tide. He knew from experience where the watery turbulence would move next as he hugged the cliff face, allowing the current to just clip Mackenzie, pushing her in his direction. He watched as the current spun her around. He saw the panic in her eyes as she was pushed just within arm's length, where she grabbed his forearm with circulation-stopping force.

Sam took her hand firmly in his and worked his way to the cave entrance. Once inside they slid off their masks and loosened their shoulder straps, lowering the tanks to the floor.

"My god, Sam, that was scary as hell! Did you know the current would grab me like that?" Mackenzie exclaimed, nearly breathless and still shaking.

He nodded. "I know the currents pretty well here. I thought perhaps I should let you have the benefit of actually feeling what these currents will do. It's one thing to be told, it's quite another thing to experience."

She scowled. "I'm not sure if I should thank you, or be pissed off. I could have been killed."

"That's not ever going to happen. This is *you* we're talking about. I'd never let you be at risk, Mac. *Never.*"

Sam walked across the grotto floor and removed a heavy chunk of angular basalt, revealing the small storage area inside.

"What's that?" Mackenzie asked as he pulled the contents from the secret niche.

"Lighting and fertilization schedules, some key seed stock, and other records from my research."

Mackenzie was still shaking off the shock of her dive and glancing around at the cathedral-like setting. She tried to focus on what Sam was showing her. "Is this where you keep the research on your cannabis that has…cancer curing properties?" Her mind raced as she tried to take everything in at once.

"Yes." Sam looked at her, a serious expression on his face. "You have to understand this is…a big step for me. No one else on the planet knows about this cave."

Mackenzie suddenly felt the full impact of not only the dive but also the revelation Sam was entrusting to her. *He loves me enough to trust me with what he holds most dear.* This thought struck her like a bolt of lightning, thrilling and shaming her at the same time.

"We need to head out. I don't want to make the swim back too taxing for either of us." Sam started to pick up Mackenzie's tank. She quickly slipped one of her arms around him; the other hand brought his face close to hers. "Thank you, Sam." The two stood for a moment, breathing in cadence with each other. She had never felt this close to anyone in her life. Sam found her lips for a moment; she relaxed into his warmth and the salty taste of his mouth.

Sam pulled away, gazing at Mackenzie with an inscrutable expression. "We need to head back. Let's take this up again when we get back to the house."

The swim back was quick and without incident. Sam stayed close by her side, making her feel much more confident in the water. He tapped her shoulder and pointed at a creature she immediately recognized as a small octopus. She noted wolf eels in the water as well, surprised at her ability to recognize sea life in unfamiliar waters with such limited visibility.

Emerging onto the beach, they removed their equipment. Mackenzie shivered as Sam wrapped a towel around her from a bag he'd left on the shore. "Let's get moving. It'll warm us up." They gathered their gear and made their way up the hill toward the house.

"You can have the shower first. I'll get the gear put away," Sam told her.

Mackenzie's teeth chattered as she hurried up the stairs to Sam's bathroom. Stripping at the door she ran the water to heat it and jumped in, letting the hot water sink into her skin.

Stepping out of the shower a few minutes later, she heard Sam coming up the stairs. Her heart thumped in her chest when he called, "Did you save some hot water for me?"

"I think so. Did you happen to bring up my bag?" She wrapped herself in a towel and stepped out into the bedroom. Sam stood smiling at her. "Right here." He gestured to the bed as they moved toward each other. They met in an embrace that seemed to gather intensity with each breath. Sam lifted her in his arms and put her on the bed, her towel dropping away like useless petals. He lay down beside her, tracing the line of her neck with his mouth, moving down to her breasts. Mackenzie's sigh of pleasure seemed to cause him to breathe faster and she reached out to unbutton his damp shirt, revealing a muscular chest. She felt his weight shift, and the warm length of his body pressed down on her as she opened her mouth to his kisses.

"Hey Sam!" a voice called from downstairs. "Where the hell are you?"

"Are you kidding me?" Sam groaned and rose to one elbow. "I'll be right there!" He looked down at Mackenzie. "I guess Marty and Vicki Jo are here."

Mackenzie laughed as she pulled a blanket around her. Sam stood and began buttoning his shirt. "We can't seem to catch a break." His eyes moved across her slender body as she pulled her clothes on. "Let's get this dinner over with as quickly as we can."

She followed him down the stairs a few minutes later. Marty, Vicki Jo, and Sam stood in the kitchen. "Sorry guys. We had to catch the tide, as you well know." Marty grinned at Mackenzie. "Vicki Jo and I know all about interruptions with regard to our private time, don't we, hon?" He gazed lovingly at Vicki Jo, who was trying to force a large, foil-covered pan into Sam's small oven.

Vicki Jo finally jammed the oven shut and looked up at Mackenzie. "Sure as shit we do. Marty's married to his pager."

Sam caught Mackenzie's eye and mouthed the word, *Pager?*

Mackenzie grinned. "It's okay guys. I need to help with dinner anyway."

"You love birds take a seat," Vicki Jo said. "Marty and I can handle this."

Mac watched as Vicki Jo pulled salad fixings from Sam's small refrigerator, obviously prepared to assume complete control of the meal.

"Sam, can I get you a beer?" Marty asked, as he stood in front of the open fridge, scratching his chin.

"Sure. I'll take one, Marty. Could you pour a glass of wine for Mac, too?"

Soon the four settled down as Vicki Jo loaded the table with a huge pan of lasagna, salad and bread. Marty appeared to have the appetite of a much larger man, heaping his plate and eating noisily.

"You'll have to excuse Marty's open mouth chewing," Vicki Jo said matter-of-factly. "He has a long history of septum contusions."

"That's because he can't keep his mouth shut." Sam laughed, looking up from examining his lasagna.

"I regret the loss of smell, but I don't regret speaking my mind, even if it elicits an occasional fist-fight." Marty grinned widely, pausing to take a drink of beer.

"This lasagna has an interesting flavor," Mac said, finishing a forkful of the meaty dish. "I don't think I've tasted anything quite like it."

"That bear went down hard." Vicki Jo was piling Marty's plate with another helping of the gamey casserole.

"Bear?" Mackenzie's fork clattered to her plate, as Sam burst into laughter.

"Yep. Shot that big bastard last summer. Male, about 800 pounds."

Sam was attempting to control his laughter as he reached over to Mackenzie and grabbed her hand. "Mac has probably never had the…opportunity to eat bear meat."

"Bear is a great meat for lasagna. It's really fatty, so you don't need to pan any cooking oil before browning it." Vicki Jo lifted her fork proudly. "It makes damn fine pepperoni, too."

Mackenzie swallowed with some effort. "It's really good."

As the evening progressed, Mackenzie found herself laughing harder than she had in years. Sam looked totally relaxed, legs stretched out in front of him. Mackenzie watched his face as he laughed; he seemed to give himself completely to the moment, engaging with his surroundings in a way she found mesmerizing.

He rolled some thick joints, and Mackenzie grew introspective. Seeing the marijuana clearly reminded her of the original mission—why she was in Sam VanDerhout's life to begin with. Today, she had discovered the very thing she had come to find. One phone call to Richard and divers would likely be sent to Sam's grotto. This would be the successful end of the story, leaving her the ability to return home to L.A. in triumph. She could probably save TH-18 with what she had seen in Sam's cave and become a rising star at Fields Pharmaceuticals.

None of these thoughts gave her pleasure, or even remote satisfaction. All she felt was miserable. She noticed Sam observing her, a look of concern on his face. She smiled and reached across the table, placing her hand on his.

Vicki Jo glanced at Marty. "Come on, Mr. Ranger sir, we need to leave these two to their own devices." She stood and began gathering up their things.

"Yeah, the tide is hitting the perfect point right about now." Marty joined Vicki Jo, picking up dishes and placing them in the sink.

"Leave that stuff, guys. I can clean up later." Sam stood as well, stretching and grinning at Mackenzie.

"Sam, I think I'm going to catch a ride back with Marty and Vicki Jo." Mackenzie felt an overwhelming need to escape. Too much was happening to her at once and she felt on the verge of tears. She ran upstairs and picked up her things, rejoining Sam, who was waiting for her.

"Is everything okay, Mac? You seem stressed, or upset or something." He drew her into his arms, engulfing her in his now familiar scent. Breaking away, she looked into Sam's eyes, placing her hands on either side of his face. "Sam, I need to take care of some things myself before…" She sighed. "…before I can be with you." She kissed him and he pulled her even closer, their kiss growing in intensity until she broke away again, gasping for a moment.

She turned and headed to the kitchen, joining Marty and Vicki Jo, who appeared not to notice anything unusual in Mackenzie's abrupt departure.

"See you, Sam." Marty saluted and headed out the door.

"Thanks Sam! Good freaking times, as usual." Vicki Jo pulled Sam into a crushing bear hug for a moment and followed Marty.

Mackenzie stood in the door, tears again forming in her eyes. She blinked them back and smiled. "I'll be in touch in a day or so, Sam. Okay?"

He nodded. "You do what you need to do, Mac. I'm not going anywhere."

The ferry ride back to Seattle was a blur. Arriving at her apartment, she pulled off her coat and sat down in front of her laptop. She would be back in L.A. soon.

Two men had watched from their boat in the twilight as a small vessel took off from the island. The larger man had thrown his cigarette into the water before reeling in his fishing line. He nodded to the other man, who started the small engine and pointed the boat to the opposite shore. Maybe they had actually seen something worth reporting, for all the hours they had been out there. He couldn't be certain.

27

Mackenzie headed directly home from LAX, calling Aiken from her cell and setting up a time to speak with both him and Mallory.

Moving about her well-appointed condo, she tried to reconnect with her life in Los Angeles. She turned up the air conditioning; it was already hot this early in the afternoon. Being up north had definitely made a difference in her ability to tolerate heat.

In several hours, Mackenzie would meet with Richard Aiken and Tim Mallory. She knew that no matter which path she chose going forward, the one behind could very well disappear.

The reality of the situation had to be faced. She opened her laptop and began checking her finances. She'd been careful with her money, but living in Southern California was expensive. She owned her well-located condo outright and the real estate market had been picking up lately. Between a quick sale of her home and her modest stock holdings, she felt she had enough to start over if needed. She glanced at her resume; it needed updating, but it held enough education and experience to land her something that would at least pay the bills.

Mackenzie jumped when her cell phone rang. "Hi Mom," she said, her voice steady so as not to arouse her mother's concern. "Yeah, I'm fine, just been working a lot of hours."

Her mother, having dispensed with her maternal inquiries, launched into a typically one-sided conversation full of her life's small details, complaints, and fears. Mackenzie interrupted her mother mid-sentence. "How is Dad, anyway?"

"Oh, you know; he's out on the boat. He's been complaining a lot about his back hurting. I've been warning him for years about all that lifting and manual labor he does. Serves him right for leaving the white-collar world."

As her mother spoke, Mackenzie was struck by how much she missed her father—his big, rough hands, his workingman clothes and gentle demeanor. As her mother was fond of saying, "He's a social nightmare."

He is Sam. The thought suddenly struck Mackenzie. "I need to get back to work, Mom. I'll give you a call later." Ending the call, she walked back to her couch. She held her head in her hands, tears streaming down her face.

Sam. His utter disregard for clothing and social convention. *He is flat out embarrassing sometimes*, Mackenzie thought, smiling in spite of herself.

She could just imagine her mother's question: "Honey, what does he *do*?" Mackenzie would answer truthfully. "He putters around his treehouse, grows awesome pot and reads books...oh, and he builds and fixes things—for himself, not for money of course." Dear God, but her father would love him.

Sam is, hands down, the best man I have ever known. Mackenzie knew this was the truth, *her* truth.

Heading to the shower, she prepared herself for the meeting with Mallory and Aiken. She avoided the rows of expensively tailored suits in her closet and selected a simple cotton dress with sandals.

"Now this is getting interesting." Doug Delaney held a set of papers in his hands. He looked up at Jonathan Thorpe, one of his best employees. "You guys kicked ass on this. The photos you took of the guy's journals printed out really clear."

Delaney continued to read, sitting at his desk; the trim, muscular, and well-dressed man in front of him waited impatiently.

"What do you think this means? '*In addition to cannabinoids' ability to moderate gli…glioma cells, separate studies demonstrate that cannabinoids and en…do…cannabinoids can also inhibit the proliferation of other various cancer cell lines.*'" Delaney paused, scanning the pages. "'*A laboratory study of delta-9-THC in hepatocellular carcinoma cells showed that it damaged or killed the cancer cells…*'

"I would bet cold cash this slacker has grown some kind of weed that—cures cancer." His ancient office chair squeaked as he leaned back, laughing. "I Googled this VanDerhout guy; he's some kind of professor or florist or something." Delaney shook a handful of nuts from a glass jar. "Does this guy seem like a genius to you?"

Thorpe scowled in reply and shook his head.

Delaney laughed again. "You don't like him much, do you Johnnie? Maybe you'll get a chance for some *alone time* with him soon. Bet you'd like that." He shook Thorpe's hand. "Good work. I want you back up north ASAP; keep on this guy's ass, keep making him nervous. We may need to step this up fairly soon."

Thorpe turned and left the room wordlessly, the click of his polished shoes fading as he left.

Delaney quickly dialed Aiken's cell number. "Yeah, Richard. You might want to get your ass over here. I have something interesting to show you."

Mackenzie had never been this nervous in her life. She knocked on Mallory's door and entered.

Aiken sat across from Mallory; he stood when she walked in. "Is everything okay, Mackenzie? You sounded unlike yourself when you called this morning."

Mallory, looking at her with concern, gestured toward a chair. "Please take a seat, Mackenzie." She declined the invitation.

"I'm here to hand in my resignation." The words came from her mouth in a surprisingly calm tone.

Mallory and Aiken stared at each other in disbelief.

"You're *quitting*? What on earth are you talking about, Mackenzie?" Mallory exclaimed. "Why would you quit Fields? You…you're on the fast track here."

"Tim, why don't you let Mackenzie and I talk in private for a moment?" Aiken said. Mallory shrugged and left the room, closing the door behind him.

"Okay Mackenzie, listen, I'm not going to try and make you stay. We just need to talk through some details. Now please sit."

Mackenzie sat down reluctantly and met Aiken's cold stare. "My mind is made up, Richard. I...I just need a change. That's all."

He snorted. "Don't try and bullshit me, of all people, Mackenzie. I believe I have an idea what's going on here. You think you've fallen for this VanDerhout guy, am I right?"

This shocked Mackenzie. She sputtered, "No! No...it's not that. I just...don't feel right about all this—"

"Stop." Aiken put his hand on her shoulder; his tone softened. "Mackenzie, I completely understand. You were pulled out of your normal life and plunged into a completely foreign situation. It's similar to what they call the Stockholm Syndrome. Your loyalties shifted from becoming too familiar with the life in Washington." He sighed. "It's my fault for not staying more in touch with you. I...overestimated your ties to us here at Fields, I suppose."

Mackenzie felt momentarily confused by Aiken's words. Could he be correct? Was she simply experiencing some kind of crazy trick of the mind? She closed her eyes for a moment, trying to still the rising panic. Sam's face then appeared in her mind's eye and she felt heat pour into her body.

"Okay, Richard. Yeah, you're right. I love Sam. And I won't be part of this thing anymore. He has a right to do whatever he wants with his research." She met Aiken's now stern gaze.

"So you're ready to give up your independence, life and livelihood here for some stoner?" Aiken shook his head in disgust. "Do you realize how that sounds? I honestly thought more of you than that."

Mackenzie felt completely certain of herself now. No going back; no way. "I know what I want, Richard. My reasons for doing this are strictly my own and do not concern you or Fields Pharmaceuticals."

"How do you think he's going to react when he finds out the truth? Do you think a person like Sam VanDerhout is going to forgive and forget such…deception as you have been a party to?"

Mackenzie shrugged. "I don't know. I just have to chance it, there's no other option for me."

"Here's what I recommend. Give it some time before you tell him anything. Let things settle down and consider for a while that you have sacrificed your career for him."

Mackenzie stood. "I'll go clean out my desk and let Human Resources know I'm resigning as of today. You're probably right about telling him the whole truth. I guess I'll wait for a while." She held Aiken's eyes for a second. "But know this: I *will* tell him eventually."

Mackenzie headed back to her office and called Sam on her Washington cell phone. "Sam," Mackenzie said, her eyes filling with tears. "I'm heading back home soon."

"Mac, so good to hear your voice." Sam sounded relieved. "Let me know what flight you're on and I'll pick you up. Lester's first shipment is going out and I wouldn't want you to miss it." He paused for a moment. "Is everything okay?"

Mackenzie took a deep breath, relief pouring through her body. "Yes, Sam. Everything's great."

28

Aiken looked up when Mallory walked back in the office.

"What the fuck, Richard?" he snapped. "You assured me this woman would be a team player. What happened?"

Aiken waved his hand dismissively. "It doesn't matter."

"What do you mean by that? She'll tell VanDerhout everything, if she hasn't already. We're fucked."

"She hasn't yet, and she won't."

"How do you know?"

"Because she thinks she's in love with the asshole. She's afraid he'll kick her to the curb if he finds out. No, Tim. We have just enough time to finish this out." Aiken looked at his watch. "I've got a few things to attend to. I'll keep you apprised of the situation."

Aiken drove quickly to Long Beach to meet with Delaney. "So, what is it?" He took his usual seat across from Delaney, declining a drink and looking impatient.

Delaney pulled some papers from his desk and slid them over to Aiken. "Take a look. My guys did good, I think. Tell me if you think this is worth anything."

Aiken spent a few moments excitedly poring over the papers. He looked up at Delaney, eyes glinting. "So your men took photos of VanDerhout's research, I'm assuming?"

"Yeah. But I think that there's quite a bit you haven't told me about this job." He nodded toward the papers. "By the look on your face, I'd say those are the real thing."

Aiken remained silent.

"Well, Richie, I have more to report, but I may decide to keep it to myself." Delaney leaned back in his chair. "I mean, if we can't trust each other after all these years—"

"Okay, fine," Aiken interrupted. "These are important. VanDerhout has, potentially, something on his island that we are very interested in. Is that enough information for you?"

"Not even close. But, just to show that I'm a team player, I'll tell you what my guys saw and see if it catches your interest." Delaney grinned, pausing for effect as Aiken tried to remain patient. "My people saw VanDerhout and his hot girlfriend go for a long dive and I'm thinking they went somewhere…uh, special."

Aiken sat up in his chair. "A long dive?"

"Uh-huh." Delaney's smile faded. "I think they may have something that any pharmaceutical company would pay big cash for…maybe some kind of…ah, cancer cure?" He indicated the notes.

Aiken thought quickly, a new plan forming in his mind. "Get a diver down there as fast as possible and report back to me immediately." He glanced sharply at Delaney. "And don't think you can do anything with what you find. You need me to make this pay off. I know what we're looking for, and I have the contacts in this industry."

Aiken rose from his seat and started toward the door. "If we play our cards right, we may both put our hands on some serious money."

29

Thorpe waited impatiently for one of his men, the only one with some experience, to finish an exploratory dive. He was relieved to see bubbles breaking on the water's surface as the diver emerged from the dark water surrounding Sam's island.

"Nelson, what did you find?" Thorpe asked nervously, as the man slid his tank to the sand and removed his mask.

"Not a goddamn thing," Nelson pulled a towel from his bag and wiped his face. "That current is a major bitch. I know there are caves down there, but if you don't know exactly where you're going, it would take a real pro just to locate each one, much less find the exact cave you're looking for."

"Great. Just fucking great, asshole." Thorpe was angry. He had been reluctant to let one of his own men go down to try and find VanDerhout's underwater hiding place, but Delaney had insisted on keeping everything within their own ranks; no outsiders.

"Fuck you," Nelson said, as he peeled off his dive suit. "Try it yourself if you think it's that easy."

Thorpe called Delaney. "Yeah, we struck out. I told you we should have hired a real diver. Okay, I'll wait to hear back from you."

Thorpe nodded toward the small boat anchored near the shore. "Let's get the hell out of here."

Aiken was pacing the floor, waiting for Thorpe to report back, when the phone rang. Delaney spoke briefly then threw his cell phone on the desk.

"Well, it didn't work. Fuck." He looked up at Aiken. "What next?"

"VanDerhout has to make the dive, obviously."

"And how do you suggest we go about making him do this? I mean, it's not like we have a lot of time here. And from what my guys say, the first pot shipments from that Podunk town are scheduled to start any time now. I've got my hands full coordinating all this shit." Delaney looked uncharacteristically stressed.

"You're going to have to abduct VanDerhout, there's no other option. Mackenzie Blake too. Make him dive."

"Blake is the good looking chick who worked for you, right?"

Aiken nodded. "Without her, VanDerhout may not be convinced enough to cooperate."

"How the fuck am I supposed to know if he brings me the right stuff? And what if he just swims off?"

"He won't, not as long as you've got the girl."

Delaney sighed. "Jesus, Richard. Try to plan things a little better next time." He reached for his phone. "I'll get Thorpe going on grabbing VanDerhout."

"Oh no. You're going up there yourself to make sure this goes down without any loose ends," Aiken ordered.

"What the fuck? Why do I have to be there?"

"I don't trust anyone but you to get this thing done properly. Listen, I don't want any of them hurt, if at all possible. But if things get out of hand…well, I trust you to do whatever you have to. Understood?"

Delaney's smile looked more like a sneer. "You got it, boss."

30

"We're fine, Tim. Relax, for god's sake." Richard Aiken, having returned to Fields headquarters, was annoyed. "We've done nothing illegal here. Nothing at all, in fact."

Tim Mallory had been pacing his office for the past hour, experiencing a case of last-minute nerves. "What if she tells him everything, Richard? What then?" He stopped to glare at Aiken. "I'm not taking the fall for this, not under any circumstances!"

"As I've said a hundred times, she's not going to tell VanDerhout a fucking thing. Not for a good long while, anyway. And, more importantly, she knows nothing substantive about our secondary plan."

"But she can damn well guess who is behind what happens. The woman isn't stupid."

"Doesn't matter. Let her say whatever she wants. We'll sue her for libel, or slander, or whatever." Aiken smiled. "We are walking away from this, Tim. Things are set in motion. Money has been paid. We may not have VanDerhout's miracle pot, but he won't be able to do much of anything with it once the dominoes fall." Aiken rose from his chair, placing a hand on Mallory's shoulder. "Forget this whole thing. It never happened."

Mallory shrugged. "I suppose you're right, as usual." He glanced sharply at Aiken. "You are absolutely certain this third party of yours won't end up bringing us into this thing if they screw up?"

Aiken laughed. "We are a major corporate entity, Tim. People like us don't break the law. We *make people's lives better.* We have the best lobbyists money can buy and the best attorneys. My contact would be laughed out of court trying to bring accusations against us. As a matter of fact, let him try. There are no loose ends here, Tim. None whatsoever."

Aiken smiled as he walked back to his office. Unlike Mallory, he had not benefited from an Ivy League education and a surfeit of charm and good looks. He had used his raw intelligence and a certain indelicacy of conscience to carve out his space in the corporate universe. Although his supervisors found him to be matchless for taking on unpleasant, ethically challenged tasks, he had found himself consistently shut out from the high executive ranks.

Using his contacts in the pharmaceutical world, Aiken could sell VanDerhout's cancer-curing pot to the highest bidder. Fuck Fields Pharmaceuticals.

31

Sam was scanning the passengers coming through the gates when he caught sight of Mackenzie hurrying his way, a smile lighting up her eyes.

Sam swung her off the ground while kissing her. "It's so good to see you, Mac."

Mackenzie slid her arm around his waist as they walked to the baggage claim. "I can't believe how good it feels to be... home."

They picked up her luggage and headed to the dock. As they sat waiting for the next ferry, Sam asked Mackenzie about her trip and discussed the excitement everyone was feeling up in Lester.

"We need to get back there right away, if that's all right, Mac. I hope you don't mind skipping a stop at your apartment."

The people of Lester had been working every spare hour they had to invest in the legal marijuana beta test for the last week. The time had passed quickly, but also with a certain ease and delight that attends those fortunate enough to be engaged in creating something new. Now, on the eve of Lester's first shipment of marijuana, virtually everyone there knew what was at stake, not only for the town, but also for the whole State of Washington—even, perhaps, for the entire future of legal cannabis.

Everyone gathered together in an atmosphere of both celebration and a certain apprehension, for the inaugural event of Lester's first, modest shipment of legal cannabis. The quality and quantity of what they had produced had exceeded their wildest expectations. Piles of neatly bagged pot sat on pallets, all finished with a beautiful *State of Washington* waxen seal. The warehouse was filled with the spicy-green, earthen scent of freshly cured marijuana plant. A second shipment waited in step behind this one, and then another.

Washington State had instigated a "back-flush" method for Lester's beta test. Over the course of two days, Lester would first send one satchel each to twenty retail stores. Once all the bags had been acknowledged at their end point, a second, larger shipment would go out. The first set of now empty bags would be shipped back to Lester and a third, larger shipment would be sent as the second set of empty bags were shipped back. It was considered to be a "no fault" system that validated each step in the process.

Greg was waiting outside the pot plant when Sam and Mackenzie drove up. "The delivery vans have arrived for the first shipment." He appeared both excited and nervous. "I told the drivers we had another half an hour or so before we were ready."

They walked into the facility, meeting up with Simon, who carried a heavy load of pallet boards.

"Mackenzie!" Simon carefully set down his load and gathered her into his sasquatch-like embrace. "I'm so glad you made it back in time for our big party at The Lodge!"

Mackenzie laughed. "I'd never want to miss a party in Lester, that's for certain."

Despite his excitement, Greg looked a bit stressed. "Sam, I think we have everyone here, ready to start this next harvest and…I asked Father Donneghy to make some kind of blessing over this first shipment to the dispensaries, but I'd like you to say something as well."

"Excellent," Sam replied. "Let's rock this thing." He felt immensely satisfied with what had taken place in Lester and had grown to consider the townspeople his extended family. He had nothing monetary to gain from this beta test; his payoff was right here, right now—in the proud, happy faces of this rugged logging town and the sweet smell of lovingly raised cannabis.

Greg put his thumb and forefinger together and emitted a shrill whistle, then yelled across the vast warehouse-cum-pot-growing facility, "Hey everyone! Gather around at this end of the building for a minute! Father Donneghy's going to offer a blessing and then Sam's going to say a couple words before we hit it!"

A few minutes later the townspeople of Lester had all made their way through the narrow aisles nestled between tall forests of green to the end of the warehouse where Sam stood.

Sam turned over a stout-looking crate as a makeshift pulpit for Father Donneghy. The priest stepped up on the crate, smiled and bowed his head as the room grew quiet.

"Our Father, we are gathered here today to join in a moment of quiet blessing for this shipment of fine, high-grade marijuana. We pray in Your name that the fragrant product that these, Your humble but highly skilled servants, have produced, will arrive safely at its destination. We pray that, in Your divine wisdom, You will guide all hands that touch this glistening shipment of weed, and we pray that You will smite all those who might try to rend our heavenly efforts asunder—or even just steal a sticky bud or two. We pray that those who purchase and use this pot will find themselves feeling closer to You than they have ever felt before. We pray that they will see their way clear, through the haze, to become repeat customers, and that they will tell all their of-age friends and associates that *Lester pot is best*. All these things, we pray in Your name, Lord God. Amen."

The room erupted in applause and a loud "Amen" as Father Donneghy stepped aside for Sam, who tried unsuccessfully to smother his laughter.

Finally composing himself, Sam began: "Thank you, Father Donneghy for that inspired blessing. Today marks the beginning of a new era for marijuana in the United States." He gestured to the bags of cannabis. "We are ready to ship, for the first time in history, *legal marijuana licensed by a State government!*" A huge whoop and loud applause rang through the warehouse. Sam continued, his bright blue eyes gleaming: "The insane propaganda campaign that has been waged against the simple plant in those bags has led many to be incarcerated like common criminals, and robbed of their liberty. In other parts of the world, drug wars have taken countless lives and toppled governments. The prohibition against cannabis has contributed violence and fear into this world and brought misery to many, many innocent people."

His voice lowered. "But, thank God, rationality has finally won out. The good people of Washington State, even many who have no use for marijuana themselves, had the courage, the good sense, to say NO MORE INSANITY."

Sam stood in silence for a moment, surveying the crowd of happy, expectant faces in front of him. "I'm so proud of all of you and of what you have accomplished here in such a short time—"

"We couldn't have done it without you, Sam!" The crowd broke out in loud applause, with whistles and whoops. Sam stood grinning, a look of genuine affection on his face.

As the crowd quieted, he continued: "For me personally, what has meant the most is that I have become a part of your community. You have become like a family to me in many ways." He stopped, looking down and clearing his throat for a moment.

"We love you, Sam!" Once again the crowd broke out in wild applause.

"Well, it's returned." He smiled, his eyes resting on Mackenzie for a moment. "The last thing I'd like to say is, thank you. Thank you for letting me share in this journey. Now, let's finish this thing!"

The entire warehouse erupted into raucous applause and whistles, hoots and hollers.

"Let's get this first shipment on its way." Greg spoke over the din. Sam jumped off the crate and the two men headed to the loading dock.

The rest of the crowd went to work on what would be the second shipment, clipping the most recent batch of perfectly mature buds.

Mackenzie joined Simon, helping to place the buds on carts to convey the harvest to curing. Beyond the curing room was a packaging line where the already cured buds were quality-checked, carefully bagged, and placed into the specially manufactured canvas satchels that were then sealed by a Washington State Department of Agriculture employee.

Sam and Greg watched as the vans took off from the loading dock, heading to their first destination, the flagship store Sam and Mac had visited in Seattle. Sam stood smiling. "I can't believe it." He slapped Greg on the back. "Can you believe this?"

The two men watched in silence as the last van disappeared. Greg shook his head, a note of apprehension in his voice. "I only hope nothing goes wrong."

Sam put his hand on Greg's shoulder, "You know the old saying? 'He that will not sail 'til all dangers are over must never put to sea.' We've done all we can do. It's out of our hands now."

32

As the well-greased machine of Lester's pot processing came to a halt on the second day of their shipments, Mackenzie began to search for Sam. She finally found him outside, speaking to Greg, who sat in his truck. Greg then took off, waving at Mackenzie as he pulled onto the road.

She had seen very little of Sam during the frenzy of the last two days. He'd practically lived at the Pot Plant. Having spent the night without him at Greg and Becky's, she was anxious to finally have him to herself for the evening.

"Are you ready to head out to The Lodge? It's party time." Sam took both her hands into his own, looking down at her with a sweet expression.

Mackenzie felt the freedom of having quit her job at Fields. She moved closer to him, wrapping her arms around his waist. "I took a room at The Lodge."

"I reserved one also. But I'm thinking now that might be redundant." Mackenzie could feel his heart beating, strong and steady, as they stood there.

"Hey Sam!" People were now pouring out of the warehouse. "Are you heading over to The Lodge?"

"You bet!" Sam walked Mackenzie to the Volvo. "Go ahead and check in while I finish up here. I'll catch a ride with someone." Mackenzie nodded.

"Are you coming soon?" She found herself not wanting to be parted from Sam for too long. More than ever, she felt the connection between them.

"I won't be long." Sam smiled before leaning in to kiss her, his mouth lingering for a moment. "Believe me, I'll be there as quick as I can." He stood and grinned, waving as she drove away.

Soon, Mackenzie pulled into the parking lot of Lake Kiutan Lodge. She sat for a moment, taking in the view as the early evening sun cast long shadows on the lawn. The immense, V-shaped lodge complex looked slightly foreboding from the outside. Enclosed by old growth rainforest and built on the shores of a glacial lake, the whole place appeared to come from another time.

Mackenzie pulled a small suitcase from her car and headed in to the Great Room. Entering through the ornate double doors, she was welcomed by the sweet scent of well-seasoned, aromatic old growth fir and hemlock logs.

After a quick check-in, she made her way to her fourth-floor room and unlocked the door with what appeared to be the original brass key. She glanced around the room, noting its walls made of smooth, polished lumber and a sizable bed with four wooden posts carved to look like totem poles. The rustic dresser and cabinet were made from old growth, knot-free fir; they opened with surprising lightness, a testament to the craftsmanship of the period in which they were made.

The sun was falling low behind the mountains and Mackenzie stretched herself out on the bed for a moment. She no longer had a job, and she was far away from the life she had lived for the past seven years. In spite of that, she felt peaceful, like expatriates who had found their true home in a foreign country. She was not yet able to face the full implications of her decision to leave Fields, and the unpleasant truths she would eventually need to tell Sam. Closing her eyes for a moment, she relaxed into the chenille comforter and listened to the hushed sounds of the hotel around her.

Sam hitched a ride with Jeffrey Floyd, arriving at The Lodge just as Marty and Vicki Jo pulled up.

"Hey guys!" Sam's voice was muffled as he spoke from within Vicki Jo's bear-like embrace.

"We're here to add to the festivities." Marty was dressed in his best uniform, neatly pressed with State of Washington insignias on either shoulder.

"Sorry we weren't able to be there when the actual shipment went out. Marty had a little trouble at the park today." Vicki Jo lifted a giant suitcase from the back of her Humvee and started toward The Lodge.

"What happened, Marty?" Sam felt a strange foreboding wash over him.

"Oh, you know. I caught a couple guys nosing around. They were near where you keep your boat. I didn't like the look of them."

"Did you speak to them?" Sam tried to keep his voice calm.

"I gave chase, obviously. But they were wilier than the teenagers I normally deal with. Whoever they were, they certainly knew how to evade the law." Marty noticed the look of concern on Sam's face. "I called in Keith and Barry to keep an eye on things while I'm here. They may be volunteer rangers, but they're pit bulls when it comes to protecting the park and its environs." Marty stopped and looked at Sam suspiciously, his small eyes narrowed to slits. "Is there something going on you haven't told me about?"

Sam didn't want to alarm Marty by telling him about the break-in at the tree house. Marty was paranoid enough already; giving him an actual reason to be on high alert might not be a good idea. "Oh, you know. That business with my impromptu trip to LA a while back has kept me a bit on edge."

"As well it should!" Marty placed his hand protectively on Sam's shoulder. "You are such an innocent, Sam. Vicki Jo and I were just talking about that on the way here."

In spite of his concern, Sam laughed. "Glad to know my friends are discussing my simplemindedness."

Sam opened the door for Marty and they entered the Great Room. "Just do us a big favor, Sam, and keep your eyes peeled." Marty clapped him on the back and headed over to Vicki Jo, who was wrangling her huge suitcase into the elevator. "See you at the party!"

Sam watched as the elevator closed on his two friends. He shook his head and headed to the front desk.

Sam went straight to his own room first. He wanted to shower and change clothes before he saw Mackenzie.

Mackenzie had spent extra time on her appearance this evening and felt relieved that she had brought some dressy clothes back from L.A. In keeping with the era of The Lodge, she had chosen to wear a sheer, pale green, drop waist dress that reminded her of something from *The Great Gatsby*. Her hair was left loose, falling in smooth curls to her shoulders. She slipped on her matching shoes and was gathering her purse when she heard a knock at the door.

She swung open the door expecting Sam; instead Vicki Jo stood there, decked out in a black, velvet floor-length dress. "Vicki Jo!" Mackenzie hugged her and stepped back admiringly. "You look awesome."

Vicki Jo smiled broadly. "This is my Renaissance Fair dress. I can barely keep Marty's hands off me when I wear this." Both woman laughed, Mackenzie closing the door behind her as they walked toward the stairs.

"So this thing is in the ballroom. They don't open it up very often, from what I hear." Vicki Jo paused and leaned over, holding the low-cut neckline of her dress and shaking her chest. Straightening up, she looked at Mackenzie and winked. "Just fluffing up my junk a bit."

A minute later they met several people from Lester heading in the same direction. Mackenzie struck up a conversation with

Becky Gunderson and Carmen Alford, the town's resident psychic.

"Has anyone seen Sam?" Mackenzie was anxious to find him. She stopped at the top of the stairs to gaze down at the beautifully decorated room, with its high ceiling and polished wood floor sparkling with lights from a series of rustic chandeliers. She saw Sam talking to a group of people near the bar and headed there quickly.

Sam turned as she approached, a smile spreading on his face. Mackenzie's heart pounded fast; Sam looked fit and elegant in a pair of olive colored corduroy pants and a black button-down shirt.

Mackenzie slid her arm into his and he pulled her closer. "How did I miss the fact you've had your hair trimmed?" She reached up and brushed his thick sandy-blonde hair with her hand.

Sam laughed. "I got some epoxy glue in it. Wallace finally had to take drastic measures and put me in his barber chair." His eyes traveled lovingly over Mackenzie. "You look so beautiful," he whispered.

Greg approached them and handed Sam a Tree Top IPA in the bottle. "And I brought you a glass of chilled Chardonnay, Mackenzie." He handed her an overly full glass of wine, looking happy and slightly drunk.

Greg walked to the stage, where a small group of musicians readied their instruments. He tapped the microphone a few times and cleared his throat. Raising his bottle of Heineken, he shouted, "To Sam! *E Cannabis Unum!*" The invocation rang throughout the ballroom and the crowd roared back, "To Sam! *E Cannabis Unum!*"

Turning to the band behind him, Greg said, "Let's go, guys!" The tuxedo-clad lead singer stepped up to the microphone and began belting out a solid rendition of "Let's Fall in Love," sounding just like Frank Sinatra.

Sam laughed. "God, they've hired a Frank Sinatra tribute band, of all things." He grinned at Mackenzie. "Shall we dance?"

This surprised her. "You can dance?" He didn't seem like the dancing type.

Sam shrugged. "I had to learn when I was in private school. My mother felt it was a life skill." He led her out onto the dance floor, joining a mix of happy couples already swinging around the room.

Mackenzie, not the best dancer herself, had taken a few lessons over the years and was competent enough to keep off her partner's toes. Sam slid his arm around her waist and pulled her close, raising her hand in his. Mackenzie found herself amazed at how smoothly he danced, swinging her around, dipping her and then pulling her close again. They were both laughing and breathless when the song ended.

"You're a regular Fred Astaire, Sam." Mackenzie fanned herself with a napkin as they sipped their drinks.

"I only hope my prowess on the dance floor doesn't raise a red flag to some of the ladies in here." Sam was looking nervously at a group of Lester matrons heading his way.

"Sam!" Leila and Lena Thorvaldsen, in the lead, each grabbed one of his arms. "We want a place on your dance card," Leila said, as her sister leaned in and added, "Preferably a nice slow dance."

"Sorry ladies." Mackenzie smiled, holding up her hand. "I'm afraid he's all mine tonight."

A collective "Awww" rose from the women gathered about Sam, who looked much like a deer caught in headlights.

"As a matter of fact..." Mackenzie disengaged him from the ladies. "...I'm taking him out for some fresh air." She led him out the tall French doors and onto the terrace overlooking Lake Kiutan.

The outdoor lights were just coming on around the lodge, tripped by the sun lowering behind the Olympic Mountains. Unlike the rest of the rustic-style hotel, the terrace was designed as an extension of the more formal ballroom, with art deco flourishes and white pillars forming a half circle around the tall, leaded glass double doors.

"The days here are so long." Mackenzie gazed out toward the lake, glittering with pink and gold lights. "It's been a while since I've watched a sunset at ten o'clock."

"It's the plus side of being this far north. As you probably know from growing up in Maine, we have the opposite effect in the winter." Sam pointed to the sky just above the horizon. "There's Venus."

Mackenzie laughed. "I think we've made some memories around star-gazing, Sam." She touched her hair. "I can still feel the bats."

Sam shook his head as he drew her close. "There are plenty of bats around the lake. Want to take a walk?"

Mackenzie wrapped her arms around his neck, wanting this moment to be etched forever into her memory. She could feel the bottom of her dress fluff in the light breeze drifting off the lake. The muted sound of "Moonlight Serenade" poured through the French doors.

"He's singing my favorite Sinatra song," Sam said, beginning to move Mackenzie to the music in a slow, graceful dance.

"Sam." Mackenzie looked up at him as they danced.

"Hmm?" Sam looked down at her. "What's up? Did I step on you?"

"No." Mackenzie leaned her head against his chest, her voice slightly muffled. "I think I'll take you up on that walk down to the lake. I…well, I need to catch you up on a few things."

Sam pulled back from her as the song ended, looking down at her shoes. "We'll have to stay on the promenade."

"Well, yeah. I wasn't suggesting a major hike." Mackenzie laughed as they walked down the steps to the long, well-lit path paved with mortared slate, which led to the edge of the lake.

They sat on a bench beside the gently lapping water. Sam pointed toward the thick forest rimming the lake. "I've spent my share of time in the southern rainforests, but I've always been hesitant to spend much time in the Olympic rainforest." He gazed into the darkness. "I think it's part of the magic, the fact it exists untouched for the most part. There's probably a wealth of undiscovered plants in there, though."

Mackenzie shivered and drew closer into Sam's embrace. He looked at her and smiled. "So what is it? You said you wanted to talk."

"I've quit my job." She sighed. She wanted to tell him the whole truth tonight; but sitting here beside him, in his arms and wholly immersed in his world, she found it increasingly difficult.

Sam gazed at her thoughtfully, saying, "Well there are worse things, Mac. Are you okay for money? I don't want you to worry about that."

"I'm fine. Thank you though." His words warmed her, but the truth of her full deception lay just beyond, threatening everything she had come to value. She pushed the thoughts from her mind, using the potency of her feelings for Sam as a shield. *I have to tell him.*

"Sam." Mackenzie stood, breaking away from his embrace. "There's more I need to tell you." She walked to the edge of the lake, wrapping her arms around herself. "When I first came to you…I was working for Fields Pharmaceuticals." She stared resolutely at the calm surface of the water. "I was sent to befriend you, seduce you, whatever it took to get Fields a sample of your cannabis research…the cancer cure research." As she heard nothing from Sam, she continued uttering her confession in a soft voice.

"If I could only explain what it's like to…to be obsessed with something, like I was when I first came to Washington." Mackenzie kept her eyes focused on the dimming horizon, feeling deeply relieved to be able to share her story with Sam, regardless of the outcome.

"Please, tell me." Sam spoke gently. "I want to hear."

Mackenzie couldn't stop the words as they poured out. "You have to understand the way I was raised, Sam. My dad left a very successful life on Wall Street when I was ten years old. We went from Park Avenue to a little seaside house in Maine. He was so happy, buying his fishing boat." Mackenzie smiled. "But my mother never forgave him." She could still feel the tension and misery in her household from those years. "My mom, she… Well, she wanted me to succeed. She and my father made sure to put me through the best college and graduate school."

"You probably felt pretty driven." Sam moved close to her again. She felt the warmth from his lean body; it took all her strength not to throw herself into his arms.

"It's like a drug, Sam. The whole corporate mentality is based on losing your sense of self. Over time, I think I just lost my moral compass. My job, my career, it was the only thing I knew."

Sam slid his arms around Mackenzie's waist, pulling her to his chest. She melted against him, unable to stop herself.

"For better or for worse, I was born into money; I've never had to bend myself to fit anyone else's paradigm."

Sam leaned away from her, looking into her eyes. "I couldn't begin to judge you for what you did, Mackenzie. I've never walked in your shoes. To be completely honest, this whole thing has caused me to face a few of my own issues, and it's not been pleasant."

Mackenzie slid her arms around his neck, finding his mouth with her own. She could feel his response, their bodies meeting hungrily. For a time they stood entwined together by the lake, wanting the moment to last forever.

Sam's body responded to the urgency of Mackenzie's embrace. He felt a passion from her that he returned, feeling it building quickly between them. He lifted his head, his breathing accelerated. "I have a confession to make as well."

"Yes, Sam?"

"I already knew you worked for Fields."

"What?!" Mackenzie pulled away, her face a mask of utter shock. "You *knew*? How long have you known?"

"It was after the break-in. I guess I went through a paranoid phase." He shrugged. "I called Fields, just the corporate number listed on the internet, and asked for you. They actually connected me to your voicemail." He chuckled. "Not what I'd call high-level corporate espionage."

Mackenzie shook her head in disbelief. "Why did you show me the grotto if you knew I worked for Fields?"

Sam sighed. "I guess I was following my heart. I wanted to put everything on the line and demonstrate how deep my feelings were for you. I trusted my instincts."

Mackenzie slid her arms around Sam's neck and rested against his body, tears flowing silently down her cheeks. He placed his hand on her face, gently tilting it upward. An old moon was breaking through the fast-moving clouds, illuminating the lake, forest and distant mountaintops. "This is what I can give you, if you stay with me, here in Washington. It's not a perfect place, and I'm not a perfect man. But it's as real as it comes."

Mackenzie felt his breath and the slow rise and fall of his chest. "It's more than enough."

"We need to get back to one of our rooms really quick, Mac." He pushed the hair from her face, laughing softly. "We're going to have to sneak past the party, however."

Sam's eyes strayed to a grove of trees near them. He saw the light from a cigarette quickly go out, as if someone retreated into the forest. He squinted in the dark, trying to make out the figure, but it was now completely sheltered from view.

"I feel badly about ditching the party, Sam…" Mackenzie grabbed his hand. Her eyes turned to where he gazed intently. "What do you see?"

"Oh, nothing. I thought I saw someone."

"We're at a hotel. There are bound to be people around." She squinted to see what Sam had been looking for, feeling slightly uneasy in spite of her words. She didn't want to alarm him, but her experience with Fields had taught her that they did not give up easily. She had no idea how far they might go to get what they wanted.

"Right." Sam shook his head. "You are right. I just feel a little jumpy lately."

Mackenzie pushed her apprehension from her mind, wrapping herself around him. "I believe I have a solution for your nerves." She reached up to kiss his neck, her hand sliding past his chest and down.

"Dammit, woman. I finally got myself presentable." He set her aside for a moment, breathing deeply. "Good thing I meditate and do yoga, or I'd have to walk through the lobby looking like a teenager on Viagra."

The two made their way toward the lodge, laughing.

"I think we should go back in for just a bit, Sam. This is an important night; I don't want to spoil it for these people. They love you."

"I suppose you're right. But stay close."

Many people had gathered on the terrace now, and the smell of Lester's marijuana permeated the air.

"Sam and Mac!" Marty jumped up from Vicki Jo's lap. "The band is taking a well-earned rest and we're enjoying some libations." He waved a joint in the air.

Sam stopped to watch the people on the terrace for a moment, his face relaxed into a bemused smile. Simon sat in a relatively small wicker chair, his umbrella-festooned drink balancing precariously on his huge knee while he spoke animatedly with Leila Thorvaldsen. Lena was taking a turn kissing Jeffrey Floyd, the baker, who was perhaps a little too drunk to know which twin was which. Greg and Becky passed a joint back and forth, laughing and looking like teenagers. People whom Sam had come to know and to love were passing in and out of the ballroom doors, their faces lit with the soft lights of the terrace; a terrace on the banks of a glacial lake, in the middle of a rainforest abutting rugged mountains and the Pacific Ocean.

Standing there, his arms around the woman he now loved, Sam could only feel the perfection of the moment.

33

Mackenzie stayed close to Sam as they moved about the terrace. She felt as if a huge, dark weight had been lifted from her body, and she free-floated in the world now, her only gravity coming from the rumpled, handsome man at her side.

Sam felt her shiver. "Are you cold?" He wrapped his arms around her. She could feel the vibration of his voice as her head rested on his chest. "We can go in for a while." He looked at her, his eyes sparkling. "I think you need a couple more spins around the dance floor."

Walking back into the thick, golden light of the ballroom, they were immediately assailed by happy revelers. A series of dance partners pulled Mackenzie from Sam's side. Simon proved a particularly enthusiastic dancer and she found herself laughing in spite of herself as he performed an impressive series of hip-hop moves, his massive body exhibiting surprising grace and mobility.

Mackenzie waited out the next dance, watching Sam have a spin with Becky Gunderson, elegantly waltzing her around the dance floor.

"Who would have guessed he was a dancer too?" Greg stood beside her, sipping water, his salt-and-pepper hair tousled at odd angles.

"He's a Renaissance man, that's for certain." Mackenzie smiled. "I'm so amazed at what this town has done. I'm especially impressed with you, Greg."

"I guess desperation can be a great motivator."

"It's more than that." Mackenzie believed that Greg deserved a serious estimation of his worth. "If I were an executive in a major corporation, I'd hire you to run an entire division."

Greg shook his head. "This is a team effort. And without Sam, none of this would have happened."

"For whatever it's worth, you have my complete admiration."

Greg was blushing when Becky and Sam returned from the dance floor.

"Are you ready to retire for the evening, Mac?" Sam's voice fell as he spoke.

She nodded, looking at the crowd. "We have to keep our departure on the down-low. Popularity has its price."

"Whoa, look!" Sam pointed toward an interior circle in the dance floor that had suddenly cleared. "Dear god," he said, delight in his voice, "Marty and Vicki Jo are going to attempt a solo performance."

Mackenzie laughed. "This I have to see."

The band struck up a lively rendition of "Fly Me to the Moon" as Marty and Vicki Jo met on the dance floor and unleashed a creative tango.

"Strictly speaking, I think the guy is supposed to be leading."
Sam appeared highly entertained as he spoke in Mackenzie's ear.

Marty had somehow lost his shoes during the course of the
evening and now danced on the polished floor in his socks, as
Vicki Jo led him through a series of intricate dips and cheek-to-
cheek maneuvers.

"I think he's losing his purchase a bit." Mackenzie noted the
fact that Marty's socks seemed to be slipping down around his
ankles.

"He's going to fall," Sam said, just as Marty's feet shot out
from underneath him during a dramatic dip. Vicki Jo, normally
vigilant, was too compromised to stop the fall as a loud *thump*
sounded over the music.

Marty lay on his back in the middle of the dance floor. "Just
taking a breather!" he shouted.

Sam took Mackenzie's hand. "Let's slip out while there's a
distraction."

They made their way out of the ballroom, heading through
the lobby and up the stairs to Mackenzie's room. Once inside,
she clicked on a lamp as Sam walked to the French doors leading
to a small Juliet balcony overlooking the lake. He sat down on
the wicker loveseat and stretched his arms behind his head.
Mackenzie grabbed a sweater before joining him.

"It's perfect here, isn't it?" Sam dropped his arm behind her,
drawing her close. A cool breeze rippled across the lake, scenting
the air with a mixture of ancient wood and young, moist green.
The moon hung just above the mountains, a carpet of stars visible
above.

"I never want this evening to end." Mackenzie's voice sounded wistful, even to her own ears.

"We have all the time in the world, Mac." Sam smoothed her hair. "We can go anywhere, do anything we want."

Mackenzie turned to him with sudden passion, her body on fire for him. She needed to be as physically close to Sam as possible. He seemed to sense her urgency, saying in a husky voice, "Let's go to bed." He lifted her and carried her gently to the four-poster.

Mackenzie dropped her sweater and started to pull off her dress.

Sam smiled. "Slow down a minute." His hands moved down her hips and thighs, grasping the bottom of her dress, sliding it up slowly as his eyes lingered over the perfect curves of her body. He draped the dress carefully over the edge of a nearby chair, and turned back toward her.

"You are so beautiful, Mackenzie." His mouth found hers for a teasing moment, pulling away long enough to slide off her bra, his hands cupping her breasts. He pulled off his own clothes quickly, revealing a form kept fit by a lifetime of outdoor activity and physical work. He struck Mackenzie as being completely at home with his body, unselfconscious and confident in his sensuality.

Mackenzie had never made love like this before. Sam seemed to enjoy every inch of her body, exploring it with his hands and mouth. When she was barely able to contain her need for him, he would slow himself and allow her breathing to normalize then continue his sensual journey, bringing her to the edge over and over again. Finally, he took her fully and she felt herself plunged into the intimacy she had sought with Sam. Their breath came in ragged gasps until that moment in which, together, they merged into the dark and were washed out to sea.

34

Sam rolled over, sensing the sleeping body next to him. The sun streamed through the windows, bringing a halo to his surroundings. Trying not to disturb Mackenzie, he carefully crawled out of the disheveled bed. He opened the double doors of the balcony and felt the scented cool of morning blowing up from the lake. Heading to the bathroom, he stopped to survey himself in the mirror, rubbing his hand across his rough chin, and smiling at the man staring back at him. He carefully brushed his teeth, happy to have beaten Mackenzie to this morning ritual. After a quick shower he stepped out and ran his fingers through the damp waves of his hair. Last night had been more than a night of pure pleasure. Sam was now, for the first time in his life, fully and completely in love with another being. Already gifted with the ability to derive joy from life, he had now realized another level of happiness. As he slid back into the soft bed, he concentrated on the wealth spread before him—laying his hand on Mackenzie's dark hair, feeling its silken texture and moving gently down her form, taking in her warmth with his fingers. Nothing more was required of the moment.

Mackenzie stirred; her eyes opened languidly. "Good morning, sunshine." She reached out to touch Sam's face, lifting herself to kiss him. They made love again, finishing in each other's arms. As Mackenzie rose to shower and dress, Sam listened to the muffled voices and smells of morning coming up through the open French doors.

"You think we should just stay here all day and order room service?"

Mackenzie laughed from inside the bathroom. "I think it's quite possible we could stay in this room for a week!"

A hesitant knock sounded at the door. Sam dressed quickly and opened it. Greg stood there, looking hung over and a bit sheepish.

"I would have called first, but the rooms don't have phones, and you never carry your cell. Becky and I are taking off and I just wanted to confirm you'd be heading over to the warehouse today. Mike called this morning and said we'd lost one of the main motors on our processing line." Greg sounded a bit stressed. "That thing's been a major bitch from the get-go."

"Of course. I'll be there shortly. I know we're on a timetable for the next few shipments to go out." Sam closed the door as he turned to Mackenzie. "I'm afraid duty is calling."

"I heard. Let's grab a bite to eat and head right over there. They can't afford to be late with any of these shipments."

Sam shook his head, loving the fact she seemed to care more about Lester's success than her own personal agenda for the day. He hugged her. "You realize I'm in love with you, right?"

Mackenzie grew quiet, her face buried in Sam's shirt. After a moment she said, "I have never felt about anyone the way I do about you. It's kind of a new sensation for me."

They headed downstairs to the bright hotel restaurant for breakfast. The sounds of silverware and plates and sweet smells of fresh coffee and morning fare drifted around them.

"I'll completely understand if you don't want to stay and help," Sam said. "I know you've had a lot to deal with the past few days."

"Of course not. I'm already here, I want to help." She kissed him. "I want to be with you, as well."

After finishing their meal, Sam grabbed their bags and carried them to the Volvo. He had a gnawing feeling something was not quite right and he didn't like it. Driving back to Lester, he couldn't shake the sense that he walked on a ledge or a precipice of some kind. It was a rare feeling for him, since he generally took life as it came along, adjusting himself gracefully to its winds and currents. But now that he was fully involved, both with the people of Lester and with Mackenzie, he no longer sailed solo in life. He realized his happiness, at least to some degree, rested in others' hands now. As always, Sam knew he would make peace with this sea change in his life. But for the moment, it was disconcerting.

Arriving back at the plant, Mackenzie threw herself into what physical labor she could find. Most of the workers showed up late, looking the worse for wear after the previous night's festivities but still eager to keep things moving. Sounds of power tools and laughter rang through the facility. Hours passed before Sam, covered in grease and sawdust and looking pleased with himself, deemed the motor back online.

"We've done a lot of good work today."

"I don't know about you, Sam," Mackenzie said, stretching her sore back, "but I feel like we moved a ton of marijuana bags today. Will there be enough demand for all this?"

Sam laughed. "You'd be surprised." They stood outside on the loading dock, entwined for a moment in their own world. A loud car horn shook the parking lot as Vicki Jo drove up in her Humvee. Marty slept in the passenger seat, a black eye visible.

"What happened to him?" Sam sounded concerned and amused at the same time.

"Oh, you know. Things get out of hand when he's around." Vicki Jo looked at Marty lovingly. "He took a couple headers on the dance floor. At least I think that's what happened." She stuck her hand out the car window. "Thanks for the great time last night, bro. I'm taking Marty home and putting him down for a nap." She laughed and gunned her engine before squealing out onto the road.

"I have a surprise," Sam said. "It might combat the aches and pains we'll probably feel tomorrow."

"What's that?" Mackenzie, exhausted as she was, still felt the electricity of Sam's body as she leaned into him.

"Well, we can take advantage of the soaking tubs that re-use the hot water circulating through the curing tables."

"They're ready to use now?" Mackenzie knew Greg had been working on this project for weeks.

"Greg and I just finished them today. Follow me." Sam led her out behind the plant.

"Is clothing optional?" Mackenzie teased.

"I'll let you decide."

As they rounded the corner, sounds of people splashing and laughing echoed off the massive trees nearby. Steam slowly wafted into the air.

The siren call of the soaking tubs had evidently summoned a good portion of the people working at the warehouse that day. Leila Thorvaldsen sat in Jeffrey Floyd's lap within the steaming water. Greg and Becky were leaning back, eyes closed.

Simon was wedged in the corner of one of the wooden tubs, his huge arm draped around his petite partner, Dennis. He called to Sam and Mackenzie, "Come join us! We're cooking off our hangovers in here."

"We just might do that." Sam surveyed his and Greg's handiwork with the practiced eye of an engineer. He told Mackenzie, "The hot water comes from a natural geothermic spring, about a half-mile away up in the woods. It comes through those pipes, then into the building, where they circulate hot water under the curing tables, and then the water exits the building and flows into the top of those three soaking tubs then cascades down from one tub to the next."

Mackenzie was impressed. "Where does the water go from there?"

"After it cascades off the spillway of the bottom tub, the water flows over to a cooling pond, and then back to the stream created by the hot springs." Sam pointed into the dark, heavily wooded area surrounding the town. "All we're doing here is borrowing some heat from the earth, and giving the water back."

"So, there's a hot spring back in the woods…up there?" Mackenzie pointed in the direction of the unobtrusive pipes disappearing into the woods at ground level, up the slope.

"Yes. It's not far at all."

"I've always been fascinated by hot springs." She smiled and wrapped her arms around his neck, whispering, "And I'm rather interested in having a private soak."

"Let's go take a look then." He winked. "We'll try and keep this to ourselves, though."

35

The phone rang early at the City of Portland, Oregon Police Department. Detective Stephen Gonzales of the Department of Homeland Security and Investigations Bureau had phone duty that morning. He took a gulp of coffee and answered tersely, "Gonzales."

Moments later, Gonzales was calling Deputy Chief Edward Sulky of the Narcotics Division. "We received an anonymous tip about a large quantity of marijuana found in the back of a van near Colonel Summers Park."

"Jesus, Gonzo, why are you bothering me with this? Call Roberts at the East Precinct."

"Ed, the marijuana was found in a bag with an official State of Washington Seal."

"What the fuck. Are you kidding? I'll go myself." Sulky hung up quickly and called his assistant. "Get me the DEA on the phone. Immediately."

That same morning, the Ada County Sheriff's Department in Boise, Idaho was dispatched to a report of a large quantity of marijuana in a vacant warehouse on the 2500 block of South Munroe Street near the city limits. Deputy Chief Bob Targa took the call in his vehicle. He arrived fifteen minutes later. Other officers had beaten him there.

Jumping out of his vehicle, Targa checked his gun. Drug busts were second on his list of least favorite things, domestic violence calls being on top.

"Kincaid, what's the deal here?" he asked one of his men.

"Don't know at this point, but apparently it's an abandoned site. We've already begun clearing the perimeter."

Chief Targa nodded toward the entrance. "Let's go. Watch yourself."

They headed into the ramshackle building, leaving a deputy outside to keep watch. Targa's flashlight cut through the dark interior.

"God, it stinks in here." Kincaid coughed as he tried to focus his eyes in the dim light.

"Over there." Targa walked quickly to a stack of pallet boards, under which sat what appeared to be a small duffle bag. He pulled on a pair of rubber gloves and quickly checked the container.

"Christ!" Targa pointed his flashlight at what appeared to be a seal on the bag. "State of Washington."

"Agent Riley, get over here!"

Greg Riley immediately recognized his boss's voice, Investigations Supervisor Jim Clark. "Yes sir."

"Give me the punch line. What the hell is going on here?"

Riley hadn't passed his first anniversary with the DEA, and he knew he had much to learn. However, one thing he knew with certainty: don't screw up in your rookie year, or you'll spend the rest of your career trying to live it down.

Riley quickly gave a thumbnail sketch of the situation. "My partner and I were following up an anonymous lead about a large shipment of cannabis coming into Missoula tonight. We were advised to start here at the Greyhound Bus terminal. Sure enough, the K-9 units we called in immediately picked up marijuana traces, and led us straight to those satchels."

He pointed to a loading dock area, where other agents from an alphabet soup of agencies stood. There, set in a neat stack, were six large, green canvas bags emblazoned with what looked like a seal.

"What the hell are those?"

"That's where this gets really interesting, sir. Those appear to be the Washington State marijuana transport satchels we've been hearing about on the news."

"I'll be goddamned," Clark said under his breath. He stared at them in silence for long seconds.

Riley and the others waited for Clark to give the word.

"Get me the Washington State Governor's office. It seems that our tree-hugging pothead friends over there in the Evergreen State have a bit of a problem on their hands."

36

Mackenzie and Sam made their way across the field to the start of a small trail. As they walked, Mackenzie could hear the dream-like echoes of conversations coming from the soaking tubs. The forest in front of them sparkled with the long light of the sun.

"I love this feeling," Mackenzie said in a hushed tone as they penetrated the cool, moist air of the forest.

Sam took a deep breath of the sweet, oxygen-rich air. "Me too."

They climbed silently up the forest trail toward the hot spring, listening to the occasional tapping of a woodpecker or the singing of other birds, each reveling quietly in the peaceful moment. Soon, however, they emerged from their common musings; they had reached their destination.

Without a thought, Sam and Mackenzie deftly removed their clothes and eased into the hot, soothing, mineral-rich water bubbling up from below into the small, natural pool.

After a while Sam said, "This is just too perfect."

"I agree." Mackenzie pushed herself through the steaming water to Sam. "I've never made love in a hot spring before." She moved against him, pressing herself into his body, allowing him to take her quickly and hungrily.

Satisfied, they listened to the sounds of the forest, Mackenzie's head resting comfortably on Sam's chest.

"This is just about the best day of my entire life," Mackenzie murmured.

Sam let the muffled sounds of the forest hang for a few moments then replied. "*Just about* the best day?"

"Well, maybe a little less manual labor and it would have been number one." She grinned and waved her hand in front of Sam's face. "Count the blisters."

About fifteen minutes later, Sam suddenly sat upright. "We better get going." A sixth sense had alarmed him. He cocked his head, lifting his finger to his lips to silence any words from Mackenzie.

Her eyes were wide with alarm. Seeing her concern, Sam relaxed. "I've got to stop this paranoid shit." He smiled. "I'm just hearing things again, Mac." He hugged her for a moment. "But we do need to get going."

They climbed out onto the soft, compressed mulch of the forest floor. Shivering, they dressed quickly in their slightly damp clothes and started back down the trail toward the Pot Plant. Both remained silent, concentrating on the trail ahead.

"Watch out!" Sam caught Mackenzie as she stumbled over a large tree root that had wound its way across the path.

"It's hard to see those damn roots," Mackenzie muttered, massaging her shin where the root had caught her.

"Let me go ahead of you, Mac." Sam moved in front. They continued walking, falling into the silence of the forest, just the occasional snap of a twig noting their progress.

What's wrong with me? Sam thought. *I've hiked through jungles at night and been less jumpy.* He picked up the pace.

They were still some distance from where the trail emerged into a field when Sam heard a muffled shriek, and words uttered in a deep male voice. He turned quickly and saw Mackenzie being held by a burly-looking man, as another pulled something over her head. Before he could charge them he felt something heavy against the back of his head. He sank to his knees as darkness enveloped him.

Sam slowly regained consciousness but saw nothing through his own hood. He realized that he rode in some kind of vehicle, traveling on what sounded like a gravel road. Clearing his throat he whispered, "Mac, are you there?"

"Yes. I'm okay, are you?" she whispered back.

"I think so."

The vehicle sped along the gravel road for about ten or fifteen minutes, when it suddenly slowed with tire-squealing deceleration and turned onto a similar road. His head throbbing, Sam felt a warm trickle of blood running down his face.

Assured Mackenzie was okay, he concentrated on staying alert and trying to judge the distance they were traveling. Struggling against shock and the ache in his head, he attempted to keep track of the time, calming himself by steadying his heartbeat with slow, deep breathing.

Sometime later, after numerous hastily executed turns that pinged gravel against the thin steel skin of the vehicle, he felt them enter smooth highway. Their hoods—pillowcases, Sam saw—were suddenly yanked off their heads. A man in the back of the otherwise empty van was holding them at gunpoint.

Sam's eyes focused on the muscular man in the passenger seat, arms crossed, a scowl on his face.

"What the fuck!" Sam tried to control his anger and shock.

"It can't be Aiken or Mallory that put you up to this!" Mackenzie exclaimed. "I know Fields is ethically challenged, but outright kidnapping is…unimaginable!"

"Let's not discuss that right now." The apparent leader glared at Sam. "We're on our way to find that fucking magic pot you've hidden away."

37

"Next on News Channel Six, breaking news about the legal marijuana initiative in Washington State. Will it be 'High Finance' or 'Down the Pot' for legal marijuana here? More news after these messages."

Greg and Becky sat in the Lester Tavern, sharing a beer after their soak in one of the new outdoor tubs. "Mary, can you turn that up?" Greg asked.

"Yeah, sure," the tavern owner replied.

Commercials over, the anchorman continued: "News Channel Six has just uncovered the apparent failure of Washington State's processes intended to ensure that the distribution of marijuana stays within our State boundaries. If confirmed, the voter's wishes for legal marijuana here in Washington may go *up in smoke.*" He looked pleased with himself over the pun.

"Oh shit!" Greg stood, spilling his beer.

"Early reports indicate the Federal Government's Drug Enforcement Agency has discovered that several satchel-type bags clearly marked with the State seal of Washington, like this one…" He held up one of the bags for the camera. "…have ended up outside Washington's borders."

Greg gasped in disbelief. "No way. No fucking way!"

The anchor went on: "These satchels have been discovered as far away as Oregon, Idaho, and Montana."

Greg pulled out his phone and called the mayor as the news circulated through the small hamlet. Within minutes, people started gathering in the Lester Tavern. They all watched as the guy on the news droned on: "News Channel Six is currently verifying sources, but if our preliminary information is accurate, the end result could be not only failure of the legal marijuana movement in Washington State, but also—quite possibly—federal criminal charges for those involved as a result of the illegal transport of marijuana across state lines."

The citizens of Lester fell silent. Greg finally awakened from his state of shock. Looking around frantically he said, "Where is Sam?"

He spun the barstool around and raised his voice so everyone in the tavern could hear: "Has anyone seen Sam? We need his help, and we need it right now."

Someone toward the back yelled, "I saw Sam's Volvo when I passed by the plant, still there in his parking spot!"

Greg pulled out his cell phone, his face pale as he attempted to reach either Sam or Mackenzie. No answer.

"I'm heading back to the warehouse." He raced to the Lester Pot Plant, the crowd following him. Sure enough, Sam's car stood in the spot the town had designated with the sign, *Hippie Intellectual Parking Only*.

"When is the last time anyone saw either of them?" Greg asked.

A woman said, "I noticed them by the soaking tubs a while ago."

"Yeah, I saw them there too. Okay everybody, form into small groups and check the plant, and around town, and the nearby woods, and call me if you find them.

"Simon!" Greg called. "I happened to hear Sam describing the hot spring to Mackenzie. Let's run up there and take a look."

Simon nodded. "I have a flashlight."

The two men started along the heavily wooded path to the hot spring. Suddenly Simon halted, yelling, "There!" He pointed into the dense underbrush along the path. "That looks like Sam's daypack!"

Greg saw it too, and not far away he spotted another, smaller one. A quick examination of the contents confirmed these were indeed Sam and Mackenzie's packs. Each contained a cell phone.

"They would never leave these behind," Simon said.

Greg took Sam's cell phone and examined it briefly, seeing no ingoing or outgoing calls in the last twelve hours. "No clues here."

"Mackenzie's phone has a password!" Simon handed her phone to Greg.

He studied the surrounding woods for a few seconds. "Well, at least we know they were headed this way, or were on their way back." Greg peered down an adjacent trail. "About the only way to avoid crossing back over the field surrounding the plant is to follow that trail to the logging road...down there."

Gathering up the daypacks, the pair proceeded down the trail. After several minutes they emerged abruptly from the shadowed woods onto a gravel-topped logging road.

Greg bent down to study the road. "It looks like a vehicle peeled out of here...like they were in one hell of a hurry." There were deep furrows cut through the gravel and into the dirt below.

"What's going on here, Greg?"

He thought for a moment. "There's a lot at stake with this whole pot thing. I think there's a chance someone may have taken Sam and Mackenzie."

"Taken? You mean *kidnapped*?" Simon exclaimed.

"It's possible. Sam's been spooked a lot lately, and he's pretty perceptive. Plus this whole mess with our pot turning up all over the fucking place...it's just too much of a coincidence."

Not only was Greg concerned about Sam and Mackenzie's safety, but the news about Washington leaking pot all over the Northwest had unnerved him. Sam's cell phone rang suddenly, causing both men to jump.

"Sam VanDerhout?" The voice on the other end sounded agitated.

"No. This is Greg Gunderson...but this is Sam's phone."

"This is Ken Silver, I need to speak with him right now."

"Ken. We're looking for Sam. We...can't find him at the moment."

"Well, goddamn find him and have him call me immediately. This is urgent." The phone went dead.

"No shit." Greg looked at the phone for a moment. He decided it was time to call Marty. Flipping through Sam's phone, he located

Marty's number. The cell rang four times and flipped over to voice mail.

"This is Officer Stout. Please leave your message. If this is an emergency, press star seven and I will be paged."

Greg quickly entered Sam's number into the paging system. Seconds later the phone rang.

"Dammit." Greg fumbled with the phone for moment. "Hey, this is Greg Gunderson."

There was a pause before he heard Marty say, "Greg? Why are you calling from Sam's cell?"

"We can't find him, Marty. Not him or Mackenzie. Have you seen them come to the island?"

"What?! No, I haven't seen them." He paused. "But I haven't been quite as vigilant as usual today. What do you mean you can't find him?"

"We found his pack and Mackenzie's with both their phones. Neither of them are anywhere in Lester that we can find. And, I don't know if you've caught the news, but Lester's pot has been found outside the state. I have a bad feeling it's connected with their disappearance somehow."

"Hold on for a moment." There was a pause on the other end of the phone then a quick, muffled conversation.

"Vicki Jo and I will formulate an attack plan and head over to the island."

"I can drive over to Manchester, if you think it would be helpful."

"No, you wouldn't get here in time. Stay where you are and keep looking for them. We'll keep in touch." The phone call ended abruptly.

"Let's get back."

Simon nodded and the two men made their way back toward the plant. On the way Greg called Becky and told her what he and Simon had discovered. "Has anyone found them yet, or heard from them?"

"No. It's like they've vanished, Greg."

Greg decided to continue the search for the time being, sending several people out in all-terrain vehicles to inspect the trails and logging roads in the vicinity. Catching up with Becky, he pulled the napkin from his wallet on which Sam had drawn the location of his island. Pointing at it he said, "We'll keep looking, but something tells me they are back here."

"So you think they're okay then, Greg?" Becky asked.

"No, Becky. I think they are in serious trouble."

38

Doug Delaney spoke quietly into his cell phone as the nondescript van, driven by Thorpe, continued on toward Southworth at an alarming speed. He lowered his phone. "Slow down, idiot. We don't want the cops pulling us over."

Seated in the rear of the van, hands tied behind his back, Sam stared at Mackenzie. "I still can't believe that this isn't Fields' doing."

Mackenzie looked miserable and frightened. "No Sam, no. Fields wouldn't go this far. It just doesn't make sense."

Delaney turned around in his seat and scowled at them. "Shut the fuck up, both of you."

Sam closed his eyes for a moment. His head ached and the zip-ties on his wrists cut into his flesh. He felt his mind going numb.

He focused his attention on the windows of the van and noticed they were getting closer to Manchester. He felt vaguely encouraged by the familiarity of his surroundings.

Delaney finished his phone call. "Okay, Doc. here's the deal. Like I said, we want your plants, seeds, and growing processes for your so-called 'cancer-curing' pot. I know it's somewhere on that fucking island of yours, and you're going to give it to me." He smiled.

"Well…for starters, you'll have to let her go." Sam nodded in Mackenzie's direction. "She doesn't know anything about this."

"Did you say something, asshole? Sounded like you thought you had a say in this shit."

The van pulled off on a side road—at least half a mile from the Manchester parking lot, Sam knew—and stopped amid a grove of low-hanging willow trees to hide it from any passing vehicles. Delaney unlocked his door and climbed out. Thorpe walked to the back and jerked open the doors.

"You keep quiet and do exactly as we say," he warned. "We know a shortcut through the woods that will get us to your boat without drawing notice. It's still a hike."

The sun dropped lower in the sky as the three men, with Sam and Mackenzie stumbling ahead of them, made their way through heavy brush toward the water. It was a difficult approach, and Mackenzie fell a couple of times. Sam stepped in front of her, trying to find good footing for her to follow. He was amazed these men knew of such a tortuous route until he remembered Marty's story about chasing strangers away from his boat. *Marty.* Sam could only hope his friend would somehow notice something was wrong.

He felt a rush of hope, seeing his boat moored in its familiar spot. His body was pumping with adrenalin, his mind clearing. He glanced at Mackenzie; she looked deathly pale, her feet and legs soaked as they now navigated the sharp boulders and tidal pools along the shoreline. He could see abrasions on her legs through rips in her pants. Their eyes met for a moment and Sam attempted to convey strength to her wordlessly.

They boarded his small boat awkwardly; Sam and Mackenzie were stuffed between the others. The smaller man of the three had a large duffle bag on his shoulder that he carefully placed beside him.

"My boat isn't meant to hold this much weight," Sam said, his eyes focused on Delaney. "And we aren't crossing at slack tide."

Delaney looked unconcerned. "We aren't going far."

The motor started quickly and Thorpe pulled out into the channel. Sam could feel the engine struggling as the boat sat low in the water. Moments later, he could tell the man was having a hard time with the crossing. The boat was being carried sideways at times, water splashing over the sides.

"Untie me and I can get us there." Sam's immediate concern was capsizing with both his and Mackenzie's arms firmly tied behind their back. If he, at least, were free, he could help Mackenzie.

Delaney looked at the water then back to Sam. "Okay, Doc." He leaned forward with a switchblade and deftly sliced through the strong plastic tie.

Sam shook his numb hands in front of him and reached across Thorpe to grab the tiller. They neared the edge of a quickly developing whirlpool but Sam managed to skirt around it. The weight of the boat restricted his ability to steer as they were pushed sideways against the current and back toward the expanding whirlpool.

"Shit, we're gonna get sucked down!" Thorpe exclaimed.

"This could more than a skirmish, Vicki." Marty moved about his house, pulling two rifles from a closet and throwing one to Vicki Jo, who caught it expertly with one hand. "We need to prepare ourselves for a full beach invasion."

"I'm taking the .44 Mag, too. You may want to pack a sidearm as well."

Marty nodded, then stopped. "We should probably only use deadly weapons in case it becomes absolutely necessary." He looked thoughtful. "I'd like to avoid breaking park rules by discharging firearms."

Vicki Jo looked annoyed. "I'm willing to try and stick with the tranq rifles, but I will use serious force if I think it's warranted."

"We have to decide whether we deploy a frontal beach assault or a pincer maneuver from the flanks, because that's going to determine our weapon selection." The two continued to argue the fine points of ballistics and range as they selected their weapons of choice.

After a barrage of clattering sounds from the checking of magazines, firing chambers and safeties, Marty emerged carrying a rifle strapped to his shoulder, and a thick utility belt around his small waist, along with a leather fanny pack. Vicki Jo had her rifle and a pocket bulging with a large handgun.

The two made their way silently down the trail. The bulging fanny pack bumped on Marty's rear as they struggled through the dense brush.

Marty took a quick left between two large trees and descended to the horsehead cove where Sam's small aluminum boat was kept hidden under the bent cedar tree.

"Just as I suspected. His boat is gone." Marty sighed and rubbed his face, wincing as he touched his black eye.

"Marty, look!" Vicki Jo pointed toward the island. They could see Sam's boat, overloaded and struggling across the channel.

"They're in trouble. Looks like the current is sucking them sideways."

"Sam can handle it. But we definitely need to approach the island undetected. I know of only one way to do that and it involves rowing." He turned to Vicki Jo. She nodded.

"I'll get us there."

They quickly hiked back to the beach. A line of rowboats was neatly tied to a small dock. Marty untied the biggest boat while Vicki Jo pulled a set of oars from a nearby shed.

"Seeing that we need the advantage of concealment, we will need to take a more serpentine route."

Vicki Jo sat, oars in hand, looking determined. "I'm on it." She skillfully navigated them out of the cove and across the saltwater channel with the speed and accuracy of a competitive rower.

39

"**I**f you think you can capsize this boat and swim away, think again, Doc." Delaney held his gun on Mackenzie. "She'll be dead before we hit the water."

"Come on, I'm working as hard as I can!" Sam kept his eyes ahead, struggling to hold a path through the swirling pools as waves continued to break over the edge of the boat. "Use this can to bail some of the water out." He reached forward with his foot and knocked a coffee can out from under the stern. "Do it now!" he yelled.

Thorpe picked up the can and started scooping up the pooling water around their feet, tossing it overboard.

Suddenly the boat seemed to squeeze forward between two opposing currents and shot toward the island. Sam had managed to work with the current instead of against it, and was now able to steer the boat with relative ease toward the sand spit.

Beaching the boat, the three men jumped out and dragged Sam and Mackenzie to shore. Delaney gestured with his gun for the prisoners to climb out. "Now, here is where we talk details. Correct me if I'm wrong, but I have the distinct impression you have what we are looking for secured, somehow, underwater?" He gazed westward at the rapidly descending sun. "And unless you want to try and find this shit in the dark, I suggest we get moving."

Sam tried desperately to think of something to remove Mackenzie from harm's way. "Yes. It's not far from where we're standing. I'll need my scuba gear. I keep it up there." He pointed up the hill.

Thorpe stepped forward. "Yeah, I know where you keep your gear."

Delaney told Thorpe, "Take him." He leaned into Sam's face. "I'm going to stay here with your girlfriend." He placed an arm around Mackenzie, who cried out as he shoved his gun into her side. "Just so you know, I won't tolerate any shit. This gal is quite pretty. I wouldn't want to hurt her. But I will, if necessary."

Sam retrieved his equipment quickly and they returned to the beach, where Delaney still maintained his grip on Mackenzie.

"The stuff you want is in an underwater cave." Sam felt his adrenalin starting to kick in, sharpening his mind and clearing his vision.

"Good boy," Delaney said.

Sam tested the scuba gear, cleared the air regulator, and checked the valve and mask. Assured the equipment was ready to go, Sam glared at Thorpe. "Thanks to this," he pointed to the dried blood on his head, face and neck, "I'm going to have a hell of a time handling the depth, especially in this tide." He indicated

Mackenzie. "She can do this dive." His eyes locked on Mackenzie, and he tried to convey what he was thinking. Letting her do the dive was the best way to get her to safety.

Delaney snorted. "You think I'm stupid? No fucking way. Having her here with me is way too nice." His hand traveled down Mackenzie's arm, brushing her breast.

Sam was seconds from lunging at Delaney and attempting to kill him with his bare hands. But he remained in control, knowing that such a move would likely guarantee both their deaths.

"I'm sure I don't need to tell you that she's dead if you don't come back. And just to make sure you return, and bring everything back with you, Nelson will accompany you on the dive."

Sam turned to see the smaller man pulling dive equipment from the duffle bag he had been carrying.

"The current is very bad right now. Unless this man has a lot of experience, it could be deadly."

"I can handle it. No problem," Nelson said as he put on his gear. "If he can do it, I sure the fuck can." He waded into the cold water.

Sam shrugged on his tank. "Don't say I didn't warn you."

"Careful, Vicki," Marty said as, a few minutes earlier, they had approached the backside of the island. "The tide's moving."

Vicki Jo grunted and swung her left oar hard through the chop, guiding them expertly around a swirl of water. They had lost sight of Sam's boat, though Marty felt certain he had made it to the island.

"We should be able to land just south of them if we're careful." Vicki Jo strained against the left oar, using the right oar as a rudder to keep the boat from being dragged sideways into a cross current.

Soon they had pulled onto a barnacle-covered spit and struggled to drag the rowboat ashore, concealing it from view in the dense underbrush.

Climbing along a rough trail from the beach they moved up the natural rise of the island and stopped at a point that gave them a view of the beach from within the trees.

As she gazed toward the middle of the island with her military grade binoculars, Vicki Jo quickly analyzed the logistical implications of the landscape before them.

"Okay, Marty. As we learned from our studies of Sun Su: '*Every battle is won, or lost, before engaging the enemy on the battlefield*'. So here's how I see it: you perform a deep penetration to the west, then pincer up from the north and take position on top of the hill. I'll hug the cliff line. Since I'll be in position first, I'll attack immediately after your initial volley."

Marty peered through his binoculars with furious concentration.

"It looks like Sam is being forced to dive. And one of the three criminals is going with him." His voice dropped. "They are all well-armed."

"So Mackenzie is going to be left alone with two men pointing guns at her?"

Marty was already moving forward. "No one dies on my watch. No one."

Delaney dragged Mackenzie to the shoreline, his gun still pointed at her. "You have exactly twenty minutes to do this, asshole. I'd get going if I were you."

Sam quickly walked backwards into the cold briny water and placed the regulator into his mouth, giving Mackenzie a final look. He disappeared beneath the waves breaking against the shore. Immediately he could feel the tug of confused currents and the pressure building against his eardrums. Knowing that he dove at an extremely dangerous time, Sam focused intently, waiting until he could reach the grotto to come up with his next step. Nelson swam close behind him. Sam knew he was fighting with the current.

As they approached the edge of the underwater cliff that formed part of the island, Sam struggled to avoid the pull of a viciously accelerating suction coming from below him. He turned his head and saw that Nelson had blundered directly into the tornado-like suction of the massive whirlpool as it grabbed and spun him rapidly in a counter-clockwise direction, pulling him ever deeper toward the seemingly endless bottom of the Puget Sound. Nelson, looking terrified, reached upward toward him. Without thinking, Sam reached out to grab the man's hand, causing him to drop rapidly. He stabbed his powerful legs toward the cliff face, trying to slow their descent. Nelson's hand slipped loose, and he was pulled into the darkness below.

Sam, now free of his watchdog, managed to hug the cliff and move into the opening of the grotto. Pulling himself up and onto the cave floor, he removed his mask and regulator, gasping and coughing.

He knew he had very limited time to return, but the game had changed when Nelson went down. He hurried to the hiding place where he kept his research and materials and carefully extracted samples and documents, leaving behind the one thing Delaney wanted: actual samples of the cannabis with tumor-suppressing qualities.

"They won't get this," he told himself. "If we have to die, at least they won't get what they wanted." He carefully put the piece of basalt in place. It blended in perfectly with the rest of the cave wall. His hiding place would remain virtually undetectable.

Sam slipped the materials into the waterproof goodie bag and strapped it to his side. He pulled on his mask and slid back into the cold water.

As she'd watched Sam disappear, Mackenzie had thought, *Swim to safety Sam, please save yourself.* She felt certain neither of them would survive. These violent men were not likely to leave witnesses behind.

"All your friend needed to do was to give Fields what they wanted in the first place; you know that, don't you?" Delaney eased his hold on Mackenzie. "Of course, then we would have never met."

Mackenzie shuddered as Delaney looked over her body, his small eyes glistening.

"Hey Thorpe, keep an eye out for Nelson and the doc. Me and this pretty gal are going to find some privacy."

Thorpe nodded without expression.

40

Marty made his way along the top of the hill toward the gnarled roots of an ancient tree. He stopped to gaze below with his binoculars, surprised to see only one man standing by the water. He stealthily wedged his small body flat as he slithered into the bowels of the tree.

Seconds later, a loud, *thuunkk!* erupted from Marty's position. He watched through his scope as Thorpe clutched at his chest in shock and dropped to the sand. Scrambling from under the tree, he propelled himself forward, over the edge of the hill, and raced toward the beach.

Mackenzie struggled against Delaney as he dragged her into the thick brush surrounding the beach.

"The more you fight, the better I like it." Delaney held her in a crushing embrace. "Here's a good spot." He pushed her to the forest floor and immediately straddled her.

Mackenzie felt his hot breath on her face as he tore at the buttons on her shirt. She turned her head and closed her eyes, hot tears running down her face. She felt herself on the verge of losing consciousness when she heard a sharp *crack*!

"All right, motherfucker. That's just about enough of that."

Vicki Jo stood above her, dangling a dazed Delaney by his collar and cocking back her ample fist like an 88mm Howitzer. She appeared ready to shove it into his face at point-blank range.

"What the fuck—!" Delaney exclaimed, just in time to receive the powerful blow.

Mackenzie sat up in disbelief as she witnessed the impact of Vicki Jo's fist shattering bone, tearing cartilage, and crushing skin as Delaney's look of surprise instantly turned to agony. His face seemed to explode into a confused gazpacho cloud in front of her as Vicki Jo kicked his Beretta into the thick brush.

Delaney fell to the ground with a muffled groan as Vicki Jo stepped beside his now prone body, pulling him back up by the collar. The thug managed to roll, breaking Vicki Jo's grip and throwing her off balance, just enough to get free.

Staggering to his feet, Delaney appeared barely able to see through his now-purplish left eye. He started to run, followed closely by a large, obviously enraged female in a red plaid wool shirt and combat boots.

Vicki Jo lunged forward, kicking his left shin and causing it to collide with his right calf, sending him face first into the ground.

Her knuckles bleeding, she hovered over Delaney, who now lay still in the rough brush.

She rolled the man over with her foot and spoke calmly: "Here's what happens next: I'm going to thoroughly kick your sorry ass. So please don't pass out yet. I wouldn't want you to miss any of this."

Kneeling over Delaney, Vicki Jo continued her beating: "I wouldn't...want you...to miss...any of...this." She punctuated her words with crushing, blood-spattering blows into Delaney's already mangled face.

Her would-be attacker now obviously incapacitated, Mackenzie's roiling thoughts turned to Sam. She rose on wobbly legs and staggered out of the dense underbrush toward the beach.

Emerging, she saw Marty standing over the body of Thorpe, rifle held high above his head. She suddenly pointed to the bubbles rising to the surface a few yards offshore. "Sam!"

Marty dropped his weapon, plunged in and helped an obviously exhausted Sam to shore. "Where's the asshole who dove with you?" Marty grabbed his rifle and turned back to the water, prepared to shoot at anything that moved.

Sam could not help but laugh at the unexpected and welcome sight. "He's at the bottom of the Puget Sound—"

"*Sam!*" Mackenzie cried.

He dropped his mask and tank onto the beach. "Mac!" He pulled off his swim fins and ran to her. She fell into his arms and they stood entwined on the beach.

Sam pushed back to look at her as she clutched at her torn shirt.

"That fucking bastard." Sam's face turned from white to red.

"It's okay, Vicki Jo got there before he could…" Her words trailed off as Vicki Jo emerged from the brush, dragging an unconscious Delaney behind her by one leg.

Sam, shocked but not surprised, moved cautiously toward Vicki Jo.

"If he wakes up, I'll keep an eye out while you take a turn with him if you'd like." Vicki Jo punctuated this with a well-aimed kick to his ribs, causing Delaney's unconscious exhale as one or more of them cracked.

"I think he's pretty well done," Sam said. "We'd better leave enough for the police to positively identify."

"No worries. The FBI can always use their fingerprint database to ID this bastard. I'm pretty sure he's a repeat customer. In any case, he'll probably come around a bit before the authorities arrive." Vicki Jo calmly examined her battered knuckles.

Marty was busy securing Thorpe's limp body with rope from his fanny pack. Finishing his work, he stood. "Well this guy's not dead, at least. I merely gave him a light cocktail of bear tranquillizer; it should provide him with a refreshing sleep for a few hours."

Sam reached for Mackenzie and again held her.

"Thank god you're all right, Mac." Sam buried his face in her hair, relaxing into their mingling warmth and inhaling the scent of her body.

"Thank god we're both all right," Mackenzie said, her voice muffled by his embrace. She tilted her head back to look at him, placing her hand on the side of his face. "I'm grateful that you didn't have to give those bastards your cannabis." She glanced down his waterproof dive bag. "That would have been unthinkable after all they put us through."

"They would have got nothing anyway. I left the real samples back in the grotto."

Mackenzie laughed in spite of herself. "You are amazing, Sam. Stubborn to the very end."

41

The police and Coast Guard paramedics arrived by boat quickly. They all gathered with the Sheriff and heard a full account of what had taken place.

"So no one can positively ID these guys?" Sheriff Krueger watched the paramedics as they loaded Thorpe onto their vessel, which sat just off the beach.

"I think I may have seen him, or at least glimpsed him before." Sam recalled the two men at Kiutan Lodge and the Hemp Daze festival. "I can't say for certain, though."

The paramedic tending to Delaney called to the Sheriff, "I think he's trying to say something."

Sam and Mackenzie walked with Krueger to Delaney's side as he lay on a gurney, his face swollen and bloodied. Vicki Jo stood nearby.

"Ai...ken. Son of a...bitching Aiken." Delaney's face contorted in pain as he forced out the words.

Vicki Jo laughed. "Yeah, you'll be achin' for quite a while, asshole."

Sam's brow furrowed as he turned to Mackenzie. "Is he saying what I think he's saying?"

"Yes, 'Aiken.' As in Richard Aiken, my former boss at Fields Pharmaceuticals." Mackenzie looked at the Sheriff, who quickly wrote the name down on his notepad.

After bandaging Vicki Jo's hands, the Coast Guard boat left the scene with Delaney and Thorpe, heading toward Harbor View Hospital. Sheriff Krueger left as well, telling them he would be in touch shortly.

The four exhausted people began walking back to Sam's treehouse. Marty suddenly stopped in his tracks. "Shit, Sam, I forgot to tell you. They've found Lester pot all over the Northwest! Greg wanted me tell you right away. It appears the Feds will be arriving soon."

Sam struggled to assimilate this news. "I'd better get Ken Silver on the phone. He's probably been trying to get a hold of me since this shit started."

Mackenzie looked close to tears. "Are you kidding? How could they...isn't trying to kill us enough for these people?"

Sam slipped his arm around her. "It's okay, Mac. I have this covered."

Inside the house, Sam used Marty's cell to call Greg.

"Thank god you're okay, Sam!" Greg sounded close to panic. "Thank god for Marty and Vicki Jo."

"Greg, I need you to tell me what's going on with our cannabis supposedly showing up all over?"

"Jesus, Sam. I'm so sorry, but I really think we have to deal with this. Ken Silver is going crazy and…I'm afraid we'll end up in jail or something."

After a quick recounting of events, Greg gave him Silver's phone number.

"I'll call him right now, Greg. And I want you to quit worrying. I've got a trick or two up my sleeve."

He called Silver, still in his office despite the lateness of the hour. The Marijuana Czar launched into a tirade. Sam interrupted: "Okay calm down. Let me talk here. Call Marianne Preston at the University of New Haven immediately. I registered the DNA of Lester's cannabis with them. Yeah, they have a marijuana DNA profile database. I worked on it myself; the Office of National Drug Control Policy set it up to help the feds determine where illegal pot growers and dealers get their product. Yes. Just call them and then get back to me."

Silver reminded him that it was late at night on the east coast. Sam retrieved Marianne's home number from a letter he had on file and gave it to Silver, then clicked off and closed his eyes.

"So, we'll be okay?" Mackenzie said.

"We'll be okay. Everything's going to be fine."

42

Within the hour, Ken Silver was patching Sam through to a three-way phone call with Marianne Preston. "Hi Marianne, this is Sam VanDerhout. Thanks for talking to us so late."

"No worries, Sam. Yes, I spoke to Ken Silver earlier. I'm in my office at the University; just got here. It sounds like you have a situation going on."

"We do. What I'd like to ask is that you guys get in touch with your contacts in the DEA for us right away. We need our sample compared with the cannabis found in Washington State containers as soon as possible."

"I've actually started the process here, though it's hard to connect with anyone this late. I reassured Ken that we're a major resource for the Feds. We have a fairly tight procedure for isolating the origins of cannabis for them."

"That's right, she did." Ken sounded much calmer. "I just had no idea your DNA bank existed. I hadn't been properly informed by Mr. VanDerhout."

"I, uh, thought I'd leave it on a need-to-know basis," Sam mumbled.

Marianne added, "Well, it's not a well-known resource. Since Sam had worked with us a few years ago, he knew the benefits of registering Lester's cannabis. We can get this cleared up for you all in Washington pretty quickly, I think."

"Marianne, do you need anything else from us for the time being?"

"No, Sam. I think you did everything up front that was required. Just sit tight for a few days and we'll be in touch."

Silver stayed on the line with Sam. "Thank god. What the hell happened to you, anyway?"

"It's a long story." Sam felt a bit dizzy. "I'll tell you another time. Bye."

"Glad to see you have things under control with the whole DNA thing," Marty said with a grin.

Sam yawned and stretched. "I aim to please."

"How are your poor knuckles feeling?" Mackenzie examined the voluminous white bandages on Vicki Jo's hands.

"Well I won't be playing the violin for a week or so."

Marty seemed puzzled. "But you don't play the violin... Anyway, we haven't had this much fun in years," he said cheerfully. His smile suddenly faded. "Sorry. I know it was traumatic for the two of you."

Mackenzie's eyes filled with tears. "I'll never be able to repay you, Marty, and especially you, Vicki Jo, for what you did for me—for us."

"I'll second that." Sam smiled at his friends. "Thank you for being there for us. Thank you for our lives."

Marty grinned broadly. "All in the line of duty." He and Vicki Jo clicked on their flashlights and waved energetically as they walked down the trail toward their rowboat.

Sam and Mackenzie stood for a moment in exhausted silence, watching their friends disappear down the trail. Barely a word passed between them as they climbed to the third-floor bedroom, undressing quickly and holding each other as they drifted into a deep, healing sleep.

43

"News Channel Six has just learned of an unexpected turn of events in the ongoing story of legal marijuana in our Evergreen State," the sharply dressed reporter began.

Vicki Jo had insisted that Sam and Mackenzie leave the island for an evening and come to Marty's bungalow for dinner. "You two have to get back on the horse that threw you," she'd told them. "The best way to fight post-traumatic stress is to engage with the world as soon as possible."

They had been reluctant to accept the invitation; they both felt traumatized—and exhausted—by their ordeal. But Marty and Vicki Jo had been insistent, and Sam was now glad they'd come. Their sprits had been lifted in the company of good friends.

The reporter droned on: "Our investigation has uncovered the fact that the Washington State drug satchels, and other security measures used in the transport of legally produced

Washington marijuana, were manufactured by a company in Tijuana, Mexico that may have ties to organized crime…"

Sam laughed. "I don't know if I'd call Aiken and Delaney 'organized' crime." He passed his joint to Marty.

"It has been determined these counterfeit satchels were used to plant false evidence in several states, including Oregon, Idaho and perhaps others."

"No shit," Vicki Jo muttered as she waved her still bandaged hand toward Marty's small television set.

"Further," the reporter continued, "forensic genetic analysis has determined the marijuana, recently seized by the DEA, is definitively confirmed to be unrelated to that produced by the town of Lester, Washington as part of the recent beta test. State and Federal Law Enforcement believe organized crime or possibly drug cartels may have been involved in this attempt to undercut implementation of legal marijuana in Washington State. The investigation is ongoing."

"Damn Feds didn't get anybody, did they?" Marty said.

Sam had his arm around Mackenzie. It delighted him that Lester's pot experiment had been proven a success. Legal cannabis production would continue in Washington State.

"I know it was Aiken, maybe even Mallory, who cooked that up." Mackenzie looked disgusted.

Sam frowned. "We've already discussed it, Mac. You're not going near that again. I don't want you implicated in any of this."

"I know, Sam, but I feel responsible. I wish I could nail Fields without getting myself in trouble too."

"Aiken, for one, is in big trouble. He'll likely do some time with Delaney for what they did to us."

Vicki Jo smiled. "I doubt that Delaney will be up to any mischief for quite a while, anyway."

Mackenzie sighed. "One can hope."

Marty raised his beer. "Well, at least no harm was done to the good people of Lester and their wonderful cannabis. All's well that ends well, I guess."

"The Pot Plant is still in business!" Sam raised his joint.

The Lester Pot Plant had been hopping with activity in the ensuing weeks. Ken Silver had informed Greg personally of the booming cannabis business the State was already experiencing. Lester had received enough orders to keep them working at capacity for a long time to come.

Greg and Sam had just finished installing a new watering system and were relaxing with Mackenzie and Becky, sitting on the shady lawn outside the warehouse. "When Silver told me how much we had made from our initial shipments I nearly cried," Greg said. "By the way, I...we have something to show you two." A group of Lester townspeople had started to gather around.

Sam gazed at the happy crowd. "Okay, what's this about?"

"As you know, we are expecting a windfall check in the next few weeks." Greg grinned broadly. "It was way more than we originally expected."

The crowd broke out in loud applause, until Greg lifted his hand to silence them. "Sam and Mackenzie..." He stood and faced them. "We here in Lester have a little surprise for you."

The couple looked at each other, puzzled. "What is it?" Mackenzie asked, a bemused expression on her face.

"You'll have to follow us!" Simon practically jumped up and down with obvious excitement. He took Mackenzie's arm and led her along. Sam followed with Greg and about fifty townspeople. They walked for several blocks and turned left down a cobblestone road, stopping in front of a small, creamy yellow bungalow with a wide, street-facing gable. A heavy roof overhang, supported by squat, white columns and braces enclosed a simple white porch with a wicker couch and a porch swing. The yard was neatly trimmed, surrounded by bright flowers in swirls of late-spring colors.

Sam, tongue-tied, looked at Greg, who laughed. "While we still haven't received our first check officially, we decided to use some city funds and bribe you with a house here. We want you and Mackenzie as part-time neighbors."

"I want them to see the inside!" Simon was already on the porch, his hand on the doorknob.

Walking up the steps, they entered through a heavy, oak door with a stained glass window. The door opened directly into the living room, separated from the small dining area by a half wall connected to the ceiling by a tapered wooden pier.

"Wow!" Sam looked around the room. The walls were covered with numerous floor-to-ceiling, stained fir bookshelves. He grinned, turning to the crowd. "I can fill these immediately!"

"This was used as a bookstore for about twenty years," Becky told him. "We knew you could make use of the shelves."

"Look at this wainscoting," Mackenzie said, moving around the rooms. "And real box beam ceilings!"

Simon showed them the fireplace, proudly pointing out the decorative art tiles surrounding the mantle. "I donated these. They were original to the Craftsman style."

"We haven't added any furniture, other than a bed," Greg said. "We thought you'd want to pick that out yourselves."

Overwhelmed, Mackenzie and Sam were led to the light and airy kitchen, painted a subtle, pale green.

"We took the liberty of stocking some party food." Jeffrey Floyd threw open the refrigerator, revealing a full selection of delicious-looking treats.

"And a few bottles of champagne!" Lena was already popping the first cork.

Within an hour, a party was in full swing and people were bringing folding chairs and more food. The house overflowed with laughter and music.

Soon the door flung open and Marty and Vicki Jo entered carrying a large box of food. Marty proudly sported a new badge given to him by the State. He had been awarded a *Meritorious Performance* medal for his part in apprehending the thugs who had kidnapped Sam and Mackenzie.

Marty touched his new bling, smiling broadly as he approached Sam. "Check it out, my friend."

"Wow, can I touch it?" Sam laughed as he hugged Marty.

Vicki Jo immediately took over the kitchen, rattling pots and stuffing foil-covered pans into the oven.

Sam and Mackenzie maneuvered their way into the kitchen to hug Vicki Jo. "Did you bring some more bear lasagna?" Mackenzie asked.

"Bear? No. I had some elk in the freezer, so I made a pot of chili with it. It really adds a tang to the beans."

Father Chris Donneghy appeared, dressed in comfortable jeans and a flannel shirt and carrying a six-pack of beer. Greg whispered something in his ear.

"Ahem." Greg called the rapidly expanding party to attention. "Father Donneghy will now say a blessing over Sam and Mackenzie's new home. Father?"

The pastor stood near the fireplace, bowing his head as the party quieted. He began his prayer in a clear voice.

"Our Holy Father, we gather here today to bless this beautiful home for Your children, Mackenzie and Sam. But first, we give thanks for the blessings You have showered upon us, as a result of legalized marijuana. This natural weed, which You have so generously provided to this world, is emerging from the dark valley of ignorance and is finally taking its rightful place on the bright pinnacle of understanding. We thank you Lord, that in so doing, pot has also brought forth a veritable cornucopia of financial abundance upon my humble parish, and the State of Washington in general. On a personal note, I thank You for the fact my collection basket overfloweth, and in thy kind graces, I am now able to enjoy the occasional brand-name beer. Oh, also Lord, if the Seahawks could win the Super bowl next season, we'd be much obliged… Sorry Lord, back to the house blessing. We ask that You bless this home, and Mackenzie and Sam, and all who enter here. For all these things, we pray to You, dear Lord, Amen."

The room exploded in applause and loud "Amens."

Sam smiled. "And thank *you* for your creative approach to prayer, Father."

As the evening wore on, the pot smoke became thick and sweet, a light breeze bending it into wisps above the people spread out on the porch and the small, tidy lawn.

Greg sat on the wicker couch, Becky on his lap. "Well, I think we did it, folks."

Jeffrey Floyd looked immensely satisfied. "I'd have to say we did." He leaned back in the porch swing, each arm encircling a Thorvaldsen twin. "I'm thinking of changing my bakery's name to, 'Jeff's Totally Baked Goods'. What do you think?"

"I think its poetry, Jeff." Mackenzie stood in the doorframe, gazing out at the quiet street in front of her.

Sam took her arm and they made their way onto the lawn, turning to face the numerous guests. "I'd like to say something to all of you!" Sam announced. The crowd quieted.

"We've been through a lot together. I can't tell you how much it means to me…" He looked at Mackenzie, who took his hand. "…to both of us, that you have given us this beautiful home. And more than that, you want us to be your neighbors." Sam cleared his throat and shook his head. "Thank you."

Everyone cheered loudly and Sam and Mackenzie were treated to a long series of hugs, backslaps and handshakes. As the evening wore on, people began drifting away.

Sam hugged Greg and Becky before they left. "I can't tell you how much this means to both of us," Sam said.

"I look forward to having at least part of my life here, in Lester." Mackenzie's eyes glistened as she took Becky's hands in her own. "You two, well, you had every right to resent me for... my part in the mess that happened."

"We all have made mistakes in our lives, Mackenzie." Becky smiled gently. "What's important is that you changed course and did the right thing. Besides, we love you."

Marty and Vicki Jo were the last to leave.

"We're headed over to The Lodge for the night." Vicki Jo kissed Marty affectionately. "We had a little tiff on the way here and we need some make-up time."

Marty winked at Sam as they piled into Vicki Jo's Hummer and sped off into the night.

Mackenzie looked at Sam, her eyes filling with tears. "I don't deserve this."

Sam wrapped his arms around her. "If you've earned something," he whispered, "it's not a gift."

They sat down on their very own porch swing. In the distance, a sprinkler started up in a nearby pot field, bringing the sweet smell of musky, dry grass finding water.

44

"Wow!" Donald Blake gazed upon Sam's house for the first time.

"I get that a lot," Sam replied as they approached the treehouse.

"That was my reaction when I first saw it, Dad. But Sam wasn't with me on the beach at the time." Mackenzie smiled as she recalled the day she had first come to this island. It seemed a long time ago.

"Sam, what a fantastic house…treehouse…home." Mr. Blake said, running his hands across the driftwood maple stair slabs appreciatively. "How did you get the risers to appear so light yet take all that load?"

Sam knelt down to point to the underside of the stair structure. "See right here, Don? I put a steel angle-iron strong back support into the groove here."

"Ah, I see. Great solution—ingenious in fact."

"Dad, just wait until you see the inside." Mackenzie watched her father and Sam together. In all her years in Los Angeles she had never asked her dad to visit. His rough, sun-burnished skin, working-man hands and quiet manner would have embarrassed her in the polished, wealthy professional circles in which she ran. She felt shame for having those feelings about the kind, honest man in front of her now.

The three proceeded up the stairs and into the house.

"This is quite an achievement." Don smiled broadly, obviously delighted to be with his daughter and her new man in such natural surroundings.

"Thanks. It was a labor of love. I had tried to build a treehouse in the back yard as a kid, but I suspect mom and dad gave the gardeners standing orders to make any such thing disappear discretely."

Mackenzie loved the sight of Sam and her father walking through the house chatting, her father admiring the expertly executed miter cuts, mortise and tenon, and dove-tail joints. The two men seemed like old friends already.

"This spiral staircase is really the kicker. Quite an achievement, Sam."

"Actually, I put in a straight staircase there at first. After a time, I had the house as I wanted it, and then started renovating immediately. The American Way, after a fashion."

"Just wait until Mac gets her way with you. You'll be putting a fourth and fifth floor onto this place."

Sam turned to wink at Mac, whom he had just caught looking his way admiringly. During the time they had been living together, Sam had proved an easygoing, affectionate partner with a wicked sense of humor. She found herself growing more in love with him every day.

The three continued a brief tour of the modest, yet organically stately home.

Don stopped to enjoy Sam's telescope, catching a glimpse of the harbor seals that frequented the island. "They really seem to love this area. Must be a lot of fish out there." He looked hopefully at Sam.

Mackenzie laughed. "Yes, Dad. I know you can't get away from fishing for more than a day."

"We can head out first thing in the morning, Don. The sockeye are still running and there's always Dolly Varden, Pollock, hake and Pacific cod."

As the three sat down to dinner, Don asked his daughter to explain what she was doing for work now that she had left Fields.

"Well, Dad," Mackenzie said, "Sam talked me into applying for a part-time teaching position at the University of Washington. I don't know if I'll get it, but it's in their pharmacy program. And," she looked at Sam, "I'm working with him on getting a certain strain of his cannabis produced for treating people with cancer."

Sam gazed lovingly at Mackenzie. "She pretty persuasive, Don. I've finally given in. She wants to find a way to get the cannabis I developed patented...the cannabis that started all the unpleasant business a while back."

"We'll figure something out and get it out there. It's too important to keep hidden away." She shrugged. "Otherwise, I'm just helping out in Lester, at the Pot Plant, and being lazy for the first time in my life."

Don Blake reached across the table and took his daughter's hand. "I've never seen you look happier, Mac."

Sam rose from the table. "Let's go on the deck for a while. It's a beautiful evening."

They sat outside the treehouse, on a small deck that Sam had built around a thick branch of the huge hemlock tree. It afforded a view of the Sound, sparkling pink and orange with the last rays of the sun. Forest flowers spread out below them, wafting their spicy scents into the cooling evening air.

"Sam can tell you every species of plant on this island, Dad." Mackenzie looked at Sam, now stretched out and smoking a thick joint, bare feet propped on the deck railing. "My dad's an enthusiastic gardener."

Sam casually handed the joint to Mackenzie's father. "I noticed you walking stiffly, Don. Mackenzie said you have chronic back pain?"

Don eyed the joint, a bemused expression on his face. "Yeah, I have a couple crushed disks in my back. It gets pretty painful."

"Try a small puff or two, Dad," Mackenzie said. "It won't hurt you."

Don took a drag, then another, and began a long coughing fit. Mackenzie handed him a glass of water. Once his coughing stopped he looked up, his face slightly flushed. "Wow. What's it supposed to do?"

Sam laughed. "Just relax you. And it's great for chronic pain."

"So it's kind of like taking a pain pill?"

"No, not really. Cannabis affects an area in the brain called the *anterior mid-cingulate cortex,* which regulates the emotional aspects of pain. To put it simply, you still may have the pain, you just don't mind it as much. That, and it's a great anti-inflammatory."

Don smiled. "Wow. I feel better already." He stretched and then leaned back into his chair, hands behind his head.

Mac cleaned up the kitchen to give her father and Sam more time to chat. The stars winked through the canopy of trees outside the window as the evening lengthened and spread before her. Her life was now here, with Sam VanDerhout, in this beautifully rugged, quirky enclave called the Pacific Northwest. *The Evergreen State.*

Or was that *The Everweed State?*

THE END

www.ingramcontent.com/pod-product-compliance
Lightning Source LLC
Chambersburg PA
CBHW051412170626
46809CB00006B/2127